Unknown Place, Unknown Universe

Lazlo Ferran

Unknown Place, Unknown Universe

Lazlo Ferran

Acknowledgments

Thanks to Ash, Derek, Gary, and Lorna.

Contents

Prologue 9

1. Unknown Place 11

2. Time's Memory...53

3. The Hunt Begins 83

4. A Great Fish in the Sky 109

5. Fuel on the Fire 131

6. Charm..165

7. Transmissions...193

8. Ignition...219

9. The Weight of a Thought 241

10. Towards the Gate 265

11. Dark Horizons 283

Epilogue 309

Prologue

It's been over ten years since Gary Enquine sent my friend Przeltski to a certain death. Not one day has gone by without the memories of that battle prowling my mind like a waking nightmare. Many times, I have woken in a cold-sweat thinking about it. I will not rest, cannot rest, until Gary Enquine has been brought to justice and been forced to pay for his cowardice. Ten years; it's a long time but I can be patient. Personal journal entry of Jake Nanden for 2101, Feb 3. 1.

Twenty-two years later … .

***

1. Unknown Place

Kek-suîxjh looked out over the hills surrounding the city, his mournful, long-snouted jackal face staring back at him from the transparent walls of his office.

In a moment of childish caprice, he tried to smile but his reflection just grinned back with a sickly parody of a smile.

It has been so long since I was happy.

His two pups had grown up, or at least one had, and even though his wife still looked as beautiful as ever, he felt the weight of age grow heavy. He returned to his desk and stared at its blank surface. He sometimes had to force himself to look away, to see the big picture, before he could remember why he had been trying to solve this problem. Religion, and his speciality, metaphysics, were not the pleasurable subjects they used to be; thinking no longer divorced from real life. Now, he yearned for one thing; to return a feeling of optimism, and yes, faith in religion and science, to the people of the planet Ito.

What if ... God allows the transgression of time-laws but only under certain conditions?

The transparent surface of the desktop filled with physics formulae to describe his thoughts but they did not produce a pattern he could accept.

No. Wipe that.

The desk became blank.

He glanced again at the sky-scape through the side of the building. A light blinked and traversed the wall; a transporter, no doubt on route to one of the many city depots.

He mourned for Isch-su. One of the last alive who had grown up on the planet Isch-su, he remembered her beautiful shores under a much milder sun.

And all that green! So much of it wherever you looked!

But they had destroyed it all. Chlorophyll, the building block of vegetation, had provided nearly everything they needed. They had become over-dependent and overproduced. The soil had become barren and the carbon-fuelled culture had destroyed the upper atmosphere with pollution. Too late, they had realised their mistake when the planet started to die. In the end, only the rich and select few other Ischians, had found a place on the escaping ships.

They had come here, to Ito, closer to the sun and much hotter but with a nascent atmosphere. This had been kick-started generations before by politicians and eager scientists looking for new horizons.

He left for home early and, as usual, walked the short distance across the plaza rather than take a rail.

As he exited the plaza, to walk towards the luscious lawn that lined the approach to the estate of the rich and successful, a panel lit up. The wall spoke to him.

"Take care. Rain due."

A smattering of rain, little more than dew, dampened his brow and he smiled.

Rain. Ha! We only arrange it for the pups so they will know what it was like on Isch-su. They don't know what real rain is!

He soon fell into deep in thought again as he walked.

The push to look for a better world, within some sections of their society, had led to political strife and ended with exile of many on two ships.

Ironically, it didn't have to be this way. Word from the colony had reached them that other suns were much richer in metals and organic life could thrive without such heavy use of chlorophyll.

This knowledge, instead of bringing hope to the younger generation, had driven the stake of despair even deeper through their hearts.

Now they seem really without hope! Mind you, we have always been a pessimistic species.

The thought seemed to revive his spirits.

He wanted to do something with the time that remained to him. He didn't want to wait passively for his own death and metaphysics no longer seemed to give him the answer he needed. He wanted to *do something*. But what?

***

The pilot of the stolen Earth cruiser, barely more than a teenager, wiggled his feet around on the dashboard and looked out at the stars beyond. The narcotic, chum, oozed juices between his teeth. An unexpected image suddenly invaded his vision, blotting out the instrument panel:

A butterfly pushed and another pale white orb joined the cluster of eggs on the rock. Pausing for a moment, she flicked her striped wings and took lightly to the air as if lifted on a breeze.

"Strange!" the pilot thought, once the vision passed. "Never seen a *real* butterfly!"

But then he saw the space compass.

"Oh! Oh! We're going off course, fast! Hey, what are those *red, flashing beacons*?"

A young woman with blue eyes and raven-black hair, just behind him, dropped the manual she had been reading and yelled:

"Correct your course!"

"I can't!"

"A third crew member yelled, "Ischian crui-... ." an instant before they were sucked into the worm-hole."

By the immense vibration that immediately threatened to rip the cruiser apart, they knew this had to be a big worm-hole, one that would take them far from their own locale in space. Stars were suddenly blinding, pale streaks of light. They were pinned to their seats with no need of belts while the ship corkscrewed around an imaginary whirlpool of space-matter.

Yells from the rear of the cabin to, "Get control," blurred into one while the pilot struggled to right the ship. Eventually, he did manage to gain some stability but moment later, they were spat out by the worm-hole into a region of unknown space and time.

The woman finally managed to reach the co-pilot seat and attempted to get a reading from the navigational console. "Navigation's screwed!" she announced.

"Great!" the pilot replied. "She's … handling like a pig too. Deceleration, not programmed … avionics damaged … . Might lose this … Planet dead ahead."

"Habitable?" the co-pilot yelled over the noise the cruiser being torn apart.

"Maybe … I see what looks like water. Can't hold this. Have to land … ."

They hit the planet's outer atmosphere far too fast for any guidance system to cope with. But they had no guidance system!

"Approach plan?" the third crew member yelled.

"There's no approach plan for this!" the pilot yelled back.

A blinding flash of white light suddenly filled the flight deck. The ship jolted, almost pulling the steering controls from the pilot's hands.

"Christ!" yelled the co-pilot. "Lighting strike!"

"Great," the pilot said to himself. He shouted, "Now we've really had it! Going to manual!"

Somehow, the pilot managed to keep the cruiser upright as strong gravitational fields within a dense layer of cloud buffeted the ship. When they emerged from the low cloud base, the only instrument left working, the altimeter, showed less than 1000 feet. A red-tipped mountain loomed, dead ahead.

By some freak of electronics, the height warning klaxon triggered all the other warning klaxons on the flight deck, creating an unbearable clamour.

"Have to put her down but where?"

"There!" yelled the co-pilot. She pointed to a patch of tan among rolling hills of green on the surface of the unknown planet below. "Desert of some kind. *Must* be flat!"

With no time to think, the pilot corrected the glide path and trimmed for landing.

"Shut down engine, anti-grav set to neutral and shut off fusion-drive!" he yelled. "I never felt so much like swearing in Christian before. Would your god mind if a heathen said, 'Christ!'"

The cruiser dipped below some high cliffs around the small patch of desert.

"Brace!" the pilot yelled. Both the co-pilot and the third crew member could help no more. They gripped their seats with all their strength and held their breaths.

The pilot saw the danger of the huge, rolling sand dunes at the last moment and turned to align the ship's path with their troughs. Just above a dune crest, the cruiser finally stalled and side slipped.

The pilot wrestled with the manual control column, the only control he had left, to pull the cruiser up level but a wing-let sliced into the crest of a dune and the ship began to skew. He did the only thing he could, he lowered the other wing-let so that the stricken ship belly bellied onto the side of the dune.

From 100 mph to zero took less than five seconds. None of the crew imagined they would live but none had time to think, thrown about as they were by the violent deceleration.

Then there was silence.

***

With its abdomen pressed down onto the lance-shaped leaf, the black and white, swallow-tailed butterfly pushed and another pale white orb joined the cluster of eggs like new moons on the shrub in the crevice between two rocks.

The rays of a red dawn breached the top of the ridge further down the east-facing valley. The light flickered on the butterfly's fluttering wings as she moved slightly to lay another egg. Hungry eyes watched her.

It would be the last of her precious eggs. Pausing for a moment, she flicked her striped wings and took lightly to the air as if lifted on a breeze, though none existed in the dry desert heat. This shrub had been the first green for miles around and she had taken advantage of its isolation as a host for her offspring.

Surging towards his prey, an adolescent lizard, iridescently blue-bellied, leapt for the fluttering black and white feast but he missed. Not interested in the eggs, he stood for a moment like a statue to take in some heat. He swallowed once as if remembering a rehearsed meal, bobbed his head and moved further up the warming rocks.

As the butterfly rose, her wings touched at the top of each beat. She passed through another shadow but she would not have considered why it was head-shaped.

Stone stood up, wondering at this moment of birth and near-death he had just witnessed in front of his eyes. He pondered the significance of the six-inch long grey-green leaves on the shrub, which had managed to survive in this inhospitable landscape.

"There *is* something growing here!" he shouted to two other space-suited figures slowly plodding up the rocky valley towards him. His voice echoed off distant sandstone walls. He spat on the ground and turned as they caught up with him.

"Fuckit!" Stone punctuated the arid silence like a scar on a pretty girl's face but he couldn't help it. He was unendingly angry, hated almost everything, and his swearing became worst when he felt nervous, or guilty. He pointed at the shrub.

"Looks like we ain't gonna die after all! Told you!"

"And that makes it okay does it, hm?" asked the last of the three to see the shrub, a female, two sizes too small for her whitish duretex space-suit.

"Can you eat it?" asked the third member of the team, a male with two dark chevrons cut into the stubble-short hair on his head.

"How the fuck should I know! I saw a lizard... Maybe we could eat *that*... You two piss me off – so negative!"

All three wore suits a few sizes too large and without their helmets, the males looked from a distance as if they were shrunken-headed talismans. Only the girl, with a full head of raven-black hair cut to shoulder length, looked vaguely in proportion. She shook her head with despair.

"If it wasn't for that haze everywhere I might know where we are," said the male with a chevron-patterned hair.

"How the fuck *could* you know, dude? We don't even know which fuckin' star system we are in, let alone what planet this is!" said Stone.

"I don't know many planets, dude, but I have a photographic memory and I remember the patterns of a few."

"Nice one! Now we will find out where we are," said Stone

"Or aren't!" said Dee

"Oh Dee, you are so negative!" said the girl.

"Just kidding. No, this feels like Earth, but supposing it's not even our Universe. Given how little we understand about worm-holes, that's possible isn't it?"

"Yes, that would really complicate things," said Stone, wryly.

"We need to get up high. Maybe we could see the stars from up there, hm," said the girl. She spoke quietly but with thoughtful authority.

"Where?" said Stone, swinging around, expecting to see her pointing somewhere.

"I was talking rhetorically fuckwit." She swore to impress him. It was all he needed to break out of the deferential etiquette he had stuck to so far.

"Ooo! The nerd swears!"

"And stop trying to assert yourself all the time. None of us knows what we are doin,' least of all *you*!" she hit back.

"Yeah! Don't talk to her like that, man!" said the chevron-haired male.

"Don't tell me what I can and cannot do Dee!"

***

Two pairs of eyes watched the three tiny white figures on the pancake of sandstone far below.

One pair, from under a scrubby bush on a promontory five hundred feet above the three figures, lazily watched a prey bird circling even higher before spotting the three figures on the rock below.

The bird of prey saw the three split into two and one, and decided to continue circling high above the lone white creature. Perhaps it would fall dead. Most things did die once on their own.

***

Stone didn't look like a hero and he knew it. It wasn't just his head, shaved to leave a single central strip of hair which historians would call a Mohican haircut. In his more self-congratulatory moments, he thought of himself as a nerd, but what he *knew* he really was, was a creep. As he toiled up the valley, fast becoming a canyon, in a suit a few sizes too large for him, he wished he had drunk all of the hi-water in the tube Jay had carried with her.

'But then … ' he thought, ' … Dee-low would have punched me, and the Jay would have said something spiteful.'

The pint he had drunk, would not keep him going long but what choice did he have? With the ship disabled and an n-gen that the stupid owners had not refilled they had nothing to drink.

"Fuckit!"

They had to find water. He got them into this mess, so he had to be the one to find water. After an hour of sweaty, gasping, painfully slow progress in the chafing suit, he relented to commonsense. Finding a shady patch between a large rock cliff and another of those stunted shrubs, he shrugged off the suit and stuffed it behind the shrubs. He trudged on. His aim, only vaguely formed in his mind, was to reach as high a spot as possible by noon and then wait for nighttime and the stars. He saw another butterfly. Stone had never seen a real butterfly before that day and his journalistic eye supplied the prose-commentary inside his head as he walked.

Golden leaf-like butterflies fluttered by while Stone trudged on feet of clay, along the lonely valley.

"Why did you give me that *look* when he offered to go on his own, hm?" said the girl to Dee while they both descended to the salt flat.

"'Cos... he feels guilty and wants to make up. You were about to stop him. I could *see* you were."

"You really think he will work out where we are, I mean, will he get high enough to see the stars?"

"I don't know. In this heat, with no water, it's gonna be tough. He's not exactly the fittest guy I know." Dee paused for a moment. "He's determined when he wants something though."

"What does he *want*?"

Dee didn't answer.

"Shit, it's hot. I really want to take this suit off, hm," she said, itching her arm after taking off a glove.

"No. Not yet! Put it back on. At least the suits give us *some* protection. Who knows what's out there?" Dee replied, scanning the horizon keenly.

They didn't talk much as they trudged on.

***

By midmorning, the pair trudging back to the crashed ship had reached the end of the valley and crossed half the distance over a vast, dry, salt lake. Ahead, through the haze, they could just see the first ridge of red sand. This marked the beginning of the dunes where the spaceship lay.

"Is there any water left at all Jay?"

"Nope. There is one chew left. You can have it, hm."

"No. Let's save it."

"My hero."

"Sarcasm."

"Of course."

The bird of prey grew tired of circling above the single figure further up the canyon just before noon. It would return and search for a carcass tomorrow.

***

Following their own footsteps, coming the other way in the dark red sand, they finally peered over one of the highest dune crests and spotted the ship. It lay, leaning to the right on the side of a sand dune.

When she had first seen it in the dock on J6, Jay had thought it looked like a large silver beetle holding two long flat suitcases at arms-length. It still looked like a beetle, but one which was losing the battle for life, its shell coming apart in the blazing heat. Steam from the overworked cooling system spiraled lazily up into the blue sky adding to the air of escaping life.

Sliding down the far side of the dune, they reached the airlock of the crippled ship. Jay pressed the code into the keypad by the hatch. It hissed open.

"Home at last!" She blew out a long sigh and flopped onto one of the loungers, which sloped at an odd angle. She felt exhausted. Dee punched the panel to shut the door and cool air from the air-con fans wafted about their sweating bodies. They both lay still for a while.

Dee licked his parched lips before speaking. "I'll get us some water from the n-gen."

"Not too much Dee. Just a cup full … for both of us!"

"Right."

***

Jay considered the situation:

'With the engines intact, flight should still be possible.'

Considering how little flying experience they had, she had been very impressed by Stone and Dee's landing along the high side of the dune. Only her first out-of-breath gasps, in a life she had not expected to have, had stopped her from screaming out her gratitude when the spaceship had finally come to a shuddering halt. She worried that the hull might not be intact

"Here you go." Dee handed her a cup.

"Thanks. First we need to find water, then food, and then check the hull, hm."

She tasted the cool liquid:

"Funny how when you are really thirsty, water tastes better than anything. Normally I don't like plain water."

Jay struggled out of her suit and Dee could not help sneaking a look at her in the skin-tight privates complete with a blue sash that denoted her blue-adept status. To his surprise, he saw that, although slim, she looked athletic. He could see every muscle and curve. He found himself lingering too long. She snapped a glance at him and he looked away.

Why do women always know when you are looking at them?

Shame quickly replaced his anger. He hadn't yet earned the right to look at her in that way.

She quickly put on the loose casuals he had seen her wearing on the morning after their graduation.

Stone's plan is well fucked now.

"Do you think we can get out of here?" She sounded surly.

"Don't know. Depends"

"You're *technical*..! Can you get the guidance system working again?"

"Me? I'm a musician. Well not even that! I'm a DJ. I couldn't fix a light socket."

"That's not true, Dee-low. I've seen the stuff you rigged for the last new rake rave you did. It wasn't cosy at all!"

"Thanks! Not cosy!" He laughed. "Wow, you really are posh aren't you? That's so lunar!"

"It's only my mum's Lunar. My dad was from J3."

"Ahh! Your mum. The great new-genderist."

"Stop it! I've heard it *all* before. Can you *try* at least and look at it?"

"Okay. Okay!" For the first time he had found a chink in her armour.

***

"How much water left in the nano-generator?" Jay asked.

They were leaning against the slowly cooling side of the ship, near the door. Their legs created troughs in the sand below them as the red sun disappeared below the horizon.

"Nano-generator! Ha! Only a *serious* nerd still calls then that! N-gen, Jay! About a pint. No more. I already have a headache. By tomorrow we'll be in serious trouble," Dee replied

"Don't whine. I have a headache too you know, hm."

They sat, silently, morosely.

Suddenly they both spoke together.

"Isn't the su-..."

"The avion-..."

They both laughed and the tension, like a thin web across the hazy sky, broke.

"Go on," he said.

"I was going to say isn't the sunset beautiful. I've wondered several times if this was Earth. It seems just like it."

"Nah! There's nowhere left like this on Earth; unspoiled like this. Don't forget Brady's postulation."

"Oh how could I forget Brady's postulation?" she laughed.

"'The closeness of an ecology to Earth's is proportional to its geophysical likeness.' *Not* 'closeness … .' Something like that."

"Congruence."

"Yeah. *That's* it. Geophysics and evolution was never my strong point. I only did it as a minor for a year anyway. Hm." She smiled.

"What are you smiling about?" he asked.

"Oh just thinking about the academy. Wondering what they're all doing back there; my friends, hm. What were you going to say?"

"Oh nothing. Just that the avionics are not the real problem."

"Oh?"

He gestured to the dunes around them. "How are we gonna dig it out of the sand?"

"Hm. Gonna have to think about that. Shouldn't Stone be back by now? I hope he's alright. I wonder if he can see the stars."

***

By now, it had grown completely dark but they could only see a dull bluish black, with slowly shifting subtle patterns, overhead. They could not see any stars.

When they had entered the planet's atmosphere, all the land masses which they could detect on the failing radar had been obliterated by a faint haze, too evenly spread for cloud cover. This is what obliterated the stars now.

After a while, sitting watching the night sky, Dee heard Jay's breathing become regular and deeper and then he guessed she must be sleeping. He had never been this close to a sleeping woman other than his two little sisters and possibly his mother, when very young. He often thought how beautiful Jay was. Her blue eyes, rounded face, pouting lips and full head of glossy, black hair were his idea of the ideal woman. He even likd her slim body although Stone complained that her breasts were too small. Ironically, Dee had never entertained the thought of having her for himself because Stone seemed to consider her his own prey, exclusively. Dee enjoyed the feeling of being next to a sleeping woman. He found himself imagining spending pleasant moments with her, walking in one of the parks near the academy, or even on J2, where he had been born. Then his thoughts turned to darker fantasies and he grinned to himself. However, he made sure to stay alert while his imagination wondered under the warm night sky.

***

Eventually, Dee became quite cold and stiff. He found he couldn't move his legs. Forcing himself up, he stamped his feet. Jay woke up.

"Have I been asleep?" she murmured.

"Uh huh." He added, "I thought I heard something a while ago. It's not far from dawn. I don't think he could find us now, even if he were out here."

"Stone?" she asked.

"Yeah."

"You think we should go inside, hm?"

"Yeah."

"Oh. Okay."

When the airlock closed, she asked him tentatively, "You don't think he's dead do you? I mean he is okay isn't he?"

"I'm sure he is. I bet he is. He's a wily bugger."

They both lay on the slanted bunks and tried to sleep. Jay slipped into unconsciousness last.

***

Jay woke first. She opened the airlock and paded around the ship's hull before she did anything else. She kept her arms folded for warmth, in the cool air an hour after dawn. She could see no sign of Stone so she went back inside and shook Dee.

"Wake up Dee. There's no sign of him. I think, maybe, we should go look for him. Find all the provisions we have – all of it. I'll wait outside."

"One Crazy-Lemon Chew, one small plastic bottle of water, and one Snookie bar, Classic," said Dee after a search.

"That's it? It's not much Dee, hm."

"No and you had to have a Classic. Not even nuts in it!"

"Sorry. I don't like the ones with nuts."

"Traditionalist."

"Not *now* Dee." He felt excited but he wasn't sure why. His face turned red.

"Hey!"

They both stood bolt upright at the sound of the familiar voice. It came from the tail end of the ship.

"It's me!"

"Stone! Jeez, you bastard. You're back. Did you find anything?" inquired Dee.

"Fuckit! I am fucked!" Stone managed to reach the welt of disrupted sand around the airlock and half-fell against the side of the ship, panting. His face dripped with sweat.

"Where's the suit? Are you okay?" asked Jay.

"Left it. Go back. Water."

***

A report of a stolen luxury cruiser had finally reached the desk of Detective Sergeant Rayburn on J6. Earlier, he had received another report of three missing kids from the Space Academy. Now he looked at both folders on his desk and chewed another pop-ice. Before long, he had put both folders together and put out an APB on light cruiser J6LCN 0067 to all sectors of the Interplanetary Police Patrol.

The missing-kids report had been submitted by the Academy. He knew that he would have to contact the parents soon but something bothered him about the description of one of the kids. He looked again at the photo of one of them; greasy hair in a slick stripe down the centre of his head and a lopsided grin. Not a tall kid, and hunched. He looked shifty, and Rayburn felt sure he had seen him before. He cast his mind back over cases going back two years, then five and then almost ten. Then he remembered the case of a kid who had stolen a small freighter and tried to reach the rebels on Earth. Very dangerous and illegal, the case had stuck out because of the sheer audacity of the trip. But the kid's explanation had stuck in his mind the most:

"I wanted to do an interview with one of the rebel leaders."

Rayburn took his feet off the desk, hauled himself out of the chair, and walked over to the rack of disks where old files were stored. Only *he* backed up his old files to disk, and when the central hub had been corrupted, his were some of the only ones left. Now he was Mr Popular at work and he had received a raise as a reward. He found the disk for the period he wanted and slid it into the drive on his terminal. He called up the case and looked at the photo.

It's the same kid. Much older, but it's him.

He thought the same thing now as he had thought then:

What would a kid enrolled in his first year at the ultra-conservative Space Academy be doing trying to interview rebels?

***

Stone had slept until the early evening when he woke, hungry.

"What's left to eat? Did you check everything?" he asked groggily.

"We have a Snookie bar, dude, but it's a Classic." Dee cast a sad glance at Jay.

"Thanks amigo," she shot back at him.

Stone caught the tone in her voice and cast a look at Dee. They let him eat the Snookie bar before admitting only the Crazy-Lemon Chew remained.

"We need food, Stone... and water," said Jay. "We desperately need *that*. Did you find any?"

"Yep. Water... lots of it. A river in fact. Didn't try it though. Might not even be water. We need that survival manual you downloaded Dee so we can test it. Food. Hm. Might be more tricky. Saw plenty we *could* eat, birds and lizards, but hard to catch. 'Course there's always fish."

"How about the stars?" Dee asked.

"Stayed up all night for those! I got to a fairly high place, on one of those cliffs overlooking the canyon, about lunch time. Fuck, it was hot! I was sweating like a pig, as they say. I holed up and waited till night. Heard lots of weird stuff. Anyway that mist or whatever kept rolling over but occasionally I would see some stars. Not enough but I waited and not long before dawn I saw it!"

"What?" Dee asked.

"Well... I'm not that good at stars but better than you Dee and I recognised Orion and Taurus. But you know?"

"What?" both the others asked together.

"It's not right! I mean Orion looks about right if you were near Earth but he's a bit thin and his leg and arm are higher than usual. And what's more, there's a really bright star above Orion, just to the left of Taurus. That shouldn't be *there*! Never seen it before."

"Oh," said Jay sadly.

"Yep. We're not on Earth."

"Shit!" shouted Dee, twisting around and striding off. "I knew it was probably too much to ask for but *not* Earth? Shit! That means we could be just about anywhere but a fuck of a long way from where we want to be. Nobody will ever find us!"

"Nope. We got to get outta here on our own," announced Stone. "I been thinking. We have to leave the ship for now. We can't dig it out on our own, least not now. We need to get supplied with water and food, and then maybe come back. We have to leave tonight. It's no good walking across the sand and salt in the day without water. We should be okay to reach the river but we need some water in case that's no good. I know where we can get it."

They both looked at him expectantly.

"Air-con condensers. I read somewhere that water collects in there from the humidity and then it's sucked in and purified and passed round again. It won't taste nice but it's water. We have to boil it."

"Yeah that's it dude!" said Dee excitedly.

Jay looked at Stone's dirty face and the stripe of black hair down the centre of his head and thought how ill he looked. She guessed they would all look that bad by the end of the next day so she didn't say anything. She had also noted how happy she had been to see this runty kid when he had come around the side of the ship, more than happy to see him alive. With his angular face, like a badly drawn cartoon, and a downtrodden attitude resulting in everlasting anger, he evinced in her the deepest protective instinct. She hated herself for it.

But he's shorter than me and six months younger. He certainly does need looking after!

After searching the ship for anything they could take, cutlery, containers, blankets, a few tools, electrical cables for tying things, some plastic sheeting, a few pocket lights and, best of all, a survival pack which included salt tablets, purifiers and a first-aid kit, they piled it all up outside the airlock. Dee and Jay went through the ship, removing panels near the ceiling until they located the condenser unit. They boiled the half-gallon of stale water they found there using the n-gen.

"Fire! We'll need fire," said Dee. "I've had an idea. Found these three heavy-duty power packs; if we disconnect one of the com units and all of the headbands next to each bunk, we may be able to get at some basic information or even get an uplink if anything comes looking for us. It will work off the power packs and we can use the bare wires to light fires. There's enough charge to last weeks!"

They packed everything they could take into some kit bags they had brought with them on the trip and gathered the rest up in the bed sheets. They then tied these into bundles and threaded the containers, which had handles, onto the cables and material strips they used as straps. Then they sat down outside the ship. Stone leaned against its side. The other two leaned against the packs, half-facing along the slope of sand. They all looked east to where the red sun would rise in a few hours.

"Honestly! Why did I ever come with you on this joyride?" asked Jay. "You two had a really bad reputation at the academy! There I was, graduated, about to become a successful woman, and I let these two good-for-nothings take me out in a ship and I end up here!"

"You were a nerd and you wanted to fit in," stated Stone.

"*Stone*?" protested Dee. "She was just bored, like we were, and wanted some fun."

Stone noticed Dee's hand resting lightly on Jay's hand.

"I guess. You're not defending her now as just a gentleman, *are* you Dee?"

"What did *you two* come for then?" Jay shot at him.

Neither answered.

"Don't worry. I know what you *both* had in mind," she explained. She looked up at the sky. "I'm not that naïve, hm!"

Dee squeezed her hand, almost involuntarily.

Letting out a long blast of air Stone stood up. "Right, time to go."

***

Detective Sergeant Rayburn waited four hours before calling the parents of the missing kids. He still had a few hours before the Academy would contact the parents themselves but the APB hadn't come up with anything and he thought they might give him some clues as to where the kids could have gone. He called Stone's parents first. He met with a storm of protest and anger coming the other way over the video link.

"Calm down, calm down. It's early days!" he replied.

He ended the call as soon as he could and called the other parents. When he put the phone down after the last tirade of abuse, he noticed the red bleeper flashing on his personal com unit, set to 'silent.'

"Space kids! They don't change. Most arrogant kids on the block and their parents are even worse! Talk about pushy!" He pressed the 'play' button.

"Sergeant Rayburn? You got a call from one of those new Interplanetary Police Patrol units operating in deep space. That cruiser that the kids took answered an ID call nearly two days ago in the Alpha Centauri region. Nothing since then." The message ended. He replayed it several times. Another pop-ice melted slowly between his motionless teeth.

***

When the space-suited figures finally reached the pancake of limestone at the east end of the valley, it was two hours after dawn. Stone felt too exhausted to continue without a break. He lay panting on his back where he had fallen. Dee dragged him into some shade where Jay gave him the last few mouthfuls of water.

When he had recovered enough to open his eyes, she asked him, "How much further to the river?"

Stone looked around him. "I dunno. Maybe... less than an hour."

"Can you make it? Dee and I can carry some of your stuff."

"Yeah. I can make it. Fuckit!"

After only a few minutes, Stone stopped and pointed to a rock to their right. He croaked, "Suit! There!"

"Leave it, Stone!" Dee called back to him.

Stone stood in the shade of the rock and looked down at the suit. "No! Look some critter's already had a peck at it. It won't survive the night and we might get away and *then* I might need it!"

His voice sounded urgent, which tugged at Jay's emotions.

"Critter? Critter? You're not in one of those old Western movies Stoney." Dee laughed.

"*Dee?*" admonished Jay.

She put down her pack in the dust, picked up the suit and tied it in with the rest of the clutter suspended from the straps. She hauled the pack back onto her shoulders and puffed out as she stepped after Dee.

Stone followed.

The sun burned cruelly and they felt like ants tortured under a kid's magnifying glass. Keeping to the left side of the canyon, they occasionally found some shade where the steep sides veered to the left around a bend. The walls became steeper, giving them more protection from the merciless sun.

Stone stopped when saw something he recognised; a shoulder of rock, which served as a ramp up on to the lip of the canyon on his left. He called to Jay and Dee, walking twenty yards in front of him with their hands lightly touching:

"Here!" He could hardly hear his own voice. He swallowed, licked his lips and croaked, "This is where I went up. The water is only another ten minutes. I didn't see it until I came back down, further along, 'cos I couldn't find the same way back."

He pointed ahead and they continued along the bottom of the canyon. For a few minutes, they were under the direct glare of the sun again. Stone tried to spit. Nothing came out but a small bead of fluid that stuck to his chin for a few moments before evaporating.

"Fuckit! It must be fifty degrees!"

***

The water-like liquid still swirled along where Stone expected it to be. The stream came out of a cave further on up the canyon but by their feet, it gathered into a pool before it slipped under the limestone floor of the canyon.

All their packs clattered to the ground as they collapsed at the pool's edge. The liquid looked deep, clear and for all the world like water.

"God I want it!" said Stone.

"Wait. Test it, dude!" countered Dee. He put the back of his hand to the surface of the liquid and kept it there for a few minutes before removing it. His skin looked slightly paler, but showed no other sign of reaction. "Feels so cool!"

"What did the manual say about trying liquids?" asked Jay.

"Put a little on your tongue, spit it out, and wait half an hour," replied Dee. Using his finger, he put a few drops on his tongue and waited a moment before spitting it out. "It's water. I'm sure it is! Tastes like it!"

They waited ten minutes but could wait no longer. Stone used both hands to cup some of the liquid and took a big gulp. He took another scoop and gulped again. His whole body felt like a knot and his head throbbed but the water tasted good. He finished by dunking his whole head under the water for a few seconds.

"You crazy idiot Stone!" shouted Dee. "Suppose there are bug-eyed alien piranhas or something?"

Stone laughed.

After tentatively drinking a few mouthfuls, Dee and Jay satisfied themselves with cautiously pouring handfuls of water over their scalps. Finally sated, they all leaned against a large rock in the shadow of the canyon wall.

"There's something I haven't told you," said Stone.

*****

The owner of the second pair of eyes that had seen the three visitors, the previous day, now watched the sun coming up. She awaited the decision of the council.

Shihu had glanced at the large prey-bird circling above the little white figures – like dolls she thought – in the valley far below. At the farthest reach of her daily forage for herbs and shrubs for the pot, she had sat down for a nibble of her takings. She looked far out over the Valley of Salt. That's when she had noticed the new tribe. She had already named them the White Tribe.

As she'd watched, one of them started up the valley while the other two turned and descended slowly towards the salt plain. Then she picked up her sadi bag and started back towards the camp. Rehearsing in her mind what she would tell her sister and mother when she saw them, she knew that she couldn't be seen to be too curious or give the impression that she might have been seen by the White Tribe. She felt acutely aware that, being of mating age, she could not take risks with tribal taboos. Her tribe forbade females to meet new tribes before anyone else. If she did, she would very quickly belong to the new tribe.

***

"*Fires*? Like *camp-fires*? Or maybe forest burning?" asked Jay after Stone had delivered his bombshell.

"Like I said. They didn't *look* like natural fires and, anyway, it was just a glow. I don't even *know* if they were fires but there were two of them, on the horizon to the North West."

"Far apart?" quizzed Dee.

"I don't *know* Dee. They didn't move all night. That's why I think they *might* be camp fires. But I can't be sure. I mean they 'pulsed' a bit. Like fires do."

"Aliens. Must be," Dee said.

"Why?" countered Jay.

"Out here? We all know there are only two star-colonies so far. And they're too sophisticated to be using fire like that."

"Fuck! If they're Anubians we are in deep shit!" she replied.

"Yeah, and suppose they are some new type of alien? Shit Stone, what have you got us into?"

"Fuckit! I knew you'd be like this. That's why I didn't tell you. I thought you would be too scared to come out of the ship if I told you. Listen we don't know *what* they are. Anyway, I doubt they're aliens. Why would Anubians be lighting fires? Anubians are even more sophisticated than we are!"

They were all silent for a while before Stone stood up. "Let's get going. It gets cooler up there." He pointed to the top of the ridge to their left. "And there are trees." They filled every container they had with the water, before starting off.

By noon, they were making better progress. They sought out occasional trees for shade and made for the top of the green-covered hill where Stone had spent the night.

"No need to go all the way up," he pointed out. "Not even sure it would be a good place for a camp. I noticed what looked like some kind of forest when I was coming down."

"Which way, dude?" asked Dee.

"Over there." Stone pointed to the south-west.

***

Now, while the camp's fires fingered the night, Shihu waited for the decision of the council. She couldn't help feeling excited. In *her* lifetime, there had never been a meeting between her tribe and a new one. All the tribes she knew were already 'momago,' taboo. Strict tribal boundaries, marked by icons and other macabre signs such as skulls, were enforced, and breaches led to war. The tribes co-operated only when the New Gods were present. Those times were long gone.

She had given them the best description she could of the three tiny figures in white near the Valley of Salt but they had gone over the details with her again and again. Looking at some of the suspicious, rheumy pairs of old eyes, balanced like worn-out old marbles on the leathery cheeks, she had become scared and prayed silently to the god B'ah as she had been taught as a little girl. All the elders smiled at her and seemed satisfied.

One of the younger men had spread his arms wide to indicate that all should be silent. A group of elders, followed by the Chief, emerged from his house to make an announcement.

***

"Fuckit! So did you see anything *at all* that we could eat today Jay? I mean besides that cactus?" Stone sat up. "I mean all those special courses you took as captain material, all those 'ologies' and 'otanies'; there must have been something we can *eat*?"

"That plant I saw earlier," she replied. "I nearly pulled it up for the tuber, but it had some reddish blotches on the leaves, which didn't look right, hm. We'll just have to eat this. I think it's some kind of cactus."

"Great!" Stone murmured.

"It's getting cold. Was it like this last night, Stone?" Jay asked.

"Oh yeah I forgot to tell you... that was the reason I was so knackered. I kept walking most of the night to keep warm. I went round and around the top of the hill. That's how I saw the fires." He closed his eyes, and his breathing soon became even, and deep.

"Asleep!" Dee observed, whispering.

"I don't like it Dee," whispered Jay. "He's getting worse, hm. I think last night may have taken more out of him than he wants to admit."

"I know. Tomorrow we *have* to find something to eat. I'm hoping we might reach that patch of green too though. Trees, if they *are* trees, have to mean some kind of nuts, or fruit, or something."

***

"Fuckit!" Stone said, sitting up. "I could do with a beer or something to smoke, chum maybe!"

Jay changed the subject. "I'm still wondering if we're near either of those two star-colonies … what were they again?"

"Oh Jay! Come on! Every cadet knows that lesson backwards. The first star-colony…" Stone started, and the others joined in. " … in the constellation of Libra, is twenty point five light years from earth and was named Arcturon. Its gravity is one point six times that of earth and it is a rocky planet but with plenty of water which can sustain life. It has a period of thirty-seven days."

They all laughed. Then Dee continued before the others joined in:

"The second colony, in the constellation of Aquarius, is fifteen light years from earth and named Thebes. It is four times the radius of Earth, rocky and hot with a gravity one point three times that of Earth. There is no natural water but an abundance of free energy in the form of volcanic heat. Its period is only two days." Jay and Dee laughed. Stone grinned.

"So what else do we know about Arcturon?" asked Jay.

"Well it ain't nothing like this babe!" replied Stone. His voice full of ironic spleen. "This is heaven compared with that! We've all seen the pictures; thin red soil, few plants that will grow, weak atmosphere. This ain't nothing like that!"

"Babe! Don't call me that!" She laughed. "No. You're right. It *is* like heaven... in a way. Actually, I am amazed just how like Earth it is, or how I *imagine* Earth anyway. The plants are really, *really* similar."

"Yeah! You're right," said Dee. "It hadn't occurred to me, but ye know *what*? *Maybe* we discovered a new world!" Both Stone and Dee looked at each other knowingly.

She noticed. "What are you both thinking? *Spill!*"

"Are you thinking what I'm thinking Dee?"

"Think so Stoney!"

"Shall we tell her?"

"Unfortunately I think we gotta."

"Aw. Well, Jessica. It just might be that we are all going to get very, very rich. I mean if this is a new planet, and we've stumbled upon it..."

"Hm. Yes I see what you... what's that?"

A bleeping sound came from Dee's pack. He jumped up and grabbed it. Ripping the top open, he rummaged for a few seconds before pulling out a flashing headband. He quickly put it on and said, "Download." After a few seconds his shoulders slumped. "Shit! I left it on. Just a software update from the ship, although why it waited until now is anybody's guess!"

"Ah well. For a second ... hm," said Jay

"Yeah." Stone closed his eyes and leaned back against the tree.

Dee switched a pocket light on and placed it the centre of their little group, with its beam pointing towards the ground. Darkness had fallen now; they could not even see a moon in the misty sky.

"So *how* did we get here Stone?" asked Jay after a long, tense silence filled only by the sound of something remarkably like crickets. "You said you thought we'd fallen into a worm-hole. I didn't think they existed, just theoretical? How do they work... compared with, say, our drive?"

Stone spat. "Ach! Worm-hole is just a slang-term. What we call worm-holes now, are nothing like people thought they would be one hundred years ago. Science isn't my thing, I'm just a damned good pilot, but I know the facts. Like any good journo should. Do you really want to hear it? It's boring?"

"Um, yeah. Tell me. I want to hear what you guys think. Although I am not exactly a brilliant scientist either, it calms me to hear it. And it helps me think. *And* we got time... nothing but time. We can have a *sing-song* later."

Dee and Stone sniggered.

"Okay! Whatever the little lady wan..."

"Little? Same age as you Stone, twenty. And don't underestimate me."

He sat up. "Hm. The universe, our universe, was once thought to contain space-time as a continuum. In 2039, Lovett and Pragurthan put forward an alternative theory that it is made of strips, which form a more or less 2-D surface. They postulated that these strips are constantly shearing and reforming and turn back on themselves to form a loop which is very hard for humans to visualise. Erm... this cannot be described in 3-D geometry. Erm... Okay I better let Dee take over. He's better at this than me."

Dee went on, "Okay. At about the same time space-time bow-waves, or STBs, were discovered at MIT, disturbances in space were also detected, which closely matched the behaviour of these STBs. This, along with the postulation and prediction by J. Schrödinger of a fifth dimension erm... which he called U_d, where U = Universe and d = something loosely termed 'depth,' led to experiments to discover the nature of these strips and STBs. These strips kinda bend and twist much like those elasticheese strips kids love so much. Generally, when you travel very fast through space you will cause these strips to resonate, and like the grain in wood, your ship will follow the path of least resistance, along a strip. Although occasionally the strip may sheer, and then you move from one to another, you don't feel this in your ship; the transition is smooth. Erm... however it's possible to distort these strips in such a way that you can travel great distances in a short period of time."

He paused and Jay interjected, "Is that it?"

Dee continued, "Just as something very light will cause only a very slight ripple when traveling over water, and yet something heavy will cause a bow-wave, so it is with something traveling very fast. A ship traveling near the speed of light will create a bow wave in time as well as space and this is because it gains a small amount of the property called 'depth,' which is not understood yet. At this point, it will cause the strip it is on to stretch and twist and because the strip is distorted from its 2-D form to a 3-D twist, time and distance for you will be distorted. You have entered the 5th dimension of U_d. This is how we travel. And if not for those lights we would still be having a nice cruise around the Universe."

"You are really clever, to understand all this, hm," suggested Jay. "Good to know we're not the only ones who get sick. But what is the inaccuracy with this method. How far off course could we have gotten?"

"Oh it's pretty good. There's about a light-year variation either side of where you want to go, for speeds up to about two-thirds light speed, which is what these cruisers are designed to go at. And we only did the standard hops of ten light years each time. We didn't do anything unusual. We weren't even in unknown space. We were near one of the colonies, about twenty light years from Earth at the time."

Jay fell silent. Stone watched both of their faces, which were lit like ghosts from below by the pocket-light. He sensed they understood each other. He wondered what they thought of him. The thought made him uncomfortable.

"So, the daughter of the famous feminist Sadie MacNamarra training to be a pilot … " he said. "I bet mummy is *real* pleased about that."

"Stone!" Dee objected.

"No, it's okay Dee," interjected Jay. "Let's get this out in the open. I'm happy to talk about this," she said. "You know although you act as if you have the intelligence your first name suggests, that of a stone, I know you're not *that* stupid! Anyway *mummy* is not a feminist. She's a New-genderist, which you *damned well know!* And *no*, she is not particularly pleased about my choice of career. She wanted me to be a designer or something. Something arty." She thought for a moment. "I'm her only child. I think she just doesn't want me to take risks." She added, "With my life."

Stone spat and laughed the bronchial laugh of a heavy smoker. "Oh yeah. New-genderism; what's it mean again?"

"New-genderism, hm: It *celebrates* the difference between men and women but seeks to *empower* women by acknowledging their role as sexual objects, allowing them to own the process of objectivisation."

"But that's so anti the original feminism, it pretty much negates it!" quipped Stone.

"Anybody would think you want to return to the old feminism?"

"Ha!" Stone laughed.

"Well it's just more realistic. Anyway it's what my mother believes, not necessarily what I believe. We talked a lot about it when I was a kid, as you can imagine, and I realised – we both realised and agreed – that I agree with some of it but not all of it."

"So that's why you're a nerd."

"It's very ambitious of you, trying to undermine my confidence by insulting me but I am not that easily led."

"Oh."

"Don't worry, hm. I know why it's particularly tough for young men now. I really do. But that's just something you have to cope with."

"Yeah. Well, to me, women putting a price on themselves, is only one step away from prostitution."

"Hm. That's an interesting point of view..." She shook herself free of a line of thought she didn't relish. "It's not really having a price, it's a sense of value and it's called *credit*."

"That's just a fancy term for a price!"

"No. You misunderstand, hm. It's a means for women to control the negotiating that *would* take place anyway in any approach to a long-term relationship, at least with a man of means."

"Yeah and meanwhile poor guys like Dee and me don't have a chance of getting near you! Do you really enjoy being pawed by old guys and only old guys?"

"That's never happened to me!"

"It will do. But what's more important is that this New-genderism is a class thing … "

"What do you mean?"

"It's taken us nearly two hundred years to virtually eradicate the class system and now you are trying to re-introduce it! Like I said, guys like me and Dee don't stand a chance!"

"That's not class! That's called 'living within your means!'"

"Hm. So how about replicants. Would you go out with a rich replicant?"

"No … . Of course *not*."

"Why, 'Of course not?' *That's* class!"

"I thought you said there was no class anymore, except New-genderism?"

"Yeah, well maybe I was wrong. I forgot replicants."

"And didn't your dad, the *great war hero* Jake Nanden, think he was a replicant once? And wasn't he happier when he found out he wasn't?"

"Hey! That's not fair! I don't like the bastard but at least he never looks *down* on replicants, now he knows he *isn't* one! He has done a lot of work to give them equal rights! In fact, maybe he's not so bad, after all. Wow! I never thought I would say that! Only an idiot like you could make me feel *that*!"

"Can't you two *stop*!" Dee cut in. "This is getting nasty. Somebody is going to get hurt!"

"Somebody already is!" Jay replied. "Sorry Stone. I was out of order. I'm *not* a snob."

"Sounds like it to *me*," Stone snarled. "Well anyway. I can't see that it's much fun mixing with men much older than you anyway. I'm not a virgin, by the way."

"Oh? Well there is only one way you could have got it," she replied.

"Yep."

"Stone!" Dee interjected.

"I am going to sleep," Stone announced.

Stone wearily rolled out some of the unused sheeting for them all to lay on and placed his pack, as a pillow, at one corner. He lay on his back, looking up at the sky. Not long passed before Jay and Dee joined him. To his surprise, Jay lay in the middle. He thought he would fall asleep immediately but he couldn't sleep at all. He lay there listening to her breathing, waiting for what he anticipated. Finally, he heard the other two whispering and then he felt Jay move slightly away from him. It made him angry.

This is crazy; after all, the whole reason Dee and I had talked her into coming was to seduce her! But I guess I thought it would be me who might succeed!

When he did finally sleep, he played the disaster that had befallen them over and over again; the two red beacons a few miles apart, blinking slowly in unison and then the feeling of falling as the ship appeared to steer itself between the lights and they lost control.

***

Stone got to his feet and opened his eyes. He felt a lot better. His sleep had been heavy, so heavy that his arm, which had lain under him, felt numb. The others had suffered indigestion from their supper.

Rather than wallow in self-pity, Jay organised them to pack and not long after dawn, they were off.

"Are we ready to go?" called Jay, hoisting her pack onto her back.

"Pass me a headband Dee?" Stone asked.

"Why?"

"Music."

"Oh. Here you go dude."

"Thanks! Fuckit!"

Setting off, Stone turned the volume up full. Jim Hendrix blasted into his ears.

Not that they will know who he is, apart from the guy who wrote the USAC anthem, which is wrong. He just played the new version!

They descended into a shallow valley and Jay led them up the other side. When they reached the ridge, they could see they were not far from the patch of green they had been aiming for. They could also see that the green was actually trees, very big trees.

"Another two hours," guessed Dee.

They started descending another shallow slope and near the bottom Jay and Dee halted. Stone came up to them.

"What's up?"

"There!" Jay pointed to a strange bush, tall, with something white on top, in the middle of what seemed like a dried creek bed. But Stone could see it wasn't a bush. When they were ten feet away, they stopped in horror. They knew then exactly what it was, the carcass of a humanoid creature leaning against a pole.

The head, hands and feet of the carcass had been hacked off. The chest had been cut open from just below the neck to the navel and by the hollow look of the body, the entrails had been removed. The slit lay wide open like a rancid grin. The whole body had been daubed with some white substance, which seemed to have preserved it, since even though it had clearly dried out, it still looked whole, like a leather, human-shaped bag.

Curiously and most disturbingly for Stone, the head had been replaced by a wicker hat, again painted white. The hat, although roughly made, had been fashioned like a pyramid.

***

Shihu's father, Makya, had started sharpening his spear before dawn.

Now I might fight, as a warrior should. There are not so many good battles these days! This might be a time to win honour.

Stationed along the tribe's border, when the single flash of a shiny mirror came from the north, Makya, and his friend Istaqa stood up and began to run towards it. They soon joined the rest of the warriors. Then, they too too looked down at the strangers in the creek-bed.

***

"What the fuck!" Stone said peering around Dee's shoulders at the white carcass leaning against the pole.

"Looks like a man," whispered Jay.

"Oh shit!" said Dee.

"What... hm... what has happened to him... it?" Jay asked.

"Fuckit! I don't get a good feeling about this place. I think it's some kind of tribal boundary marker. Unless he did something really, really wrong."

"Bad!" whispered Dee. Neither Jay nor Stone were sure if he just thought the scene bad or wanted to correct Stone.

"Fuckit! Well we can't go any further," declared Stone.

"We go up this creek-bed," said Jay, "which seems to come from the trees. That's where we want to go and I'm guessing it forms the boundary for this tribe, whoever they are. Also, there might even be some water. Maybe we'll be safe if we don't cross the creek."

The others fell in behind her. They moved along the creek-bed for a while.

"Jay?"

"Yeah? What is it Dee?"

"I think we should stop. Don't do anything sudden. I think they've found us."

They looked up to the top of the bank on their left. Two round, red-painted faces were peering over the top at them.

The two red-faced men stood up. One held a spear, the other a crude axe. They didn't speak but seemed almost to look through the space-travellers.

More men joined those on the bank, coming from the north and south. Finally, several came cautiously up on their bank, behind them, and so they were surrounded. Still nobody spoke, each party assessing the other.

A taller man than the rest pushed through the group on the far bank and stood proudly, holding his axe out to the side. His face had two horizontal white stripes, one below and one above his fiery eyes. He said something.

"What did he say, Jay?" whispered Stone.

"I don't know. How should *I* know?"

"Well *you've* done the basic language skills course."

Each of his words seemed to hurt the silence so Stone said no more.

Jay's training, forgotten until that moment, kicked in and she held her hands out, palms upward, in a gesture that she had been told would be universally accepted as one of peace. The big man didn't move or say anything although he watched her gesture closely. She tried again.

"You try, Dee," she suggested. "I'm a female. Maybe they don't allow females to parley."

"What?" he asked.

"Just do it!" she hissed.

"Okay, okay." He tried the gesture and the big man took a step forward. He crossed his arms on his chest, still holding the axe. Then he carefully replaced it in a strap at his waist. He held both his hands out, mimicking Dee's gesture.

"It worked!" Dee said.

The big man spoke again.

"Just say hello, Dee!" suggested Jay. "Neither of you are going to understand each other at first, but that will come later. Just pretend you understand him."

"Okay. If you *say* so." He projected his voice and tried to sound commanding. "Hello chief. We greet you!" He repeated the hand gesture. The big man smiled and his warriors grinned. Dee went on, "We three..." he said, pointing to Jay and Stone, "welcome you. No, I mean we greet you. We come in peace... from Earth."

"Idiot!" said Stone. "He won't know what that fuckin means, will he?"

"Doesn't matter Stone. Be quiet. We don't need your arrogance right now." interjected Jay.

The big man laughed at something and descended to the creek-bed. He stood only a few feet in front of Dee and Dee felt scared.

"Oh shit. He has an axe," he murmured.

"Don't show any fear!" Jay suggested.

The big man gave her an irritated look.

"I think you're on your own Dee," she whispered.

Dee had an idea and slowly took off the pack. He made the 'peace' gesture again and slowly pulled one of the headbands from the top of the pack. He held it towards the chief and pointed to Stone. "Show him what to do Stone."

Stone put the headband on, the lenses covering his eyes, like old-fashioned sunglasses. The chief looked proudly at the other warriors, ostentatiously took the headband and clumsily put it on. He laughed, looking at the world through polarizing filters for the first time, and took them off again. He beckoned for the space-travelers to follow. The warriors, with weapons pointing at the three travelers, led them north along the creek bed.

***

Forcing herself to gaze straight ahead, Darda walked briskly along the bland corridor towards the yellow double doors at the end.

That's nice. Somebody at least has tried to brighten the place up.

She tried not to look at the guard to the right of the doors, hoping he wouldn't bother her, but he thrust forward his laser just two feet in front of her so she stopped. She looked at him.

"ID please Miss." His voice sounded even younger than her soprano.

She hesitated and then held out the plastic for him to read. He snatched it from her, checked it and then stared into her eyes. His eyes seemed to hold utter doom within their dark irises.

She felt like holding her breath.

Suddenly he snapped, "Please go in. When the bell sounds, the time is up. Do not pass anything to your relative. Cameras will be filming you."

He sounded bored.

She pushed open one of the doors and started to breathe normally again.

Scanning the room, she saw perhaps fifteen USAC Ionian Citizens but couldn't spot the one she wanted.

She put her headband back on and checked for messages; none. She switched to 'mirror' and looked at the reflection of her face.

One of man's handiest inventions, I think!

Tiny sensors around the lenses' edges, picked up the minutest reflected light of shiny surfaces nearby, allowing her to see her own face from any angle. She licked her bottom lip to spread the gloss more evenly and add a bit of sparkle.

My mother's blonde hair ... nice face, full lips, blue eyes! One of man's handiest inventions, I think! Not bad! For an IM girl!

She hooked the headband around her neck. Walking to an empty seat, she sat down, just as the double doors on the opposite side of the large meeting-hall opened and a man stepped in.

It's him!

Her heart fluttered and she struggled to get it under control. The tall, good-looking man with blonde hair looked just as she remembered from the vid calls.

"Adam!" She waved her hand above her head and he spotted her. He smiled and walked quickly over, before sitting down facing her.

Under the harsh light high above them, his features looked more sculpted than on the holocam. He still looked calm and kind. She wondered for an instant what he thought of her, but then he spoke.

"You made it! I wondered if you would *be here*. Isn't it great! I feel like a criminal!"

"We are criminals. This is scary, and let's not forget it. I shouldn't be here."

"But you are!" He laughed at his own impertinence. She smiled.

"God, you're more beautiful than I thought!" he added.

"Always what a girl likes to hear, although I could interpret that to mean that you thought I was ugly."

"Ha! Ha! Sorry. I'm not good with words. Anyway you know that isn't true. It's just so good to finally meet, I mean see, you."

"Aren't they both the same?"

"Yes but I like to think that we've known each other for a while. It feels like it."

He put his hand flat on the table and touched the tip of her middle finger with his, startling her. A feeling like an electric shock went through her but she didn't pull away. She instantly felt connected to him, as if by an electrical circuit.

"You must thank Ryeduxi for me, from the bottom of my heart!" he said.

"I will, but she knows. She's a good soul."

They were still, silent.

There seemed too little time for words so they just looked at each other, sharing little flirtations and half-hints of smiles.

She broke the silence after some minutes, looking at her polished nails. "So... so do you feel the same way, now that you have met me?"

"Dear Darda. I think you'll always be the braver of the two of us. Yes, I do. And I want to do what we've talked about."

"Well that's it then! We've taken the first *step*."

"Yes, *cousin*!"

She laughed.

The bell sounded.

"Ten minutes!" she exclaimed. "It's not much! I'll have to go! It's all over. Have a safe journey back."

"Don't forget to say thanks to … To Ry-oo … . Oh I give up! How *do* you pronounced that name?"

"You mean Ry^duxjhi?" She pronounced the name, 'Ry-yiduchi.' "Well, you've seen it on paper. The caret, or 'tent,' the upturned 'V,' you use to extend the vowel in a descending tone and where there is a hyphen, you pronounce it like a hard 'T.' But Ischians don't seem to mind if you ignore *this*! In Ry^duxjhi's name, because the caret is over a gap, you just extend the vowel longer."

"Wow! You're an expert!"

"Not really but I studied Ischian at Uni."

"And their years? Different to ours."

"Yes. Each of our years is forty of theirs. They frequently live to 3200 years!"

"Okay. I have to go! Take care!"

In the instant before her hand left the table, he held it and then let it go. She felt herself redden. As she walked away it felt like she walked on water.

As she pushed open the double-doors, back to her usual life, she saw the sign on the wall, 'Worlds Treaty Organisation: Relatives' Repatriation Service.'

She laughed.

Thank God for it!

***

Ambi-xjhu stared at the black screen, astonished. He couldn't move. If his mouth had been open it would have stayed open.

On the screen, a blue image appeared, like a negative of the food he had eaten the day before, complete with the funnel of his favourite hranî drink.

I've done it!

He repeated the thought out-loud. "I have done it! Yes! Whoo!"

He whacked the desk top with his paw, which hurt. He felt jubilant but he forced himself to take stock.

"Now calm down Ambi. We need to be sure about this. You know how pedantic the council is. Anything dodgy about the discovery and they will attribute it to somebody else. Have to... document everything carefully."

He noted the time, stored a time-stamped image of his desktop, including the screen, and backed up his work immediately. Finally, he said to the security image-recorder, "Discovery made at 03.14," as if defying the image-recorder to prove him wrong. Then he needed witness.

He walked calmly to the portal, peered through it and called the first unfamiliar technician into the office.

"Look at that!" He pointed to the black screen of the strange looking box on the desk. "What do you see?"

"Um. Just an image, a picture of food. Why?"

"Doesn't matter," Ambi-xjhu replied. "Just please note the time and place. It's all recorded. You are my witness. You are looking at the first moment of a great discovery!"

Ambi-xjhu had finished his first prototype screen several days before but in all that time, nothing had shown up on the screen.

Finally, in a moment of sheer reckless speculation, he had wired it up to a good power-source, crammed the whole apparatus into a carrying-case, closed the lid and wandered nonchalantly around the company recreation field on the ship during a lunch break. The risks of radiation-leak alone would be enough to get him sacked if he caught. When he opened the case again and looked at the screen, it still looked blank.

Now it had something, an image of an event that occurred a day before in the room before the screen had ever been there. He didn't yet know quite how but it had captured an echo of an event in history.

***

Unknown Place, Unknown Universe

2. Time's Memory

Somebody called Ambi-xjhu. He didn't want to open his eyes.

"Ambi?"

"Umm?"

"What time do you have to get up? It's nearly 02.00."

"For you baby, I can stay in bed all day long."

"Um hm. That's very flattering." She fell silent, drifting off to sleep again, before a sense of duty forced her to probe again. "But you need to get up, don't you? You told me you were expecting a reply to your holocall to Dr Kek-suîxjh."

Ambi-xjhu craned his neck and forced his eyes to open. He looked at the bland sun lighting the sky, through the panoramic window in the cabin.

"Look Ho-hi. It's gorgeous. I often think it's more beautiful from up here."

She put her face next to his on the pillow and looked at the mountains of Bek-su far below, and then at the sun rising above the planet's curved horizon.

"I sometimes wish I was down there with them but not today," she replied.

"All those fierce, hard, little green soldiers. So angry and so like the toy soldiers I played with as a kid. With their fascist leader! Surely you don't want to be down there with that? Better to be up here, floating in the clouds, invisible. On Ito they don't have armies any more. Did you know that?"

"No war then? Tell me about Ito and the Professor. Will you take me there one day and maybe I can meet him?" It had been a playfully rhetorical question. Visiting Ito would probably be impossible now.

"I only met him after we escaped to Ito. Mine was one of many families split by the selection process to leave Isch-su for Ito. The Selection Council had decreed in the final days that if a selectee was a parent, then in many cases, up to three children under five could accompany them but not the other parent. The thinking behind this seems to have been that both parents would have already passed their genes on to their children, making them valuable too but unless the other parent had been selected separately, there could be no reason to retain them anymore. My mother had been selected, but not my father.”

“Yes. You told me.”

“Did I? Anyway that’s when I met the Prof. He took me under his wing but he wasn’t... like a father figure. I was far too rebellious for that.”

“You still are.” She nuzzled him.

“I saw him more like a partner-in-crime. I don’t know what he saw in me but he seemed to *think* I had talent. He told me so.”

“He was right. Oh he was so-o right!” She pulled the sheets off him and lay on top.

“Now Ho, I am not sure there is time for that!”

“Oh there is! I will be quick.”

He let her take him, and enjoyed giving in to her.

***

Kek-suîxjh’s wife, Hri-hu, leaned over to nuzzle him at the entrance to their apartment. Although he smiled at her, he was still deep in deep thought. Then she licked his ear and he forgot all other thoughts.

How incredibly lucky I am that my partner is still so beautiful and affectionate after over 2500 years together. None of the males I know, get that kind of attention.

She turned and he followed her into the main sunning-area. She pointed to four large funnels of jzu-serinî on the large table.

“Oh I can see there is a lot to do!” he told her.

Oh no! I had forgotten we are having a dinner party tonight!

"Actually dear," he said, "I *had* thought we might do something different; order a take-away, something nice like roasted katahh with a lavish side-salad? I thought I would sacrifice one of my holiday days to pay for it."

Smile. You know she loves surprises.

"Dear Kek! You don't have to do that. We have plenty of money and I think it's a great idea. You do the ordering and I will just polish my nails and preen my ears."

"Your ears are still the *most* gorgeous dear. So *long* and silky! They were always the best and still *are!*"

"Oh Kek! You sweet-tongued rogue, you!"

She does still look great.

A few days later Kek-suîxjh and Hri-hu were invited around to dine with an old friend, Sos-yrîxjh, and his wife. Kek-suîxjh itched to talk to Sos-yrîxjh, besides himself almost the only senior religious person left on Ito.

"Kek! At last the females have gone off to do what they do best, eh? Waffle! Ha! You haven't found any way yet to break the laws of time?"

"Well, we have made a few dents and bends. But actually breaking a hole through it … . That would require not just me but most of our great minds working together and that's just not going to happen now. But as you know we do at least have rudimentary time-travel."

Sos-yrîxjh leaned close to his host and whispered in his ear.

"And how about that bright student of yours, Ambi-xjhu Dilvvyrîxjh? Have you heard from him?"

"I have, but you know it takes many days for messages to reach us from Bek-su. It's rarely more than the bare minimum of information. I don't think he has made much progress with his experiments."

"Hm. I see. And what of the rest of the colony?"

"Yes. There is much to tell," Kek-suîxjh whispered. "The great religious project that almost precipitated the Rift; it has been re-started! Long ago in fact, but I couldn't tell you. A new species, known as the Bekians, has been synthesised from the DNA of Ischians and the higher canine species we kept in captivity since our days on Isch-su."

Sos-yrîxjh's eyes widened. "I wish I had known."

"The new species has been left alone to colonise Bek-su and, with a life-span only one-fifth of ours, there has already been three generations. I hear that they have fascist tendencies already!" He chuckled and his friend smiled. "The Ischian scientists, including Ambi-xjhu, are living either on one of the orbiting space-ships or in one of several ships floating silently and invisibly in Bek-su's sky."

"Ah it must be like Vîu's House! To think of it! To not have a government based on Martial law, no matter how moderate, would be like walking on Isch-su's green velvet skin once more!"

"Ah Sos! You ever were the poet!"

"Why thank you Kek!"

"And of course you know of the new species; humans."

"Ah yes! The humans. What news of them?"

Kek-suîxjh leaned very close to his old friend, so close that his nose touched his friend's ear. His friend raised his ear to pick up the faintest of sounds.

"I tried to contact one of them. Not long after I last saw you. Using the old Paths of the Universal-mind."

His friend slowly nodded but Kek-suîxjh sensed, from scent changes, that he was greatly interested.

"Did you succeed?"

"I think so... though I don't think it did much good. I *did* sense, though, a great yearning for spiritual freedom."

Again his friend nodded slowly. "You took a great risk Kek. We must not speak of this again. Hm. Is he religious, your student?"

"Ha! I have done my best to convert him but, like most youngsters these days, he sees it as part of the problem and not part of the solution."

Both Sos-yrîxjh and Kek-suîxjh relaxed, now they were safely onto the subject of religion.

"I want to do something Sos! I don't really know what but I am old and my hind-paws still itch. Somewhere out there is the planet of our … former God, Vîu, and I want to find it." He looked at Sos-yrîxjh's face. "You don't look so sure."

"No Kek. I am sure you are right. But that's the problem. You can understand why the youngsters have lost faith. We have given them nothing but mirrors! Behind one God lies another and so on, forever!"

"Not forever! But you know Sos, finding the First Planet would be a start..."

"Please!" Sos-yrîxjh held up his hand to pacify Kek, now getting excited. "It's fantasy Kek. What can you do? Steal a spaceship?"

***

Standing up, Ambi-xjhu walked out onto the small stage to deliver his presentation. Never before had he felt so alone. Knowing how conservative most scientists actually are, he expected vilification.

"At 03.14 Bek-su time, twelve days ago, I saw for the very first time an echo through time from the past. Now I would like to share with you the method by which I achieved this."

Tell them you know how hard it will be for them to believe it! No, I mustn't. Keep going.

"As an isotope of the dominant atmospheric gas on both Ito and Isch-su, Helium4 had long been used as a medium for calculating the age of both planets. Its decay allowed this. However, in several abstracts published towards the end of the Common Scientific Period on Isch-su, geo-historians noted that a side effect of using helium4 in the lab was an occasional disturbing 'flash-back,' sometimes, seemingly, from millennia ago. It wasn't uncommon during this time for scientists to be advised to 'take leave' for psychological exhaustion."

He looked up to see the reaction of the small but prestigious audience. They were silent. He cleared his throat.

"However, the consistency of these occurrences had led me to wonder. For my thesis at the end of my major in physics I had experimented with applications for metallic hydrogen, a material that only recently has become possible to manufacture and store easily. Using a plasma field 'frame,' I had been able to mould the new material into shapes, although I had not been able yet to find any practical application for them. Now I think I have."

He looked to one of his arch rivals in the front row and saw a smile creep onto the Ischian's face, a kindly smile.

"First we created a very thin sheet of metallic hydrogen, oh, about the width and height of a paw-wear box. Using laser cooling and using a small power source, we set up an electrical field to layer an extremely thin coat of Helium4 on the front, or 'detector' surface..."

A murmur, repeating the word 'detector,' rippled around the small auditorium. Ambi-xjhu paused.

"Hm... and to keep it there. Of course the super-cooled Hydrogen keeps the Helium4 super-cooled as well and at these temperatures Helium4 is a super fluid. This means that it flows without losing any energy. In effect, even though it is in contact with the metal, this is a frictionless contact. Now the phenomena with Helium4 and flashbacks made me wonder if something is going on at the quantum level within the brain. For those of us not familiar with this, there are some interactions within the brain, some thought processes, which have been proven to take place at the quantum level. Helium4 has some very interesting quantum properties. The total spin of the nucleus, zero, is an integer, so it is a boson. This makes it very, very stable under extreme conditions, which is very useful to us for reasons that will become apparent in a moment. The important thing here is that it flows without losing energy and the metallic hydrogen keeps it at a temperature where it can do this. Now this is the interesting part. My idea, just a hunch, was that quantum events might leave a trace, when they 'decay.' Again, the concept of decay is not one widely accepted so it amounts to a hunch. Now, if some substance were sufficiently sensitive and stable enough, it might be used to record such events by being 'bumped' by the bow-wave of such quantum events."

He looked up. "Are you still with me?"

There were some smiles in the audience and lots of nodding heads.

Ambi-xjhu went on, "Now, not long ago, many physicists ignored the fact that quantum events are going on around us all the time but that this is not natural. What I mean is that this is not the natural state of things. The natural state is for there to be nothing going on and everything else is 'noise.' This idea has only recently started gaining wide acceptance. The main corollary of this is that we believe quantum events can 'decay.' As I said, it is a hunch but my experiment has added weight to the idea. For the experiment, I assumed that this *was* so. I further assumed that, as Hjukrek-suîxjh Ammaadiîxjh postulated, that all quantum events move in unison within the influence of large gravitational entities. That is to say that for the purposes of small-scale experiments, you could assume if an event left a trace, it would remain in place as it decayed relative to its surroundings. Hm, the large gravitational body in this case being the nearest star and perhaps even the planet it is on. Here I was actually wrong. It turned out to be a rather serendipitous error as you will see."

The audience watched his gesturing paws in rapture.

"The last part of this jigsaw is the Helium4-coated metallic hydrogen. I speculated that if the Helium were bumped by a quantum event, it would momentarily leave its super fluid state and lose the characteristic of flowing without losing energy. This might cause it to actually interact with the metallic surface and leave a trace. I was using the model of the old technology behind image capture; the image plate. So I produced my detector and what do you think happened?"

Faces in the audience looked right and left, but then to him again, rapt.

"Nothing! Absolutely nothing! I waited two days, and still nothing! And then I saw it. An image on the screen of my meal from two days before, complete with a funnel of hranî."

There were smirks in the audience.

"But the interesting thing was thatI set up the detector up in the lobby of my office and not the lab. The meal had been placed on the lab work-surface and had never been on the lobby table. And the detector had not been in the lab since before the meal with the hranî. And just to clear things up, I had not had a meal with hranî in the lab or the office in those two days since!"

The audience broke out into a roar of discordant conversation.

"Now I can... I can... Please..!" He waited a moment. "I can tell you now that if I had left the detector on the whole time, there would have been a moment when an image of the blank office wall would have hit the detector and this would have left a blank image."

"You see, I had been wrong when I thought that the quantum effect would remain essentially static in local space. In fact, quantum events drift slightly because of the movement of local space relative to the theoretical absolute space. It's not much of a drift actually, just enough to move ten or fifteen feet in two days. To return to this specific event, as I said, there would have thus been an image of the blank office wall at some point, and when the decayed quantum event of the meal had passed through the detector, it wouldn't have left a trace at all.

This is because, as I had speculated, the minuscule quantum event of the wall passing would have bumped the Helium, which would then have left its quantum state for an instant and 'etched' the surface of the metallic hydrogen. The later event would not have shown. So you see, it had been sheer luck that I had turned the detector off for hours before the successful detection."

Ambi-xjhu didn't mention the fact that he had taken a walk around the recreation field with the detector in a carrying-case.

The murmurs of astonishment were reaching a climax. Finally, the Principle Scientist had to stand up and raise his hands from the front row to calm the audience.

"I hear you asking; why did it only detect the meal and drink and why did it take two days? This is something I have pondered quite a lot. At the moment, I am not sure. It needs more experimentation. But I believe that the quantum decay levels impart a certain energy to the Helium and this reduces with time. It just happened that this particular charge, from a small battery, had been exactly that needed to detect an event that happened two days ago. Again, I very fortunate. If I had used a bigger charge, I might have run the experiment for a month and concluded that it didn't work. For the rest of it, basically, I have used a kerraline casing to contain and insulate the extreme cold temperature and, as I mentioned, a small battery, all I needed to maintain the right kind of charge. Then all you need is a weak laser-beam to scan the surface of the plate for any deviation that indicates an image has formed. This is then passed to the monitor screen on top. The weakness, at the moment, is that the plate can only store one image before needing to be wiped clean. I think this is an easy matter to fix though. The metal surface can simply be momentarily melted to remove the image. Well gentlemen, there you have it. The galaxy, and perhaps the Universe's, first event-echo detector."

There followed a long silence, during which Ambi-xjhu's heart stopped beating and his career flashed before his eyes. Then the Principle Scientist stood up and started clapping. His claps were swamped by a sudden storm of clapping and shouts of approval from the audience. Ambi-xjhu was a star.

***

"We're getting near the trees!" whispered Dee to Stone. "Do you think their camp is there?"

"I don't know but they look awfully human."

"Yeah. I am thinking something different to that thought that we had before. And it's not such a pleasant one."

"Fuckit! I know what you mean."

"Wow! Will you look at those *trees*?" Dee exclaimed. "They must be three-hundred feet tall!"

"My mum talked about *really tall* trees once and I asked her about them; dad had told her about them." Stone said.

After demanding Stone put on his space suit, the tribe's leader instructed a young woman to teach Jay the word for 'Moon and 'Sun' in their language.

"Her name is Shahkyo. It means 'Mink.'" An exhausted Jay explained, lying down next to Dee that night. "I had to tell them you are our leader Stone."

***

Stone woke with a start. He had been dreaming about something which scared him. He couldn't recall it but, as he lay there, a vision came to him.

He stood in a long, brightly-lit corridor in some building, many stories high. Out of the large windows to his left he could see a landscape perhaps half a mile below. The corridor seemed like that of a hospital; beds on the left and doors on the right. At first it seemed pleasant, well lit and brightly painted, but an air of melancholy and decay belied this. Then he noticed the patients. They were headless, some missing limbs. There seemed to be something where their heads should have been, a shimmer as if of something lost. They all seemed confused and were murmuring. The one word he could pick out was, "Why?"

Dee was leaning over him. "Alright mate? Time to get up. Make it quick. Jay and I need to talk to you before they round us up."

They huddled around Stone's bed.

"Jay thinks we should say we came from mountains over the desert. That way they won't look for the ship. We can't risk that."

"No, you're right. Okay. That's our story then."

The question and answer session in the morning took only a few minutes. The first question was, as they had expected; where did they come from? They gave the answer they had rehearsed and after some mutterings, the perplexed red faces accepted this. The second question hadn't been expected.

"They want to know where our suits are, Dee," Jay translated.

"I dunno! Tell them we buried them somewhere."

Jay spoke to the young woman slowly, pronouncing new words awkwardly.

"I told them we buried them in the sand before we reached the salt because we didn't need them anymore."

"Good."

"Yeah but they are asking why Stone still has his."

Dee looked stumped.

The young woman said something. It sounded like a question and Jay answered.

"What did you tell her?"

"I said he still has the suit because he's the leader."

"The leader!" Stone laughed.

She replied tersely, "It was all I could think of."

***

Shihu finished combing her long brown hair and hurriedly braided it while walking towards the back of the gathering crowd. A chant of "The visitors are coming!" rose up.

Shihu's mother and older sister were still frantically preparing food. Shihu had only just enough time to grab her little nephew and run to the stream with him under her arms for a quick bath. He struggled and told her she was the, "Worst auntie in the world!"

She could only catch glimpses of the visitors between the shoulders and arms of others as they entered the village. Two men and a... woman! It was a very strange thing for a woman to be openly traveling with two men to meet a new tribe.

The crowd, in a semi-circle around the entrance to the village, obscured the activity as the other villages laid out the last of the food and drink on long mats between the huts.

Shihu glanced at her sister and mother and giggled. She hadn't seen her sister move so fast for years.

When they had all finally sat down to feast, the Chief spoke to them. In a loud voice he told them where the visitors had come from and then their names. The names sounded strange to her ears:

The Chief smiled at each in turn. "The visitors' names are Dee-Low, Stone and Jessica. They are to be treated with great honour. They shall eat and drink as much as they want."

He pointed to the three hastily restored huts. Each hut, made of something like wattle and daub, had only one opening, facing east, and the entrance, with an awning, lay on the north side. "These houses, we give to them for their use. Now let us feast into the night!"

A great whoop went up from the men and the women ululated. This lasted several minutes before the sound of laughter and gourd crashing against gourd replaced it.

After only a light snack, the drummer started beating the rhythm to the Life Dance. There was much pounding of dust and as Shihu stamped down the line, she caught her first proper sight of the visitors. She noted that two, a man and the woman, leaned towards each other.

They are the couple talked about.

She glanced at the man on his own.

He is not bad looking. He has the typical young warrior's hair. He is short but looks intelligent.

Although they were strangely dressed, the visitor's faces looked friendly. In fact, they looked overawed by the spectacle put on for them. The chief seemed in an ebullient mood, getting quickly drunk on the strongest kech.

Only late that night did Shihu came really close to the strangers. As was the custom, during great feasts, even the women would drink a little kech. They drank away from the sight of the men and from gourds secretly charged. One of Shihu's friends, Honovi had gained notoriety from her fondness for alcohol. Shihu had seen her merrily filling the gourds of other girls behind a hut whilst leaning against a doorpost for support. Even Shihu had tasted a little that evening and so, when asked to serve the guests, she felt not the slightest bit nervous. She carried a large gourd of kech to them and then three platters of meat.

"Serve us!" the Chief said to her. "Be quick girl!"

She lowered her head before each of the guests when she approached, them, as befitted her lowly station within the tribe. In the flickering firelight she stole a quick glance at the young woman only a few feet from her, the woman's mate and then the one who stood alone.

She is pretty. Her mate is the better looking man.

Aware that men within the tribe considered her attractive, Shihu had been taking her time agreeing to settle with any of the men. In fact, she wasn't really attracted to any of them and secretly wished for a chance encounter with another tribe. Women rarely married outside the tribe unless during wartime but she couldn't help being hopeful.

She smiled briefly at the man who stood alone. He smiled back for a fraction of a second and then looked away. Shihu felt something move in her. Her heart fluttered and she felt as if she had been suddenly heated by a fire.

The chief said something to the guests and nodded towards her.

I shouldn't have smiled at him. I am too bold. Now the other women will think I am a fool!

She lowered her eyes even further and quickly backed away from the guests.

"What are you looking at Stone? Like what you see?" said Jay.

Stone looked away from the girl who had served him, prettier than the rest of the girls he had seen in the village. Prettier even than Shahkyo.

"She is the Makya's daughter," said the chief. He paused for a moment. "She is the one who first saw you in the Valley of Salt."

Jay translated in a whisper and the chief obliged by not looking at her.

The chief fell silent. He looked at Stone for a long while. Stone held his gaze and, when the solemn brown eyes finally looked away, he understood that the chief had been sizing him up for something.

***

Stone felt like a fool when he knocked on the door of Jay and Dee's hut, late the following morning.

A strange dawn chorus had passed. Stone had listened to the tribe murmuring incantations from within their houses while facing east through the openings in their huts.

*Bloody weird, all these flowers all over our porches.
Makes it seem like some tiny bit of suburbia!*

His neighbours took some time to answer.

"Who is it?" answered Dee eventually from inside.

"Me!"

"Oh. Wait! Okay come in!"

Stone felt a pang of jealousy, like pain, seeing Jays' bare back in the pile of furs. Dee held her close to protect her nakedness from Stone's eyes. With his other hand he rubbed his eyes.

"What is it mate? It's a bit early!"

"It's nearly midday. Anyway are you two gonna get up. Like *ever*!" He wanted to say something about Jay's apparent abandonment of her self-imposed celibacy but held his tongue for his friend's sake.

Sitting cross-legged around a low table, the three drank an infusion of herbs, not unlike tea but with the aroma of pine.

"Have either of you ever met a medicine man?"

"What! A doctor?"

"No Dee. I mean a medicine man, like a witchdoctor. I met one once on one of my drug-fueled joy-rides. Before your time Dee. Mexican. Anyway, deep, he was. He told me lots of strange things but that chief last night.... I realised he is some kind of medicine-man. He has a powerful medicine. He knows things! He sees things!"

"Oh. *Now* I know what you're talking about, dude! You mean like those American Indians."

"Yes, and you know what I've been thinking? I think that these guys are just *too* like American Indians. In fact I'm starting to think this *might be* Earth." He waited for the expected intakes of breath and wasn't disappointed. "Oh, I dunno, maybe twenty, maybe one hundred thousand years ago. Hard to say."

"Jeez! You really think so dude?"

Jay said nothing.

"Been thinking. There's a way we can test this. Dee, do you still have some power left in those headbands?"

"Yep! Not for much longer though."

"What we need to do is measure the length of a day, *exactly*!"

"Oh, I see what you're getting at!"

"Yes!" Jay exclaimed.

"If it's exactly twenty-four hours by the time on your headband, then it's a near certainty this is Earth. Add to that the gravity, which feels damned like Earth's, and I think we could be certain. 'Course, we could measure the gravity but I don't think we need to."

"No. You're right. There's a problem though, measuring the length of a day. We can't see the moon and can only see the sun's glow through the haze. It won't be precise."

"It will be accurate enough. We should start tomorrow morning. Evenings, there's always too much going on. I'll come with you."

***

A short time later, Stone and Dee wondered aimlessly around the village, waving at villagers who made a fuss of them.

"Dee. I've realised something."

"Go on mate."

"I realise what a scum I have been. All this journalism is the ultimate career for a dude like me who wants to lay the blame on others and avoid all responsibility themselves. And the joy-riding is just an extension of that. It's what has got us into this mess and you know what?"

"What made you think this?"

"Never mind. I'm going to get us out of here, make sure you two don't take any blame, and I'm going to make a success out of all this. Somehow!"

"Phew! That's quite a lot of thinking you've been doing there Stoney. You sure you're okay? You haven't even sworn since last night."

"Yes. I feel good. I feel like I know what I'm doing. I have something *worthwhile* to do at last. Changing the subject, how is it going with Jay? I'm not jealous. One of us *had* to win!" He elbowed Dee-low in the ribs.

"I reckon you *are* jealous Stone but thanks for taking it this way. She really is *cool*."

"So what does she look like in the buff then, eh? She looks better than we expected don't you think? She doesn't look like a nerd at all now!"

"Oh Stone, don't embarrass me."

"Heh! It's cool."

***

Packing her small sadi bag, Shihu wondered what else she should do or take. Her father had only just told her she would be going on a mammoth hunt with the visitors and they were leaving before the sun had climbed to his highest point in the sky. She felt that the very greatest honour had been bestowed upon her.

Not long after dawn, Stone and Dee had sneaked out of camp with the excuse that their tribe too had a ritual which had to be performed at dawn. They climbed to the top of the nearest bluff. There, they waited for the lip of the sun. Dee had packed one of the headbands and a power pack, just in case.

"Store: Oh five, seventeen and thirty. Finish" he said. A red light flashed once on the headband he held in his hands. As they descended, he placed it back in his pack. Small spurts of dust swirled into mini clouds behind them. They made tiny figures in the vast landscape.

"Dee! Stone! We have to get ready." Jay came up to them when they returned to their houses. "Shahkyo says we're going on some kind of hunt with the Chief. It's a great honour and we can't get out of it! Also Stone, I am going to have to teach you the language. The Chief wants to talk to you about a few things and I won't be allowed to translate. Dee is no good so you will have to learn!"

"Wo! Hold on Jay," Stone replied. "Hunt? What sort of hunt?"

"I don't know. They've spotted some kind of large animal, I think. They seem very excited!"

Shihu carried her sadi bag over one shoulder and a heavier bag with some supplies for the party over the other. She glanced at Stone shyly as she passed and he smiled at her. She looked down and smiled to herself. But when she looked up, she saw Stone, looking at Jay.

Shihu felt disappointed.

She thought, 'That's the second time he has done that. He likes her! What is it my sister who told me once: if you have a rival and she is prettier than you, be nicer than her; if she is nicer than you, be more clever than her; if she is all three, find another man? Hm. I guess the New Gods might think she is prettier than me. Therefore I will be nicer than her.'

Jay turned to Stone. "Stop smiling at her Stone. She'll think you're interested in her."

"Maybe I am. She *is* pretty!"

"Hm. Where do you think we are, *if* this is Earth? Shahkyo told me that her forefathers spoke of a lake that is as wide as the eye can see and it's many miles west of here."

"Those big trees; I remembered more about the story my mum told me. She said they were called Giant Somethingsorother and grew near somewhere called the Mojave Desert. The sea must be the West Coast. I wish I had studied geography more but there didn't seem any point on J6. You could see everywhere from your back garden! I think it's Mexico... somewhere."

"Could be!" added Dee.

Before long, they were off. There were about twenty men but Shahkyo and Shihu were the only women from the tribe. There were also some dogs; called 'sadii' by the tribe. Stone couldn't help noticing that Shihu glanced at him several times furtively. He also noticed her strong, but shapely legs through the slit in the waist of her tunic.

As they walked, Jay started to teach Stone the basics of the natives' language. But she seemed irritable to him. Before long she left him alone to practice his first basic vocabulary.

During Jay's sleep under the giant trees, she had an uneasy dream. Forced to choose between two white fish again and again, each time she heard herself saying, "No," to both. Her sleep the night before the hunt hadn't been much better.

She looked at the two young men accompanying her, then at the warriors all around her and berated herself silently.

I've abandoned my principles! The daughter of Sadie MacNamarra sharing a bed with a man my own age! And he's seen me almost naked! And yet neither Stone nor Dee is really what I'm looking for. Look at all those warriors. They're real men! They probably know more about life than we'll ever know. And yet I would still choose one of my own kind, either Stone or Dee; two delinquent nobodys with bad reputations and no thoughts beyond sex, junk-food and raves. I sometimes wonder how a woman's sensibilities work!

When the sun had started to descend in the western sky, they halted under the canopy of a forest for a feast. Though not many, they had seen some of the giant trees in this forest too.

Preparations for a feast began. A rhythm struck up on the drums, the rhythm to the first dance Stone had seen in the camp.

"It's called the Dance of Life," Shahkya explained to Stone, at Shihu's prompting. Shihu then made it clear that it was her favourite dance.

"Ah! What's the dance about?" Stone asked Jay.

Shihu leaned close to Jay and so did Shahkyo. With their help, Jay explained to Stone:

"The dance of life represents the four stages of life. Sometimes, the bolder boys' noses touch the girls, usually out of sight of elders!"

Shihu's hand brushed Stone's. He took her hand in his. He raised a gourd to his mouth and took a long draft.

***

When the chief stood to make a toast, he urged Stone to his feet. Stone found, to his surprise that he stood taller than the chief.

"Biaichi' danape,'" the chief said, grinning. All the tribe on the hunt grinned and whooped.

Stone glanced at Jay but she shook her head.

"Tsaa'," Stone replied confidently using the only word he knew of their language, the word for 'good.'

The chief slapped him on the back and they sat down to drink more.

The chief said something else and Stone only caught two words he recognized, 'talk' and 'night,' but he smiled back and said, 'Tsaa" again. He found he could get by quite nicely with just this word.

Stone guessed they were close to the rock promontories overlooking the dried salt-lake.

'Perhaps this is significant,' he thought.

After some feasting on rabbits shot by bow on the hunt, the Chief indicated he wanted to talk seriously with Stone. During the afternoon Jay had done her best to increase Stone's vocabulary to cope with the conversation Shahkyo had warned her were coming.

Placing his hand flat against Stone's chest, Chief Cheveya repeated the gesture on his own chest, and then waited for Stone to finish his mouthful. Cheveya had placed five eagle's feathers in the band around his head, whereas normally he had only one.

Stone noticed Shihu in shadow, some distance away. Only her face alone lit up in the firelight. She had marked a horizontal red line on each cheek with paint. He wished he had something to symbolise the gravity of the occasion but decided a serious expression would simply have to do.

Stone understood about one tenth of what Cheveya said; enough, until a long sentence followed by a long pause and the enquiring gaze of the Chief stumped him.

Stone was stumped. Jay had foreseen this however and had taught Shahkyo a few rudimentary English words. She sat just to Stone's left and had the trusty stick and a patch of cleared earth just in case.

She whispered to him, "Ask exchange women. T'ha'adition."

Stone whispered back, "Ah. Hm. Err, you mean how many?"

Shahkyo didn't understand this so he held up his hand and showed first one finger and then five and nodded, encouraging the Chief.

Cheveya shrugged his shoulders and held up eight fingers.

Stone's street-bargaining instinct cut in and he held up six fingers. The Chief appeared to see this as a very serious matter for consideration and after a long pause, deep in thought, he also held up six fingers.

"Stone! We don't have six women!" whispered Dee from further to his left, exasperated.

"Don't worry. He doesn't know that."

The Chief said something else Stone didn't understand and Shahkyo whispered, "Make big deal tribes. F'ha'iends."

Stone repeated his favourite and most powerful word, "Tsaa'!"

The Chief grinned and the serious business of drinking and eating resumed.

Stone leaned in Shahkyo's direction. "No dance tonight?"

He watched Jay and Shahkyo, heads bobbing up and down for a moment before Shahkyo whispered, "No dance. Big danger."

While they were drinking, Stone's eyes often strayed to Shihu and the Chief whispered something to him. He repeated it to Shahkyo, She clasped her hands over her mouth and squealed with laughter before translating it:

"Shihu good woman... Sometimes wild like female deer kicking. Um... like Stone."

Stone swallowed once and smiled at the Chief. He took a long draught of the kech.

"Tsaa'," Stone said, earnestly.

They drank on into the early hours when beds were laid for the visitors. They crawled under the light skins gratefully. Even though it seemed to be high summer, it grew quite cool at night.

"Hey, you two," said Stone quietly before the others could fall asleep. "You know what I said this morning Dee? About getting us out of here?"

"Yesterday Stone. Yes, I remember."

"I been thinking some more. Actually I didn't mention it at the time but there's something else."

"What's that?"

"God!"

"But you don't believe in God."

"No I don't. But that's not the same as knowing for certain that God *doesn't* exist. I really want to know, now, if he exists or not. Oh I know... A few weeks ago, if you had asked me, I would have said, 'Ask my dad.' He's the one who believes in God. And he's real cosy. Well, he's still cosy. He's cosied up to everyone in high society that you can think of. I haven't changed my stance on *that*. It's something else."

Do you know we might be the first real time-travelers in human history? That may change the way people see God forever. Who knows? Perhaps we might even be able to get right back to the beginning of time one day and see if he's there! Anyway for some reason, coming here has made me more inclined to believe in him. I don't know why. I mean, I have never believed he existed but that doesn't mean I am *sure*. Now I want to be sure! One way or the other I want to be sure. That's all.

"Okay dude. Sounds like a big challenge on top of everything else you've got."

"Seems to me you are going to have your hands *too full* to think about God," added Jay.

"What do you mean?"

"Well that girl, Shihu. As far as I can make out, the Chief is pretty keen that she should be a token of the two tribes' alliance that he is planning."

"Oh! Yeah. I know what you mean."

"Go to sleep dude," added Dee.

Stone drifted off, listening to the sound of the sentries set around the camp. They called to each other with brief howls like wild dogs, which Stone later learned were called coyotes. An air of great excitement pervaded the camp although Stone still didn't know what animal they hunted.

***

Stone lay on his back, looking up at the thatching of the hut's roof.

Only the say before, he had thought, 'I haven't had any of those strange visions recently!'

Now, another one burst into his brain. He seemed to be piloting the cruiser, somewhere in space:

"Any idea how to trigger the beacons yet?" Jay said.

"Nope! Working on it!" Dee replied.

"Incoming above!" screamed someone behind Stone. The voice sounded familiar; the voice of a woman with a strange accent. The ship immediately went into a teeth-juddering, up and down vibration. The main burst of light seemed to be outside the cruiser but in the main cabin, hundreds of little points of light turned into ripples.

Where these made contact with objects, these exploded or became pocked with empty craters up to a foot in diameter. Even the floor and partitions had holes in them. Only the skin of the ship seemed to have escaped the disruption.

"Phew! That was bloody close!" shouted Stone, looking behind him.

Stone's mind suddenly cleared and he found himself staring at the roof of the hut again, sweating and panting as if he had really been in a battle.

'I have to tell Jay and Dee about these visions,' he thought. 'But hell, they will just think I am getting madder by the minute. No, not a good idea.'

"Stone! We took the reading! I couldn't wake you."

Dee shouted just before pusing open the door to Stone's hut.

"What?"

The sun's shafts of light were not yet probing through the trees on the hill above them, when Dee shook Stone awake.

"And guess what? It's exactly twenty-four hours... as near as we can make it anyway," added Jay.

"Oh, great! That's good. I mean, it's what I expected, but at least it means we're... *time-travelers*!"

They both laughed.

"Did the chief get suspicious?"

"Nah! They're too busy doing their own praying." Dee laughed.

"And we're all looking for God!" Stone replied.

"Eh?"

"Never mind."

That morning, the dogs were again set to hunt, and this time their pleading howls were answered by some of the men when they ran off to investigate.

"Mumaki," Shihu said to Stone when the men returned.

The dogs were very agitated and strained when they were leashed.

"What's mumaki?" Stone asked Shahkyo. She drew a picture in the dust.

"Elephant?" he ventured.

"I think she means a mammoth," suggsted Jay. "Look at those tusks. Haven't you heard of mammoths in your vast journalistic experiences Stone?"

"No. I don't think so."

"Prehistoric elephants... with long fur. Dangerous... I would think, hm."

"Oh. Wow! Sounds interesting! Are we going to hunt them?"

"I hope not," said Dee from the comfort of his hammock, now strung between two saplings of the great trees.

Preparations for the hunt commenced immediately. From long pouches, each of the warriors took a few small metallic objects. Stone was curious and asked a man if he could look. The man hesitated. Then, in his upturned palm, he held up the metallic objects but he wouldn't let Stone touch them. Until now Stone had only seen the tribesmen using flint arrow-heads but as he looked at the three, crudely made spear tips in the man's hand, he knew what they were made from; iron. They glinted in the evening gloom of the forest as the man turned them. Little flecks of rust contrasted with the highly polished metal of the sharpened edges.

The Chief explained to Shahkyo, who translated for Stone, that the mumaki had moved on to the east. Two of his men would track it until dawn and then they would be ready to attack it.

Late that night, in the cool air under the forest canopy, Dee came rushing up to Stone.

"I can't find Jay!"

Immediately the two split up to search for her.

It took Stone a few minutes to find her, some distance beyond the large tree, in amongst some shrubs and ferns.

"Jay? It's Stone. What's wrong? It's dangerous for you to be out here on your own. Come back to the camp."

"No! I don't want to. I am not crazy about killing an almost extinct animal but Shahkyo told me I won't be allowed on the hunt *because I am a woman*! I'm just angry, that's all. I need a few minutes … ."

"But … ."

"It's not really that anyway. Fuck it Stone! Don't you see? How the fuck are we going to get back home from *30,000, or 100,000 years ago?*" She practically screamed the last few words in his ears and screwed her hands into little fists.

He wanted to touch her shoulder but he knew she would push him away.

"Oh." At first, he didn't know what to say. Then, like an angel of mercy, a single word came into his head: 'spear.'

"The spear heads."

"*What?*"

"They're made of iron."

"So?"

"Well, if there's iron, then they must know how to work metal. If they know how to work metal, they'll be able to help us fix the ship."

"Oh great! So they're experts on soldering and testing quantum computers are they?"

"No, but they can learn. Also, they understand basic astronomy. That can help."

"Well. I'm just pissed off, that's all! I haven't had a proper bath in days, I have no make-up and I'm sick of dried fish … and meat. But most of all I want to *believe* we can get out of here!"

"Yes, so do *I*. And I *do* believe we will."

"Well … when you going to speak to them about it Stone? Now you're the leader, you're gonna have to say something... and soon."

"Yeah. I know that."

"And I hope you're not going to get so settled with that native girl, who is probably just about ready to serve you like a slave and do whatever you want, that you lose the urge to actually *leave* here!"

"Believe me, that's not gonna happen. In fact, part of the reason I'm doing my best to be so amenable is *so* we can get out of here."

The hint of anger in his own voice mollified her a little.

"Sometimes I wonder why I told them you were our leader. I thought I saw something in you, Stone, but now I'm not so sure."

"Saw something in me? I'm not sure what you think you saw, but I can tell you I *will* get us out of here. Even if it kills me."

"And one other thing. I want you to persuade them to let me go on the hunt tomorrow. If *you* can't persuade the chief to stop the killing, I want to try. Okay?"

"But you know what they're like with women. They'll never let you go."

"Well I want you to persuade them."

"Hm."

"Okay? *Okay*?"

"Alright. I'll try, but I am not promising anything."

With that, the tension seemed to go out of her and she accompanied him back to the fire.

***

Kek-suîxjh's world had been turned upside down, not even his original world, which was a dying planet, many million miles away but after over three thousand Ischian years he had come to expect things to be a certain way. Now, they weren't.

The first shift in his paradigm had arrived with a message from Ambi-xjhu. As usual, he'd had to make up a suitable excuse to leave work and then take a circuitous route, doubling back on himself several times, to reach the house of his friend Xi-yrîx. Xi-yrîx still held the Faith and also an amateur deep-space electromagnetic-com hack. Kek-suîxjh suspected that Xi-yrîx didn't actually pick up messages himself from the Outcast colony on Bek-su very often, he didn't have powerful enough equipment, but somewhere, somebody did. Xi-yrîx passed these messages on to Kek-suîxjh and anybody else brave enough, or stupid enough, to be interested. Kek-suîxjh didn't know how they hid their traffic from the authorities and he didn't want to know.

When the great strife, known as the Rift, had started on Ito, which eventually led to the Great Wars, Ambi-xjhu had been one of the religious hard-liners who had refused to recant, and had been condemned to exile in one of three space-ships. Hidden deep within Kek-suîxjh's heart had been the desire to go too but he could never leave his wife.

To make matters worse, the exiles had been incredibly fortunate. Starving and beginning to contemplate cannibalism, one of the scientists made a discovery. Kji-jshxjh finally found a way to harness worm-holes so that the would-be colonists were able to travel great distances in a single hop. After nearly twenty years of traveling, at a distance of nearly one thousand light years from Ito, they had found an inhabited planet which they called Bek-su, the 'blue one.' Named for the dominant colour of the plants and trees, it had abundant life which could sustain a thriving colony of Ischians. Within just a few years they made their greatest discovery; another advanced species on a planet only 100 light years away. These aliens called themselves 'humans.'

Strange, that unlike the Ischians, they did not name themselves after their planet, or the planet for themselves.

These humans, the males being called 'men' and the females, 'women,' also inhabited two other planets near the first but their home planet lay a further 20 light years away and called Earth. Of course it hadn't been long before contact had been initiated. But a great mistake had been made.

Watching safely from a distance, the Ischian outcasts had observed how the humans did not manufacture most of their tools from chlorophyll but instead used derivatives of iron, an element very rare in the Ischian solar system. Hungry to get access to this latter element, the outcasts had bypassed the two colonies withss of the metal. They had gone straight to a moon of the home star-system called Io, where great quantities were mined. Indeed the whole core of the moon consisted of iron, something Ischian scientists had long predicted could occur. But the humans themselves were fighting over the iron, and the Ionians, whom the Ischians had befriended, were the faction that were losing. Ambi-xjhu had told him there had been much ear-pulling in the Council of Exiles over this mistake. Of course the High Council, back on Ito, had been blue with envy once they heard about the new species and the source of iron. The colonists kept their exploitation of worm-holes a secret and some time passed before those on Ito learned about this. The other discovery, that time-travel of a sort was possible and that they did not have access to the technology, also irked the High Council.

* * *

3. The Hunt Begins

Kek-suîxjh put the contraband pod in the player and watched the screen. The face of Ambi-xjhu came on the monitor, a little older and looking more confident but more subdued than last time.

"Hello Master. How I wish we could talk freely without it seeming like a long-distance game of kluxii. Not that I am in anyway trying to outwit you. It's just that every nuance of what you say to me has many months to be reflected upon and turned over in my mind, as if it is some strange game. When is some talented young scientist going to invent a way to send messages through time-space distortions economically? Excuse me for rambling. I had practiced all day what to say but now I find my mind spewing out all sorts of rubbish. Ha! Ha!

"What news? Well the big news, and as big as news can get really, is that I have done it! I have discovered a way to detect time-echoes! Yes!"

The young student's ears were erect and his eyes opened wide. This, together with the wild, sweeping gestures of his hands that often disappeared out of the camera's view, told Kek-suîxjh instantly that his young Protégé felt very excited.

At last. Thank my God. This is really big news!

"Well I won't go into too much detail but I already demonstrated it to the community here. I took every precaution, as you said I should. And you were right. If I hadn't done that, there would have been all sorts of problems. But the Principle Scientist stood up and applauded me! Anyway it involves Helium4, quantum events and metallic-hydrogen. I would send you the paper if I could find a way to do it safely. But more of that later. Anyway, now, perhaps, there is a chance I can find out how time started and where! As you know, this has always been the question that most fascinated me. What is it our God said; the beginning of time is not at the end of a line."

Affection for the young student almost overcame Kek-suîxjh. A tear slowly formed in his eye and soaked into the fur on his cheek.

"The other thing I have to tell you is that I have met somebody. An ischian!"

The young Ischian male grinned artlessly.

"She's a Bekian. Wo! Don't be shocked. It is not like you think. She doesn't look like a dog-female. Ha! No. You see for each generation we had to keep some pure stock as a control and hers would be the last pure-stock. Her family would be one of the last to be introduced and just by accident I met her on the surface of Bek-su! Yes; pure coincidence. Anyway she lives with me now up here on C-One. It must be very strange for her to be looking down on her brethren. Anyway, her name is Ho-hi and she looks just like any normal ischian except that she is very beautiful. Her fur is light, almost a gold colour. She is quite bossy too! I will tell you more about how I met her, and more of the Fascist regime taking hold on Bek-su, in my next message. For now, I have something more important to tell you. For some time now many of us have wondered how news of us reached the High Council in Ito when we tried so hard to conceal it. Oh, I know it's not you Prof! So who is doing the talking? Well anyway, it's the subject of much discussion among some of us... more liberal scientists..."

Strange that he is not laughing at his own jokes. This must be serious!

"Well, I had gone to a party with a lot of drinking and somebody, I won't name him, blurted out that we would be a lot better off without spies among us! Of course we thought he might be drunk and mouthing-off but he named one of *us*! The one accused, whom I know very well, laughed it off. When pressed, he became aggressive and proposed a toast to the High Council! Imagine *that*!

Of course we questioned the accused spy later and he acted very surly. He left early and now has become withdrawn. We questioned the accuser further and he told us that not only do we have High Council spies among us, but some of them are actually among the colonists living with humans!"

Kek-suîxjh felt the hairs stand up on his neck and shoulders.

His young student went on, "I couldn't get this out of my mind and last night I thought more and more about some things I have seen this person, this possible spy, doing; places he shouldn't have been doing them, or times he shouldn't have been doing them. I think it's true. And I think he might know about my secret messages to you. You need to take care Master, and from now on my messages will be... only of domestic things. It is just too dangerous for you otherwise."

Kek-suîxjh walked through the plaza. Then he called Xi-yrîx, punching the 'encrypt' key. By the time the call got picked up, Kek-suîxjh stood outside, on the lawn.

"Xi-yrîx? Is that you?"

"Who is this please?" answered an unfamiliar voice.

"Who is this? Where is Xi-yrîx"

"Wait a minute please." The voice sounded rough, but patient. "Hello."

"Yes. Please can I speak to Xi-yrîx?"

"I am sorry. You cannot speak to him."

"Why not?"

"He has been arrested." There seemed a note of satisfaction in the voice's course tone.

Kek-suîxjh ended the call.

My God! I have to get Hri's help. She will be able to get him released somehow!

The old Ischian thought it too early to be going home but then he thought his wife might be home already; she often was.

He strode across the lawn and up to the elevator-pod which rose to their apartment. He reached their door on the fifth level and stopped in his tracks.

Outside the green door, neatly aligned together, were Hri's favourite red foot-ware. This perplexed Kek-suîxjh.

She would not normally be leaving home at this time and she never leaves her shoes outside the door unless she is leaving. And then only for a moment. They are too valuable.

He pushed on the door cautiously and it whooshed open. He peered inside their entrance-way and could hear Hri speaking to somebody. He stepped inside. Edging closer to the door at the other end, he could hear Hri apparently talking to one of her loyal staff, whose name he had heard before. Since he could only hear one side of the conversation he knew she would be talking on a com.

"Yes Sjî. Do it. Arrest Professor Sos-yrîxjh now. He knows about Project Arcadia too. Yes. And his wife too. I want them both for questioning. I never liked her anyway. Ha!"

Kek-suîxjh felt as if somebody had kicked him in the stomach. He felt like retching.

Sos-yrîxjh! Our friend! Our dinner guest a few days before! How can this be!

It didn't sound like the Hri he knew at all. His first instinct had been to push open the door and confront her but a cold mote of fear somewhere inside him kept him from doing so. He turned, walked briskly out of the apartment, and headed back towards his office. He didn't know where else to go. He felt as if his feet weren't touching the ground. He last felt this when he had first been in love with Hri but this seemed a grotesque contortion of that feeling.

At the last moment, he turned away from his office and headed for the nearest bar, a cheap one where his colleagues would never go. He sat in a darkened alcove with a long glass of inexpensive and bitter, choa-î and twirled the funnel on the mat. Periodically, he tapped the biomium-funnel with his extended thumb-claw, as if to warn anybody off who might want a conversation.

Where should I go? What can I do? I have been such a fool!

His anger matched his anguish. Then, one word sprang into his mind; Arcadia.

Arcadia? What is Arcadia? Only one thing I know of that is called that.

Suddenly a light came on in Kek-suîxjh's mind.

Yes! Yes! It was a long time ago but yes! It was Sos-yrîxjh who first told me about it. The expedition of the archaeologist Dr. Piloxxrîxjh back to Ischi-su, shortly after we escaped from Isch-su. Funded by the newly founded Martial Council, the funding had been inexplicably and abruptly cut, and Dr. Piloxxrîxjh and his team were never heard of again. I researched it... yes! And all I managed to find; one copy of a news article. Cost me a packet too! I have it still in the office!

Instantly Kek-suîxjh felt energized and went back to the office. He felt as if a thousand eyes were watching him while he paced down the dark corridor. The office somehow felt crowded and malign when he entered. He went over to his com tablet and punched in the security code for his archive. After a struggle with his fading memory, he located the folder with the Arcadia news article in it. He opened the folder and stared at the screen. The article had gone!

The net is closing in, isn't it?

Kek-suîxjh felt naive, and very alone.

***

"Kuia! Degai!"

"Kuia! Degai!"

The cry had passed between the hunters every few minutes, like a chant. They pursued their prey though the forest the following morning. Jay had been allowed to accompany them as far as the forest's edge but there she would have to stop.

Earlier that morning, Stone had dropped back in the line of men to talk to Shahkyo. He had some burning questions

"Shahkyo, what … red stripes on Shihu's face?"

"Means she see man she like. Old custom. Ve'hay not much now. Shihu please Chief."

"Ah. Shahkyo. Erm … not sure how to ask this... Shihu in my house … ? Erm, under stars … ?
What … erm … first step?"

Shahkyo cupped her hand over her mouth and squealed with laughter. "Shihu ask Chief … she sha'hae bed with Stone."

"Really?"

"Yes."

"And … ."

"And?"

"Chief say yes?"

"No."

"Oh."

She cleared her throat. "Custom man sleep with woman th'haee times" She held up three fingers in case she had the number wrong. "Hen he say *'yes'* or *'no.'* If he say 'no' he must say yes umm … other woman."

"Ah. Seems reasonable – I mean good."

"No." She wagged her finger. "Shihu and Stone, no sleep in bed."

"Oh. Why?"

She pondered how to answer this for a moment. "Big..." She mimed wiping sweat from her brow and climbing a steep hill.

"Hard? Difficult?" Stone tried.

"Ah yes. Difficult. Umm ba'hother of Chief, Avonaico, he like Shihu. Give to Chief two ummm … ." She ran over the names of animals that Jay had taught her.
" … bea'ha skin."

"Oh. I see." Stone fell silent while he pondered this new angle.

***

The visitors were told that the tribe had cornered the mumaki in a clearing.

Then Stone saw it. Long, whitish tusks, which crossed at the ends, emerged from the overhang below him followed by a great, flat head. Reddish-brown, coarse hair hung from the great head. The beast had been cornered and swayed from side to side, agitated. Stone heard a deep rumbling sound, almost subsonic, coming from the beast's belly.

Probably had many fights, poor bugger. Just one more. He looks like he's ready for it.

Without warning, the warrior in front of the beast, lunged forward and drove a spear straight through the beasts shoulder, narrowly missing its eye. It howled a thundering, raging roar, which seemed to shake the very trees around the clearing. Stone crouched down further behind the rock.

Two warriors jumped down from rocks to face the beast. Each held the last fifteen feet or so of a vine-rope with a large loops on the end. For a moment Stone thought they were going to try and lasso the mumaki but they spun the loops around their heads to build up momentum and then launched them onto the ground either side of the beast's front feet.

Traps! Nooses for their feet!

A warrior threw a spear which hung from the beast's shoulder. Two more men jumped down to help corner the mumaki.

Blood already matted the fur of the beast from the first spear, which still hung limply from its shoulder. Blood stained the grass, smeared by the beast's stamping feet.

A chant of "Baika!" went up from the warriors and joined with the thundering deep roar of the beast to cause a confusing clamour in the clearing.

The warriors were using rope lassoes, anchored to trees, to snare the feat of the mammoth and they soon had two of its feet caught.

The beast, in its frustration, put its left, front foot on another loop. The beast stepped back for a moment, while a warrior tensed to pull the loop tight. Unbalanced, the mammoth stepped further forward this time and trod fully into the loop. The man yanked the loop with all his might.

The warriors on the ropes attempted in vain, with great heaves and shouts, to each other, to pull the mumaki's legs apart. The rope on its right slipped on smooth bark and then snapped. Instantly, a man with spare rope rushed forward to tie in a new length but the man at the front of the rope lost his balance and fell near the beast's feet.

Seeing how desperate the situation was, Stone took a deep breath and leapt down into the clearing. He grabbed the frayed end of the rope and pulled it tight. The mumaki seemed confused and had little space to move. Nevertheless each time it took a step backwards Stone's arms were almost pulled from their sockets. He felt a man grab his wrist and hang on to him. Stone saw, out of the corner of his eye, the furious activity behind him. Several hands tried to tie the lengths of rope together with a crude knot.

For a moment, the rope slacked and Stone had to watch the beast in case it moved towards him. The great tusks slashed the air and a mixture of blood and dust clouded the air as it struggled to break free.

Somebody shouted something in Stone's ear and he returned his attention to the rope. He could see the knot, now securely tied, and a man slapped Stone's wrists hard to make him release his hold on the rope. He let go and ran around the base of the rocky wall, away to the trees and safety.

Stone saw the chief's brother, Avonaico, jump down from a rock and take aim at the beast's head. The chanting of, "Baika!" grew in intensity. Avonaico took aim and let loose the shaft of the spear. It flew straight and drove right in to the beast's skull behind its left eye. The mumaki trumpeted with pain and shook his head to try and release the spear.

Stone felt horrified but fascinated. The beast waded through fronds of grass, wet with blood from its wounds.

Its eyes were wide open with anger and fear. Then it saw an opportunity and lunged for Avonaico. A warrior, to the right of the beast, anticipated the move and lunged again at just the right moment, just as the beast put its right leg forward. This time the spear went right into the beast's body, burying itself perhaps four feet deep in flesh. The beast moaned deeply and shuddered. But at the same time it caught Avonaico's head with its tusk and twisted its head to send him flying across the clearing. The warror lay motionless on the floor but other events in the clearing quickly took Stone's attention. The mammoth dropped slowly to its knees and bellowed at the warriors now surrounding it. Chief Cheveya himself strode up to the mammoth and climbed onto its left flank. It raised its great head once to peer at him but couldn't see its assailant from the pierced and useless eye. It tried to get up and for a moment it looked like Cheveya would lose his balance but he steadied himself and prepared the fatal blow. The mumaki reached for him with its trunk. For a moment, it gripped his waist delicately with the lips of his trunk. It seemed a pathetic gesture and then Cheveya drove his spear deep down into the side of the beast, right through its heart.

The beast bellowed one more time and lay silent. Both the beast and the men were red with blood; a scene of absolute carnage, cruelly and coldly delivered. The air seemed electrified and although Stone could only hear the murmuring of the leaves in a gentle breeze, his ears were still reverberating with a roaring cacophony. He could still hear echoes of the beast bellowing and the shouts of the men in his head. The chief and his men began whooping with victory.

Stone felt the tension release from the pit of his stomach.

Fuck! I never want to do anything like that again.

When they met up with Jay and Shihu, Shahkyo told the two young women what had happened excitedly, making great gestures with her arms. Jay stood up, fists clenched and paced up and down.

Stone avoided talking to her but pulled Dee aside, whispering:

"I saw one of those marker poles. We killed the mammoth *outside* Naxa territory." Dee nodded.

Avonaico took advantage of his condition, beckoning for Shihu to come and help him. She pursed her lips and looked the other way.

***

During the feast that followed, three tradesmen visited the village from the south. One showed Stone a beautiful cowrie-shell necklace.

"Wow! It's beautiful."

When he tried to think of something, with which to pay, Chief Cheveya closed Stone's hand around the shell and announced to the tribe that Stone had fought the mumaki well and that, like the New Gods who had been unarmed too, Stone had won honour and respect from the tribe.

"Did you hear that you two?" Stone whispered to Jay and Dee. "These New Gods sound like astronauts to me."

Must find out more.

"They visited a few other tribes locally before this one," Dee said. "Apparently they do the same route most years. Anyway they said at least one of the other tribes already knows about us, knows we're here!"

"Really! How the *hell*..."

"Word travels fast apparently. Anyway that's not *all*! Think about it. These guys are turning round and going back. Today! That means they will talk and soon everybody will know where we came from. Need I say it?"

"The ship! Shit! Somebody will find it."

"Pretty soon, yeah."

"You got to say something Stone. Soon." added Jay.

"Yeah. I know."

A hand touched Stone's shoulder lightly; that of Makya, Shihu's father.

Stone held out his hand and Makya clasped it firmly.

"Tonight, Shihu stay Stone house if Stone want. Now with fight mumaki, you are brother."

Stone nodded slowly.

***

Shihu's look seemed so open and innocent that Stone felt moved. They were alone at last in his hut and the music outside had become just a murmur.

"I have never felt like this about anyone before Shihu," he told her, facing her on the bed of furs. She sat side-on to him. She looked into his eyes.

"I have been with other women," he went on. "But not like this. In my land, it is unusual for a man as young as me to... have a woman." He suddenly knew how futile this line of confession was. Her open innocence disarmed him and, for the first time, he opened up his deepest feelings to somebody.

"My own mother was away for most of my childhood. I was raised mostly by a replicant nanny, I mean, another woman. I only saw my mother on her rare leaves, or when she sat reading bed-time stories to me in the body of a hired blanker. A blanker is... oh, never mind that. The touch of a blanker is a cold one. Anyway, like I say, I have been with women before but I have never felt as close as this."

He felt the pull of her warmth and longed to touch her but he wanted to clear his conscience.

"You won't understand all of this but you get my point," he snapped.

Shihu smiled, reached across and touched his hand with her fingers. Her simple affection touched him deeply. He leaned over and touched her nose with his nose. Then he kissed her. She giggled. Then she tried to kiss him. Their lips met, and for a moment they were motionless, suspended in a moment of sensual delight. Then their lips pressed firmly together and they kissed until they were out of breath. Shihu untied her tunic, pulled it over her head and fell upon him, kissing him hotly.

***

Stone woke to the sight of Shihu's back, while she saying whispered her morning prayers through the opening in the east side of the house. He could pick out a sound something like 'Ha'ah' several times. When she finished, he saw her take something from around her neck and replace it in a small wooden box. She came over and kissed him. He noticed that she no longer wore the cowrie-shell necklace. His disappointment showed in his gaze. Shihu felt her neck with her fingers before darting to a low table and picking up the necklace. She asked him to place it around her neck again. He felt touched that she had noticed his feelings.

"What do we do today, darling?"

"Da'aling? Who is *da'aling*?"

"You are. It's our word for somebody we care very much about."

"Ah. And I can call you *da'aling*?"

"Yes. If you want but we don't say it in front of Jay and Dee, or your people, okay?"

"Okay?"

"Ah. Another word. 'Okay' is one of our best words. You can use it a lot. It means 'You feel same?'"

"Ah. We not say."

"Good. You can also say okay when you mean 'good.'"

"Ah. Okay?"

"Yes. Good."

They both laughed and kissed.

"So darling, what do we do today?" Stone asked again.

"Stone say."

"Oh okay. I want to see a Sky House."

The day dawned hot. The couple set off. Stone wore one of the makeshift hats and a light poncho to cover his over-browning shoulders. Shihu delighted him in a tunic with a very short hemline. She wore moccasins but Stone had noticed that she seemed equally comfortable in bare feet.

"We go the'hae?" Shihu said uncertainly pointing to the west of the village.

"Yes, there's is fine."

"Good. Wind. Nice, cold."

Holding his hand Shihu guided Stone out of the west end of the village and down a long, gentle slope between derelict houses. Stone had noticed them before but never asked about them.

"Why so many old houses with... no people, here?"

"When Shihu little, many people. No food. People die or walk a long way."

"Oh. The tribe must have been much larger then."

She smiled but said nothing and held on to his hand. They were walking very slowly, as lovers do in their first days together; it didn't seem to matter where they went or when. They reached the last of the old houses, not much more than a pile of thin timbers and mud. Beyond, the slope steepened and Stone looked out over the green plains which stretched out to the far distance. The morning's hazy sun cast no shadows but Stone shuffled quickly from side to side, wondering if he might cast a shadow miles across the plain. He could see none.

"Shihu. What are the New Gods and when did they come? I heard Chief Cheveya talk about them last night."

"New Gods? Come... sky when Shihu's g'ha'ndmoth'ah young woman. Make big houses. Sky houses. Naxa help them."

"Your tribe? Naxa?"

She nodded, turning to face him and shielding her eyes from the sun with her hand. Stone thought, in that instant, that he loved her.

"Did they have white clothes like ours? Did they look like us; Stone, Jay and Dee?"

"No. Not like Stone or Jessica."

"Did they walk on legs?"

Shihu's tribe had not encountered horses yet and had no concept of riding an animal so Stone felt at a loss to describe a spaceship or any other type of transport.

Shihu laughed. "Yes."

The gentle zyphyr ruffled Stone's hair as he and Shihu wandered onto the plain. Stone reveled in the sensation of cool air through his Mohican, which had become greasy and itchy.

Shihu led him towards a kind of headland; a buttress of bare rock that penetrated through the rough scrub on the slope. He thought perhaps she wanted to show him a view or a favourite place of hers. He held on to her hand.

But she continued on around the base of the buttress and led him into the cool shadow on the other side. She stooped every now and again to pick little white flowers, which she gradually laced into a bracelet. When she had finished, it she asked Stone to tie it around her wrist.

"What is that, Shihu?"

"Oh... Where?"

"There!" He pointed and checked that she saw what he saw, but she seemed disinterested.

Feeling his heart quicken Stone found himself wanting to run.

Whatever it is, it's been there for a long time. It's not going anywhere. Calm down Stone!

Slightly below it still, and only perhaps one hundred yards from its edge, Stone couldn't believe what he saw. He let go of Shihu's hand and ran the last fifty yards. He stopped ten feet from the structure. He put his head back and looked up at its lip against the hazy blue of the sky.

Wha...?

Stone walked gingerly forward and placed his hands reverently on the cool stone block in front of him. A sloping wall, five blocks high, spread out either side of him for perhaps five hundred feet. The rows of blocks were set back from the ones below slightly, giving a stepped effect. The blocks, pale yellow in colour, smooth and cool to the touch, were about ten feet long by eight feet high, giving the wall a total vertical height above ground of about forty feet. Stone's history wasn't good but even he could not mistake what this was.

It's a pyramid! A fucking pyramid! Unfinished!

In old colour history programmes, he had seen pictures of the great pyramids at Giza in Egypt and at least one diagram of the pyramids during their construction.

Those diagrams looked just like this!

"Stone!" Shihu had come up behind him.

"What is this Shihu?" he asked.

"Sky House," she said, disconsolately.

"Wow! Wait till Jay and Dee see this!"

Stone ran along the base of the pyramid until he found a few lose, uncut blocks, upon which he could climb to reach the top of the first course. By similar means, he reached the flat top of the pyramit and he could look out over the whole extent of the structure. Only it wasn't quite flat. In places there were spaces in the blocks, and running over to the open spaces, he found himself looking down into unfinished corridors and tunnels, some sloping down at a steep angle. In at least one corridor, the walls were painted with a great frieze but he couldn't wait. He ran back to the southern edge and jumped down, course by course, until he landed in a cloud of dust next to Shihu.

"It's a *pyramid*! A *pyramid*!" He took her hands in his and danced, spinning her around. Taking her in his arms, he kissed her. He laughed. Shihu joined in, happy that he looked happy.

Stone imediately started off towards the village, towing Shihu behind.

"Did you build these for the New Gods?"

"Yes. I think."

"Uh huh! Come on!"

"Wow!" Jay exclaimed, seeing the pyramid for the first time.

"*Isn't* it? *Man*, we *are* made. This is *so* cool! Come on! I'll show you the way up."

Stone took them back to the base of the unfinished pyramid, where he had gazed on it with awe. Now he saw the same look on their faces.

Dee placed his hands on the stone. As if talking to it, he murmured, "Limestone. Not as well worked as those at Giza though. Much cruder."

"Yeah! Still pretty cool though!" added Jay. "Stone, did the villagers build this thing?"

"Yeah. Shihu says so. Oh yeah, I found out the tribe's name too. The *Naxa*! Here! This is where we go up. Just stand on that stone."

"Smaller blocks than the big pyramid at Giza." Dee observed, standing on the first course.

"Come on babe!" called Dee from behind Stone, half way along the side of the pyramid.

Soon all three were standing on the flat stone plain on top of the structure, looking down into one of the spaces that would have become a corridor.

"Can we climb down?" Dee wondered, out loud.

"Not today, Stone. Let's go back, hm." Jay replied.

***

News spread fast around the village that the guests had been looking at the old Sky Houses. They were not taboo but regarded with wary superstition.

Shihu explained to Stone and the others:

"People not talk about them because of sadness. Most people not go the'ahe now."

However, some of the villagers gave them dark looks and Avonaico's were the darkest of all.

"He does not like the new ways, the ways of the New Gods," explained Shahkyo. "The'ahe a'ahe othe'ahs that feel like him."

That evening, after politely sharing a meal with the chief and Shihu's family, the visitors retired to talk over what they had seen. They had already asked the chief for permission to revisit the pyramid the following day and he had agreed without much concern.

"Don't you see?" said Stone, impatiently "The pyramid is out of place here. I don't know exactly what time it *is* here, but I'm sure as hell that mammoths did not exist when they built the pyramids. Also the iron arrow-heads? Did you see those? There's some kind of intervention going on here. Whoever it *is* has a way on and *off* this planet, and so we can find a way out of here *too*!"

"That's a lot of assumptions, Stone, hm."

"Well Jessica, there's a lot of evidence. And it's mounting up!"

"Maybe there were *earlier* pyramids than the ones in the history books," suggested Dee

"In *North America*?"

After a pause, Jay cut in, "Anyway Stone, if there is this other... higher race here, do you think they are just going to offer us a lift? Anubians don't exactly have a reputation for friendliness."

"They do with Ionians, apparently. They have been allies for years, since my father was young."

"Oh, everyone knows it's just a pragmatic thing. They would probably eat the Ionians if they had no use for them."

"Ha! Anyway it might not *be* Anubians. It might be humans, time travelers. Had you thought of that, hm?"

"This is all very interesting chaps, but I am going to bed. You coming Jess?" Dee declared.

"In a minute. I won't be long." she called as he left the porch and entered the house.

"Oo! *Jess* is it now?" Stone murmured. "We all know why he wants you in bed *right now!*"

"Are you jealous?"

"No. Not at all."

"Stone, there's something I have been meaning to talk to you about. Now seems as good a time as any."

"Go on."

"I have decided, Stone, that I need to do something for these people. And there is something I *can* do."

"What do you mean?"

"The kids. Have you seen some of the little kids? They are suffering badly from malnutrition; big bellies, crying all the time. We can help them. We have a medical..."

"Wo! Hang on Jes... I mean Jay. We can't just go laying in to these people, changing their way of life! You know the rules; nobody must intervene with any kind of life, anything at all, on any planets that are explored. It's against the Law. Every space-traveler knows that!"

"When did *you* obey the Law? Anyway, I don't care Stone. For one thing, we haven't just traveled in space but in time too. How do we know that man, modern man, has not already intervened in their way of life? Somebody certainly has. You heard them. Their whole religion has been changed."

"Doesn't matter. We have to set an example. If it *was* aliens then we don't want to lower ourselves to their level."

"That's weak in this case. And you know it!"

"Jessica! No!"

"My mind's made up. I'm going to teach them, first about hygiene, which *actually* they're not too bad on, and then do some proper education with them."

"No way! Does Dee know about this?"

"Yes. He says it's up to me."

"I bet he does! He may be easily-led... and in love with you … but even he cannot agree to this! *Dee!*"

"Don't Stone. It will only lead to an argument. I'm telling you the truth. That's what he said."

"He really is crazy about you, isn't *he*?"

She said nothing.

"I have to think about this Jay. Don't do anything until I have spoken to Dee tomorrow. I'm going to bed."

***

But Stone didn't get the chance to speak to Dee about Jay's ideas the next day. Nor did he get a chance to explore the pyramid further, until much later.

He woke with a start, to the sound of yelling and screaming.

"What the fu..." He sat upright in his bed of furs and then peered through the opening in the side of the house. Dawn had broken but even in its rosy light he could not see anything for a moment. Then, a warrior, wearing an unfamiliar style of headdress, ran across his field of view.

The warrior aimed his spear at something.

"Attack! Jay! Dee!" he shouted.

Dressed in just his underpants, he sped to the house next door, dodging an arrow which whistled past his left ear.

Shit, that was close.

"Jay! Dee! Get up. We're being attacked!"

He pushed aside the wicker screen which acted as a door and pushed aside another screen to the bedroom. Dee and Jay sat upright, furs pulled up to their chins protectively. Dee's mouth and eyes were open wide. It seemed to Stone as if everything started to happen in slow-motion. He had plenty of time to notice Dee, staring past him, not at him. He threw himself over the top of his two friends just as he heard a primeval scream from behind him. He buried his head in the furs, expecting to feel the thud of an arrow, axe or spear at any instant. A thrill, at once hot and ice cold, shot through him but the moment passed and nothing had hit him.

"Stone! Look out!" he heard Dee finally shout.

"Aahh!" came an animal sound behind him. Stone had to look. Twisting round he saw the face of an enemy warrior falling towards him. The face had been daubed a ghastly yellow, striped with red across the cheeks. The eyes were highlighted in circles of white. The whole gave the effect of a ghoul from the very pit of Hell. The face landed with a thud on Stone's half-exposed chest. The hand, clutching an axe fell harmlessly to Stone's side, on the floor-matting.

Another face in the doorway grabbed Stone's attention; Avonaico's. The two men looked at each other with a deep recognition of respect.

"Kuia! Baikai!" Avonaico shouted and threw Stone a spear.

Then the chief's brother left.

"You two, stay here. You're not dressed!" Stone picked up the spear and ran out of the house.

"But neither are..." Jay's fading plea followed him out of the hut but became lost in the clamour of battle.

Stone awkwardly held the spear and aimed at a pair of yellow-faced warriors on the other side of the clearing. He aimed the spear uncertainly, first at one and then then other, but both saw him and parted company to circle around behind some huts. His chance had gone.

Another warrior ran from Stone's left and for a moment he pointed the spear at the man's body before recognising him as one of the Naxa. One of the enemy pursued the warrior, wielding an axe. Stone took aim and for an instant before he released the spear, the thought passed through his mind that he might be about to kill someone. The thought made him hesitate for an instant and the spear flew wide of its mark. Stone felt relieved but then angry with himself.

Shit! Gotta do better than that.

He steeled himself and ran to recover the spear. As he ran he felt that he might never reach it before the battle ended.

Everything seems to take him too long!

He had to search for the spear in some shrubs and then pull it out by the tail end. He turned to look for another target and saw Jay and Dee, emerging half-dressed from their house. To their left, Stone saw a yellow-faced warrior lying in the dirt and pointed in that direction to his friends. Then he returned to his own task.

It seemed to him that most of the enemy had been running to the west end of the village so he followed them. He saw several of the village men, in a circle and surrounded by the enemy. The Naxa were defiant but losing. The enemy jabbed at them with spears and the defenders were awash with their own blood.

Stone felt something primitive course through his veins which made him yell, despite himself, as he lunged at the side of one of the attackers. His howl gave him away and the man turned, just in time to fend off Stone's blow with the haft of his axe. Stone swiveled the spear's shaft under the arc of the axe and drove it into the man's side with cry. The man went down and Stone had just enough sense to withdraw the spear's shaft before it became trapped under the falling body. Two of the attackers swung to face Stone. The distraction gave the surrounding warriors just the chance they needed. With renewed energy, they pushed forward and a melee broke out.

Stone quickly felt out of his depth but his allies moved to defend him and overwhelmed the enemy. The enemy survivors ran from the scene of the bloodbath. Stone stuck the point of his spear in the ground and leaned on it, out of breath, and exhausted.

"I think I need some coffee," he mumbled.

Several of the tribesmen patted him on the shoulders before they too sat down.

Jay! Dee! Gotta find them!

He found them both, sitting on the porch of their little hut. Dee nursed a nasty cut to his hand. Jay tried to find something clean to bind it with.

"Did you get one of them?" Dee shouted.

"Yes." Stone found the word hard to say. He wanted to spit. "You?"

"Nah. Just a cut. He got away. Jay did though. Nice shot."

"Where?"

Jay didn't answer.

"There!" Dee pointed to a man lying face down. The shaft of a spear protruded from under his lifeless body.

Stone stared and then noticed that he had started to shake – violently. He clenched his fists but couldn't stop it. He gritted his teeth. Jay looked up from where she had been picking up shards of broken pots by the side of the hut.

"The shaking stops after a short while," she said.

***

Kek-suîxjh had decided to leave his wife. There was one last thing she could do for him.

The night he drank in the bar, he finally found the courage to return home, well after the middle of the night. During their long marriage he had never once stayed out so late without having first warned her.

"Where have you been Kek? I have been worried. Darling? You are drunk aren't you?" she said, sitting up in bed. Kek-suîxjh knew her capable, even under great stress, of sounding calm. Her voice now sounded even and gentle.

He had to swallow some bile before answering. "Yes dear. I am drunk. I had a bad day. Did you know Sos-yrîxjh has been arrested?" He couldn't resist baiting her.

"Yes dear. I heard about it on the news. It's an awful shame. I know you were both close. Wasn't it over some illegal documents that he had?"

"I don't know. Actually I know nothing about it. I wastoo busy getting drunk. I am very tired now and I need to sleep."

"Okay dear. You rest and we can talk about it in the morning."

During the long night that followed, he formed a plan which provided him with a single point of calm in his chaotic thoughts.

Over the following weeks he started to prepare a complex plan and every detail had to be worked out precisely if it were to succeed. After all he, had married a member of the High Council, somebody with access to all the intelligence channels.

His sense of betrayal from his wife led him to focus his considerable analytical mind for the first time on matters devious enough to outwit those closest to him. His one advantage, he told himself, had to be that his wife did not suspect that he knew her real character.

After nearly a month of planning, his first move would be to withdraw a huge amount of currency from their joint account. He would need every bit of it. He also needed a cover-story.

"Darling," he said that evening, stealing himself. "I have booked a surprise holiday for us both."

Her jaw froze, half-open, but he pressed on.

"You know that new resort at Skyblue Lake? The one on the lake filling a volcano crater, and completely covered over? The brochure says you can't even see the transparent dome and that the beaches are of real sand. They say, 'On a clear day you can believe you really are on Ischi-su.' That's the advert isn't it?"

He watched her eyes. She had been caught off-guard but didn't seem to suspect anything.

"Well, it's a lovely idea, dear. I will have to think about it."

"I have already booked it." He wanted to grit his teeth at his own audacity.

"Well... well, we have said for some time that we needed a holiday together. I... I guess it will do us good. You really should have consulted me first, though." With that, she left the room and Kek-suîxjh breathed out.

The next part of his plan was the most cunning but also the simplest. Hri-hu had always been a heavy sleeper; once she fell asleep, she would be out cold until the wake-drug that she took brought her back to consciousness. It did this at precisely the right time for her to eat breakfast and make the limousine that usually picked her up. He only had to slip the security-pass from her wallet in the middle of the night and sneak out to the side door, where an agent he had paid would be waiting to swipe it and take the image to a counterfeiter.

Although it seemed ridiculously expensive, within two days he held an exact duplicate of the pass in his hands.

He knew of nobody loyal to him left at the Institute so he had to use the same agent to carry out the next part of his plan.

Taking one of his days off from work, Kek-suîxjh waited at home on one of the days when Hri-hu came home particularly early. At a pre-arranged time, he asked Hri-hu for access to her com.

She hesitated and in that moment he knew she suspected something. But he calculated silently that she would not want him to know that and would feel forced to give him access. He made himself breathe evenly and started counting to one hundred, hoping he would not be tempted to say or do anything stupid.

"Fine!" she said, when he had reached fifteen.

She logged in before handing it over to him. The com's laser detectors, using object-recognition, fixed two points on the base of his skull. The sensitive detectors picked up the minutest variation in electric field below the skin to detect Kek-suîxjh's thoughts and intentions. The cursor on the screen reflected these, allowing him to start searching for scientific news articles.

A few minutes later, the agent, using Kek-suîxjh's pass, entered the lobby of the High Council offices where Hri-hu worked. Most middle-ranking civil servants had access to the lobby but not any further. Security was lax at the offices and Hri-hu had let slip that there were too many cameras for the security guards to watch all of them. The agent worked his way up to her office on the third-floor and then opened the door to Hri-Hu's office, using the pass. Instead of entering, he simply left. Within minutes, an alarm sounded and a call had been made to Kek-suîxjh's wife at home.

****

4. A Great Fish in the Sky

Kek-suîxjh had made another excuse to use Hri-hu's com in her little office, next to the bedroom. Since he didn't have his own, she often let him use hers but he knew she changed the password to both that com and also the one for her most secret documents. This would be the last thing Hri-hu could do for him. In there, of all places, knowing, as he did now, how devious she was, would be the document he wanted.

He also suspected that she used a mind-logger to record her sessions. After Hri-hu gave him access he just thought of some inoffensive news articles on SkyBlue Holidays and worked his way through them. He spent quite a bit of time looking at the sky-trains; balloons shaped like pointed ellipses which plied the narrow, protected corridor through Bek-su's violent atmosphere to and from SkyBlue Lake. One of them, the Imperial Cruiser had once belonged to Ischi-su's royal family, before the wars took hold, and had been renovated at great expense for the tourist route. It's heavily decorated superstructure, with royal-red filigree around the friezes of royal life on its hull, were a complete contrast to the utilitarian look of High Council vehicles. Some said it looked like a great golden fish, floating over stormy Ito.

How ironic! It would have been nice to go.

But Kek-suîxjh would never go on that holiday now, or any other holiday, with his wife.

He hoped Hri-hu's mind-logger wouldn't notice the little blip when he had inserted the hack-devise into the memory slot on the side of the com.

That was yesterday. Now, he forced himself to think of fish in the holiday lake while he inserted the device but he had little doubt that there would be a moment when the mind-logger would record a moment of increased activity. Would this be flagged up as suspicious or not? He wasn't sure. After taking the advice of a very expensive hacker, he felt confident that the device insertion itself would not be recorded because he had been told most officials were busy and used the slot a lot. They turned off the tracker to avoid filling up the logs, and their own time, with long scans. Hri-hu was just such an official.

***

"How bad is it? It looks bad," said Stone.

Blood bubbled out of a slit between two of Avonaico's lower ribs. He gasped, fighting for every breath.

"Punctured lung," Jay whispered to Stone. "Dee! Do we have anything we can use as a hose? A tube? It's a broken rib that has punctured the lung. It must have broken during the mammoth hunt. No wonder he was in pain. He says he was hit in the chest with the side of an axe. That must have driven the broken rib into his lung. The tear is not big. He could survive... I think. We need to insert the tube so that the air can escape and with some luck, a lot of luck, the lung will re-inflate by itself."

Dee returned holding something long, thin and black.

"Stone! You'll have to help me. This cable, it has a polymer outer sleeve. If we can slit it down one side and then use tape to seal it back up, we can use it."

They slit, gutted and re-taped the cable to form a black tube. Jay inserted the tube into a slit in the gasping warrior's chest. Avonaico's eyes widened with the pain, but he made no sound other than a slight gasp.

"One of the most painful things you can ever, *ever* experience," Jay said, under her breath.

A faint gurgling sound could be heard from the end of the tube, a sound which made Stone feel like vomiting. Avonaico's head slumped to one side as he slipped out of consciousness. Anxiously Jay leaned over to lay her ear against his rising and falling chest.

"It's okay, he's sleeping," she pronounced.

***

While Dee and the rest of the tribesmen drank in celebration, Stone slipped away, to wash himself in the stream. He stripped down to his trousers and waded into the cold water.

"Ah. Feels good," he told himself.

"You can't wash properly like that," came a chuckling, female voice from behind the reeds. Jay suddenly stood up so that he saw her head peering over the reeds. Her dark hair had been slicked back with water. He thought she looked incredibly beautiful.

"What are you doing there?" he asked

"Same as you," she said sheepishly. He heard another voice giggling.

"Who's that?"

Jay spoke to somebody beside her and then stone saw Shihu's face appear beside Jay's. She too looked more beautiful than ever. Her hair looked almost as dark as Jay's, slick too with water, but as the afternoon sun shone from behind her, it made the hair around her head glow like a halo of gold.

"Why don't you come over?" Jay asked.

Stone didn't reply at first, wondering what to do.

"Don't be shy. We can't see anything!" They both giggled at his sudden modesty.

He felt strangely challenged by the two girls and waded around the reeds, at one point up to his arm-pits, to reach them. Their two heads bobbed in the little waves like pretty buoys. He could see their clothes, neatly folded on the bank.

"The chief has accepted you as one of the tribe now," he said to Jay.

"Yes. So it would seem. Shihu tells me he calls me his daughter now."

"Ha! What do you think of that?"

"He does his best. He's hardly a modern man by my standards but still, at least it's something."

"Yes."

"Why don't you take off your trousers and underpants too? Then you can really get clean."

Nervously, Stone waded on until the water came over his waist.

Shihu smiled at him, slightly red-faced. Her hand appeared from the water and scooped something from a wooden bowl on a floating basket-weave tray, wedged into the reeds. She put the viscous liquid in her hair and started to lather it.

"Ha! That's cool. I like the tray!"

"Take some!" said Jay. "It's aloe, same as modern shampoo. They make it from the plant which grows locally. The other bowl is for your body."

He scooped some aloe from the first bowl and rubbed it into his hair.

"Ah! Feels good." He rubbed it in and rinsed his hair with scoops of river water. "Now if only I had a razor!"

Shihu took another scoop of aloe and worked her way around his body until she stood behind him. She poured the liquid onto his shoulders and started rubbing it gently into his skin. Slightly embarrassed, he raised his arms to aid her and grinned artlessly at Jay. She took another scoop and started on his chest. Shihu said something he didn't understand.

"Trousers!" Jay translated.

The heat of battle had left him and been replaced by a sense of deep sadness and quietude. It seemed as if his own morals were of as little consequence as a puff of air in the sky. He acquiesced and threw the trousers and underpants onto the shore.

Both women worked with complete and disinterested concentration. Stone felt anything but disinterested. When he felt Jay's leg touch his under the water, he became aroused. Her eyes flicked a glance at him and then she carried on as if nothing had happened.

Perhaps all women are just plain practical!

When she reached his groin, Jay spun him round so that the decision would be Shihu's. His lover, understanding the gesture, began again at his thighs and worked her way downwards. He glanced at her with a glint in his eye. She returned his glance, reprovingly. He reminded himself that Jay too had killed that day.

I can't expect absolution from these two women.

He took one last scoop of aloe and washed his groin himself. Both women giggled.

"There! Now you're clean! Like us!" Jay said. She executed a few clumsy back-strokes to pull away from him and examine their handiwork.

"I could get so used to this," he said.

"Yes. I know what you mean. But today, I wondered if we're not becoming more like them, bit by bit. If we're not careful, we will never leave here!"

"Tomorrow, I want to go back to the pyramid."

"I don't think that's a good idea. Wait for a while."

"But..."

"Be patient. Now, more than ever, they will need to pull together as a tribe. We shouldn't interrupt their rituals."

"Do you know what will happen to the two men who were captured?" asked Stone.

"Shihu told me. The other tribe, the Gjanga, are cannibals. I'm sure you can guess what will happen. I don't need to spell it out."

"What the... Are you serious! That's disgusting! We have to do something!"

"No Stone. That's not the way it's done around here. Let them do it their way. Do you want to start a war? We were attacked because of the mammoth. We killed it in their territory. Our tribe was in the wrong, Stone, not theirs. Soon it will be the phase of the moon for a special ritual. Shihu's told me about it. We must let them carry on Stone. But on the way we will pass near the house of the witch-doctor, Enkoodabaooh, so you can visit him if you want. Now turn around while we get out."

That night would be Stone's second with Shihu.

After talking for a while, he suggested they sleep. She knelt, facing away from him and undressed. As she pulled her tunic over her head, he nearly moaned at the beauty of her bare back.

She clutched her hands over her breasts, which were fuller than Jay's and climbed onto the pallet with him.

"Look at our skins!" Stone remarked. Her arm and legs were so much browner than his, which were so white that they seemed to shine in the darkness.

Shihu chuckled and put her hands around his torso.

Stone still struggled to get used to her unrestrained affection. Sometimes it took his breath away.

"I love you," he murmured. "You don't have to worry. It seems like you think you will lose me!"

"You will leave me … ." she murmured.

"No I won't!" But the words didn't sound right to Stone.

He opened his mouth to speak again. Shihu suddenly lifted her head and kissed him on the lips. She climbed on top of him. He cupped her heavy breasts and watched her heaving shoulders as she began to gasp. He felt himself becoming hard and pulled down his pants. Shihu rolled away to copy him and then they were entwined, planting wet kissed all over each other's body.

Stone took her from behind, ferally. He felt nothing complicated about it but deeply satisfied after.

Shihu immediately seemed to fall asleep in his arms. But she caught him looking at her when she opened her eyes. She smiled but caught something else in her eye. She knew something that he didn't. Afterwards, she traced the features of his face with her finger for hours before he fell asleep.

***

Stone, impatient to see the pyramid again, he satisfied himself with the promise of seeing the tribe's witch-doctor.

On their way to the site set aside for the moon ritual, they took a side-trail to meet the witch-doctor.

Three small, naked children with dirty faces ran to greet them. The children grabbed the visitors' hands and dragged them along the path towards the huts.

"Stop!" Shihu yelled. She took off her moccasins and pointed to their shoes. They all removed their shoes and carried them the last leg of the journey.

"Sign of respect," Jay suggested.

While the children dragged them to the porch of the largest hut, an old man with a huge pot-belly walked towards them holding a small wooded bowl in his hands. He had a plume of long feathers and grass tied to the back of his head with a band. He flicked tiny splashes of water at them from the bowl with practiced skill, splashing their faces, cooling them.

Shihu dropped to her knees and could not be persuaded to stand up. When the old man beckoned for them to approach the hut, she edged forwards on her knees. Stone could see something he had never seen before in her eyes; fear.

Jay asked Shihu if they should do the same and the tribes-woman muttered something in reply.

"She says the village women must not stand in the presence of the witch-doctor," Jay translated.

"Go on then. Down on your knees!" Dee laughed.

"I'm not doing it! I'm not a woman of *this* tribe, hm!" She walked calmly towards the hut and the old man laughed good-naturedly.

The shaman greeted them with an expansive gesture of his arms and a gaping mouth almost devoid of teeth. The vistors found his speech difficult to follow but, between them, Jay and Shihu managed to slowly translate it. Shihu kept her face down and never once made eye-contact with Enkoodabaooh.

"Greetings." the witch-doctor said.

Stone studied the old man's features while the old man studied theirs. His age seemed impossible to guess but he was prodigiously old. His few wisps of white hair clung to his temples like stringy mountain-climbers. His pallid eyes were sad, almost mournful. When he laughed, his large mouth, framed by rubbery lips, opened like a chasm and his eyes glinted like meteorites coursing across the night-sky. A single, white front-tooth hung from the top of his gums like a precarious stalactite in the cavernous mouth, although there were still enough back teeth to crunch his food with. He peered at them with barely concealed curiosity.

Stone cleared his throat. "I have come to ask you some questions." Jay and Dee winced at his forthrightness.

'It's his nature,' Dee's shrug almost seemed to say.

Enkoodabaooh laughed. He clapped his hands, which seemed to be a signal, because they were each handed a green leaf with some sweet-tasting pastry on it.

"What is your question, Chief of the White Tribe?" He laughed again and glanced at Shihu, whose downcast face glowed red with embarrassment.

"We have seen arrow-heads made of a shiny material... erm... which we call metal. Did you make them?"

Enkoodabaooh chewed his sweetbread slowly and sadly, before his eyes crinkled in amusement and he said, "Yes."

Stone looked at Dee. He asked hesitantly, "Where did you learn this?"

The old man chewed some more and then opened his great mouth again. A piece of pastry hung from his upper tooth and Stone watched it, transfixed, while he waited for the next words of this enigmatic, old man.

"Ah! Yes. That is a very good question."

For the first time, Stone noticed that Enkoodabaooh's own feet were adorned by very large and ornate slippers, made of leather and decorated with plumes of feathers. They gave him somewhat the look of a large, bronzed chicken, what with the plumed feather hat as well. Stone wanted to laugh but bit his lip.

Two beautiful young women came to the door-opening of one of the other houses.

"My youngest wives," Enkoodabaooh said, indicating them. Two of the children ran up to the women and took shelter under their arms. These women too, were ornately dressed in many colourful layers of finely woven tunics.

"Clearly Enkoodabaooh is a rich man!" thought Stone.

"Where is the fifth wife?" he asked. "Is she ill?"

"No. She is working," He indiced a woman working at what looked, to Stone, like a crude iron-furnace

"My first wife," said Enkoodabaooh. "Actually she is not my first but she's the oldest one still alive!"

"Look at that Jay, Dee! A furnace. Wow!"

"It's too early for one isn't it, dude?" Dee pointed out.

"Exactly what I said when we saw the arrow-head Dee. But there it is."

"Now I will answer your question. When I was very small I lived in the village with all the other children. But I was a restless child and went to live with the old shaman."

Enkoodabaooh told them of his youth and the years until he had seen the visitors:

"Then one night, there were very bright stars of many colours that moved across the sky. The old shaman was afraid but I was not. The following day a great white bird, shaped like a fish, landed over there, near the village."

"I ran to the village and saw tall men, with heads like dogs, talking to villagers. But they would not listen and fired arrows. I saw a terrible light, flashing everywhere, and many of our people died. I ran to fetch the shamam.

When we returned to the village, do you know what we found?"

His guests slowly shook their heads, rapt.

"Everybody in the village fell silent... but the tall dog-men walked among them. It was as if the Naxa had become children. Each of them wore a small amulet around their neck. I tried to take one from a young warrior but he hit me. The magic of these amulets was very powerful. One of the dog-men, the leader, whose name was Anx-duschi'a, walked up to me and talked to me. At first I felt scared but he did not point at me with his fingers or give me an amulet. He explained that they were from a place very far away and that they were friends. They knew how to build tall houses and make food from all the things around us. They would make our tribe very powerful if I would talk to the others and stop them fighting. I said I would. They gave me great baskets of food, arrows and spears with shining points which would not break. They took the amulets away from the children first, then the women and then the old men. Each time I explained that we should be friends and each time there were even more baskets of food so that most listened to me and accepted the new tribe. Eventually we were friends with them."

His audience had their eyes fixed on the strange old man, as he illustrated his story with gentle hand gestures.

"They told us they came from a land in the sky and they called themselves the Bekians. But we believed they were gods and so we called them the New Gods. This made them angry. They forbid us to worship them but as the tribe became more powerful, nearly all secretly worshipped them. We fashioned amulets in the likeness of those they had given us."

His eyes opened wider as he continued to talk about the strange visitors

"But not all believed that they came from the sky. Some believed they were jackals which the Gjanga tribe's shaman had put a spell on. The Naxa chief did not believe them. He secretly organised a small hunting party of warriors and attacked the great white fish-bird, one night. But they never returned. His son also did not believe but he was more cunning. He watched and waited. He was still waiting when he was an old man and when his spirit flew into the sky with the eagles!"

He cackled at his own joke.

"Meanwhile, the Bekians organised us men to build a great white temple to the stars, great house with a pointed roof, near the village. You have seen it." He said this with certainty. "We had so much food, water and drink that we had nothing else to do so we were happy to help. We learned how to cut rock with knives that sparkled in the sun. For a while, everyone felt happy, even the dog-men who could be angry at times... They also made the Itchik and Gjanga tribe allies so that they would help with the sky-temple."

Stone put his hand up politely as if he were still in school. "Excuse me but were the dog-men black?"

"Yes. Some of them but not all."

"Did they have long ears?"

"Yes and sometimes their ears stood up like a dog when it is hunting."

"And they looked like jackals?"

"Their heads, yes. Their bodies were like a Naxa warrior but they were the height of two Naxa."

"Um. Thank you."

"Ha! Ha! You are curious, Stone. Have you seen them before?"

Stone answered hastily, "No!"

Enkoodabaooh's penetrating gaze searched Stone's eyes for the truth.

"How do you know our names?" asked Jay.

"I know much about you. A shaman must have eyes everywhere. Otherwise he wouldn't be a shaman would he? Let me continue," he said. "It took many years to build the first level of the great sky-temple. Chooveyo, the cautious Chief of the Naxa was an old man and his children were already young men. The old shaman had died and because I had learned all of his magic, I had now become the shaman. The Beka'ns, as the tribe called them, told us to paint the rooms of the great house with strange symbols and designs. Few of us could paint well enough for them but one, Hotoato, had great talent and they gave him the job of making the altar painting. They showed him the design but he was one of those who passionately believe the Bek'ans really were the New Gods. One night, he painted over the design they had shown him and painted the likeness of Vinu, the God of Bek'ans, instead. When Anx-duschi'a saw this he became very angry and all the Bekians left for a pow-wow. They did not return for days and then only Anx-duschi'a came, alone. He talked to me and told me that they were leaving. He told me that he felt sad to leave but that the Bekians had wanted us as friends and not worshippers. He told me to look for the coloured stars in the sky. 'One day we will come back.' Then then left. We felt very sad on that day."

Enkoodabaooh shook his head sadly.

"Hotoato himself didn't want to, but many tried to carry on building the sky-temple. But without the Bek'ans we had to hunt for food again and before long nobody had time to work on it and we abandoned it. The other tribes drifted away and we became enemies again. I don't know if it was because the old gods were angry too but it rained little the next summer and each summer since seems to have become worse. Many have starved. Chooveyo's two sons, Cheveya and Avonaico grew up, and when he died, they had to fight to decide who would be Chief. Cheveya, who believed in the New Gods, won but many of the tribe followed Avonaico who did not believe in the New Gods. Cheveya said all the tribe should worship the New Gods, but he knows many secretly worship the old gods and to keep the peace, he allows this."

"Are you sure Cheveya believes in the New Gods?" asked Stone.

"Yes."

"I am not sure he does."

"I remember both Cheveya and Avonaico sitting on my lap when they were little and I know what Cheveya believes."

"Oh!" Stone replied.

Jay laughed at the thought of the great Chief sitting on Enkoodabaooh's lap.

"Well, that is the end of my story. Now if you will excuse me I have many things I must do..."

"Wait!" said Stone. "You haven't told us about the … the arrow-heads. How you learned to make them … ."

"I believe I have, haven't I?" the shaman said with a mischievous glint in his eyes.

"No."

"Oh. Well … I spent a lot of time waiting around in the camp of the Bek'ans, trying to learn as much as I could. There were lots of young women there too. For some reason, which I could never understand, the Bek'ans were very keen to have women around the camp but not, generally, the men. They always chose the prettiest girl. And they were always talking about a secret girl; Ee Em forate ninifive. It's a strange name for a woman. I guess they must have kept her in the great white fish-bird because I never saw her. I looked … ."

He looked sad for a moment.

"Anyway, they didn't want men. I was an exception. I even climbed inside the great white fish-bird; it was hollow, you know. And they taught me how to make the shiny 'iron.' They showed me how to beat it to make simple objects like the amulets, not magic ones but the ones the Naxa use today, and little sheets that reflect light."

"It's a great skill to have," said Stone.

"Yes. You know, I saw the many-coloured stars a few nights before you came to the Naxa."

"Really?" Stone tried to sound disinterested.

"Anx-duschi'a once told me that the land of the Bek'ans was on a star very far away. I believed him."

Enkoodabaooh's sadness, combined with his curiosity, cut Stone to the core. He found it very hard to look at the old man.

"We have to get going Stone," Jay whispered.

"He knows, Stone," she told Stone when they were out of earshot. "Enkoodabaooh knows about us."

"I know."

"Do you think he'll talk to Cheveya?"

"Tonight? I doubt it."

"No, I mean later."

"I don't know."

"You're going to have to tell Cheveya."

"I know. I'll tell him when we get back to the village."

***

The Red-Earth Moon Ceremony involved all the women passing into a dark cave, from which they didn't return for several days. While in the cave3, they stripped completely and painted themselves in red ochre. Outside, the men also stripped and painted themselves, including Stone and Dee. They also at powder from a mushroom, which stone guessed to be of the soma variety. He took a pinch, put it on his tongue and then held the bowl of kech to his mouth. Enkoodabaooh seemed just about to move the green leaf away when Stone grabbed a handful of the powder and shoved it in his mouth, washing it down with the milky liquid.

"Ewww! Tastes foul! Ha!"

"Wow... that's a lo-..." But Dee was interrupted by the shaman, who was hopping from one foot to the other, shouting something in Naxa which they didn't understand. All the man looked gravely at Stone but he laughed back at them. Enkoodabaooh looked very agitated and indicated with a wagging finger that Stone had eaten too much. He then mimed putting fingers down his throat and retching, to show that Stone should try and vomit it out.

"Nah! I am fine!" Stone wagged his finger back and Enkoodabaooh slapped his hand on his forehead.

Woo, this is fun! Powerful stuff!

All the stars he imagined above him, seemed to expand into spheres of light as he looked at them and he found himself looking for Earth. At the very moment he thought he would find it, among all the trillions of stars within his view, he found himself being drawn back to earth. Three lights; green, blue and red, dancing over the hills to the east caught his attention. They came straight over the top of him and shot away over the western horizon.

Our ship? Was that us? No.

***

When they returned to the village, Jay began organising an infirmary. Stone could see she was manipulating him into making a move so he told Cheveya about the cruiser. Cheveya seemed excited and immiately agreed to help dig it out of the sand. However, when Stone readhed the crash site, he couldn't find it.

"Perhaps the sand has buried it," he suggested to the Chief.

They dug for a while just over the crest of the tallest dune but found nothing. They moved to the next dune and then Stone saw something shiny protruding from the sand.

"There it is!" he shouted

They could see the top of the ship's hull. They began to dig.

"Stop!" Dee held up his hand, hours later. He peered into the hole that the men had dug. He instructed the tribesmen to dig a trench all the way to the main hatch.

Cheveya and the Naxa men were silenced by the sight of the great, metal ship. Their mouths hung open.

Cheveya asked, "Can I touch her? Will it hurt?"

"No! Go ahead," Stone replied.

"She is so smooth!" the Cheveya said, running hands along the smooth contours of the ship. "And beautiful!"

The tribesmen dug all day to reveal the port winglet, which Dee feared most might be badly damaged. When the tribesmen finally uncovered it, t looked to themas if the front wing-let, used for steering in planet atmospheres, had been purposefully bent up to the vertical from its original horizontal position.

"Well, at least it's a neat bend," Dee announce. "That's lucky! We should be able to straighten it, with a tree or two."

"Yeah! Heh! Heh!"

"Well..." Dee's voice echoed in the alloy-shelled cavity. "Actually the wiring and instruments are basically intact. If the atomic-gyros are also intact then we might be okay. Of course the engine is probably a mess, judging by the pylon, but it doesn't have many working parts. We might have to get old Enki to build a bigger furnace."

"Cool. That's a relief. So we have a chance then?"

"Well, no."

"Huh? Why not?"

"Well. Like I said when we crashed, the lightning that hit us when we entered the atmosphere shorted out most of the avionics equipment that still worked... It's why we had to land manually and why we crashed. Up until then, the main problem we had seemed to be the violence of deceleration coming out of the worm-hole. But that screwed the navigation. Dunno why, probably 'cos it lost its orientation or something. It just seems to have gone haywire and then shorted out. *Now*, it looks like we can probably fix the avionics but I don't know about the navigation. Without that we'll never even *find* the wormhole, let alone get *through it*!"

Darkness was falling. Cheveya took the decision that they must stay for the night so Stone showed them vids about life on Earth.

Then there were many images of animals from around the world; horses, tigers, bison, lions, kangaroos and whales. When they saw the bison the men all pointed excitedly shouting "Moosto!", and when they saw the tiger their mouths dropped open in admiration.

***

Two events interrupted the trip back to the village. The first occurred just as they reached the cliffs on the edge of the salt flats.

"On the hill... Up there," Stone told Dee, nodding towards the shoulder of rock to their East. "They see movement... Itchik."

"We're being watched then."

"It's not good. Suppose they follow our tracks back to the ship?"

"Yeah."

The second event was more traumatic. One of the Naxa men, at the head of the column, suddenly held his hand up and yelled. He ran forward and knelt down next to a bundle by the path. They were at a point where the territories of the three tribes, Naxa, Itchik and Gjanga, met.

The kneeling man lifted the linen tunic wrapping from the bundle and held it up for his companions to see. Under it lay a pile of bones. They recognised the tunic at once.

"Hototo! Hototo!" the kneeling cried. Lifting the two femurs for all to see, he stroked them affectionately.

"It is Hototo. They took him in the attack on the village," Cheveya said sadly. A tear rolled down his cheek. "They were very close friends... We knew it would be so. Still, sad when you know that their spirit is gone."

"We're sorry," offered Stone.

The man ahead of them gathered the bones and wrapped them in the Hototo's tunic. He came towards them and the other warriors gathered him into their arms.

That night, the whole tribe fell into mourning. When the wailing had been done, Stone asked Cheveyo what would become of Hototo's spirit.

"When the New Gods came, we believed that you walked the earth at night as a spirit until you had learned to be at peace and then you could choose to be born again. Some believe what the Sacred dog people told them and no longer believe that but I do."

"What did they teach you, the New Gods?" asked Jay.

"They said we should worship their God. But when we asked his name they would not tell us! Well, we were very confused. We asked how they worshipped this god with no name and they told a very strange thing! They told us that they had worshipped one called Vinu for many, many lives of men on their world, but then they had found that they were wrong! Now they knew that Vinu was not a god but only the first of their tribe. Of course we wanted to help but we asked them where we should look. They said that we would find the answer inside us. That is why they wanted us to build the Sky House. They said they would show us how to paint images in the rooms which would help us. But that led to a sad end... Anyway I have spoken enough for tonight. I must leave you to think on Hototo and then I must walk around the village and talk to my people. It will be a long night." With that, he left.

"Stone doesn't have a god," Jay said.

"No?" said Shihu. "None?" She looked sadly at Stone.

"Not yet," he said cautiously.

***

Work continued to dig out the spaceship. A crew of about ten men and twenty women would go out to the ship in the morning and some would return in the evening. Others would stay inside the ship to continue digging the following day. Naxa men posted a lookout on top of the cliffs near the promontory. They were watching for Itchik.

Stone sat with them one night, looking up at the night sky. He watched a point of light streaking across the hills ahead of him, from right to left, not really thinking about what he saw. Then a second streak tore him from his reverie. He wondered what it was.

Shooting star?

Moments later, he had completely forgotten his thoughts.

Red, green and a blue points of light streaked across the hills covering his whole field of view in perhaps two seconds before disappearing, in formation, to the north.

What the fu...!

The men with him didn't understand what he tried to tell them. He hurried back to the village at dawn.

Arriving at Dee's house he burst in without knocking.

"Dee! Jay! Guess what I've just seen!"

"Oh Stone... not again! You really should knock," Jay exclaimed, grabbing one of Dee's shirts to cover herself.

"A blue, green and red light streaking across the sky!"

"Where?" asked Dee

"Across the hill I climbed when we first came up the valley... over the Itchik village I guess and then way up to the north."

"Three lights, you say?" asked Dee.

"Yes!"

"Are you sure?" quizzed Jay.

"Yes! Yes! It can only be one thing!"

The two faces looked at him expectantly.

A spaceship!

He strode around the room as he spoke.

"They must still be here! Do you think we could ask them for help? No. No. I guess not. But it's *something*! We can find a way back. I'm *sure of it*! The only thing is though, why didn't Enkoodabaooh mention it? He must have known. It flew straight over his house..."

"Calm down Stone," Dee said. "Maybe it's the first time. Maybe it was just one ship. And maybe it wasn't even a ship. Have you thought of that? There are other things it *could* be."

"No, no. I am telling you, it was a ship. It..."

"It could be a plane," interjected Jay.

"Yeah... I guess *so*! But even that's good. Technology...! Parts...! But why didn't Enkoodabaooh tell us. Now I am getting really quite angry! I have to go and speak to him. Maybe he knows more than he's saying."

Stone's visit to the old shaman had to be short. Busy with his furnace, the old man had little time to talk. Stone told him of the lights and Enkoodabaooh told him the aliens ships were still there.

"But why didn't you tell me!" said Stone, astonished.

"You didn't ask me."

"Have you seen them, the ships?"

"No, but when I was a boy I saw one on the ground, in a long valley. You won't want to go *there*!"

"I do! Where?"

"It's deep within Gjanga territory, in their old sacred valley. Avonaico knows it. It's very dangerous to go there. Twenty of us went, four came back … . We lost a lot of good warriors."

***

When Stone returned to the village from his visit to the shaman, he excitedly told his friends about the crashed alien spaceship. They were as surprised and excited as Stone.

"But is it *alien*?" Dee asked.

"Yeah. Has to be, doesn't it?"

"Shit. I mean it's cool, but it doesn't help us, does it?"

"You're not thinking man. Think. What can the alien ships do that ours can't?"

"I dunno … . Go through worm-holes?"

"Yeah … and?"

"I dunno Stone. Stop torturing me."

"What do they use for that? Navigation equipment. They can *navigate* through holes."

"Shit yeah! But wait. We can't use their equipment. It's probably not even made of metal, it'll be that gooey bio-stuff and there's *no way* I'll understand what it *does*. I won't even understand the language. How will we read it?"

"Yeah. You got a point. But you'll figure it *out* Dee!"

"You're always saying that!"

"No, he's right Dee. You will!" added Jay.

"We gotta go there... But it needs careful planning. Enkoodabaooh says he's been there with twenty warriors and lost a lot of men," Stone told them.

"Why?" asked Jay

"It's deep in Gjanga territory."

***

Hri-hu's com-pod bleeped in the apartment.

"Yes? Um-hm. Okay. I will be right there. Don't touch anything and get the security-recordings."

"What is it dear?" asked Kek-suîxjh, pretending innocent ignorance.

"Oh nothing. My office door alarm went off. Probably just a cleaner who left it open. If I am not back in time, eat without me."

"Fine. I will cook something for you to eat though."

"Thank you dear. You are so sweet! Log out when you are finished."

She nuzzled him and left for the office.

Now is my chance!

The hack-programme Kek-suîxjh's device had installed, not only blocked the mind-logger from logging his activity, replacing it with dummy activity, but also retrieved logs of Hri-hu's activity. All Kek-suîxjh only had to look for an out-of-context phrase which looked like a password.

There! What is that? '125u1xjh2259.'

He recognised his own name and the date of their marriage.

Very slack! She never was very technologically-minded! Now all I have to do... is... type this in... and then... there we go! Access! Ha! Ha! Now just do a quick search for A-R-C-A-D-I-A... and there it is! That was easy! Mm, fascinating.

He decided to print out the documents. There were just too many documents for him to digest right there and then. Of course the printer would log this but he would be long gone before she would ever check and find out what he had seen.

***

5. Fuel on the Fire

Ho-hi wandered lazily down the country lane towards her home-town of E-îx-eej. That familiar feeling of security from childhood swept over her as she took in the blue fields, speckled with early-spring flowers. A few black specks circled above her; eîtch-uns looking for an easy meal. Ambi-xjhu often told her that his home planet of Isch-su also had blue sky but had green vegetation.

Imagine that? Blue trees and green grass! Something about the crystals of some metal, strontium or magnesium or something, that caused the green colour, Ambi-xjhu. Bek even means 'blue'! But wait, wasn't it actually named by the Ischians?

Ho-hi frowned. She still felt still confused about her culture. Once it had seemed simple; there were Bekians and the Sky-Gods. But now that she lived with a god, things were not so simple. She shrugged.

So good to be home!

Apart from scientist, Ambi-xjhu's had another role as chief-statistician and he had asked her opinion on the people's mood at the moment. Not being sure, she now made her way to a political rally to assess the mood for him. It would be a good opportunity to do something useful for her lover and catch up with her family at the same time.

Lover! Can you believe it? I have a Sky-God as a lover! I wonder if I can ever be something in the world of Sky-Gods. After all I have the ischian drive for organisation and I must have the right genes, I look right for the part. I am sure I could do it. I must talk to Ambi about it some time.

"Passing!" called a mechanical voice from behind and then she heard the crunch of biomium on gravel as a robot, with wheeled foot-ware, passed her. She watched, admiring its smooth motion as it shrunk to a dot and then vanished around a bend ahead of her.

Not far from where I first met Ambi!

She recalled how she had first met him:

She had been out for the day in the country with her brother's family and had wandered off after lunch to be by herself. She felt her skin go cold so she instinctively looked up to the sky for signs of a Sky-God ship. Bekians only whispered among themselves of the mythical Sky-Gods, whose great floating ships were invisible but blocked the heat when they passed. Could it be that one was passing?

Soon the air grew warm again. She plucked a flower delicately using her first and second claw and put the stem to her lips to suck it experimenteally but she became distrated by a good-looking Ischian male, walking towards her. She stood still, waiting for him curiously, watching an elegance in his stride that she found attractive.

"Hello. I am lost. Can you help me?" he said, smiling.

Now she could see blood, seeping from a small cut above his left eye and that his clothes looked strange. These new facts made her nervous. But the element of danger just made her more curious about the stranger.

"Have you been in a crash?" she asked

"Ha! Yes. Sort of."

"Are you alright? Is anybody else hurt?"

"No. It was just me and I am alright. I just need to get to the nearest town as soon as possible. I believe it's called E-îx-eej?"

"Yes. I live there."

Oo! I shouldn't have told him that.

She remembered being cold, earlier.

"Are you from a sky ship?"

"A sky ship? What is that?"

"It's when something passes between the sun and the ground and cuts out the warm air. Just for a moment!

Some say if there is cloud about, you can see the ellipse of a ship disturbing the cloud but I haven't seen that. I thought I felt something cold just now though!"

His eyes widened.

"Really. Well... I... er. What is your name?"

"Ho^bixjhu."

"Well Ho^bixjhu, I would like to know more about what your people whisper among themselves. Would you be my guide for the day? Or... or are you too busy?"

"Ho-hi. You can call me Ho-hi." She looked at him and considered what her feelings told her about him. She decided she liked him.

"It will cost you a meal in the best restaurant in town?" she announced.

"Ha! It's a deal!"

How he had resisted in the restaurant before telling her more of the sky ships and Sky-Gods!

Now, nearing the rally, she began to see more signs of activity; white banners fluttering in the distance, large tents and bobbing heads of Bekians above the hedges.

A waist-high sales-bot, green and rusty, waddled up to her from the verge to wave a programme in front of her.

"Cheapest programmes anywhere! You *can't* go in without *one!*"

"Oh yeah?" she replied. "Watch me."

Ho-hi saw a large queue ahead. It snaked towards the gate of the rally, on her right. She smiled at a young Bekian male, with very short ears, near the front of the queue. He grinned artlessly at her, then edged backwards to make space. She joined him. An old bekian, heavy and with badly applied face-adornment, glared at her from the queue ahead but said nothing.

They passed under the banner that announced 'Worker's Liberation Party Rally' and through the gate to a muddy field. Ho-hi quickly released herself from her guileless male and wandered off into the crowd. There were stalls selling food and clothes as well as books about the 'struggle' and other Isch-suian philosophical works. On the central of three stages, a band played loudly and young Bekians swayed and gyrated to the music as only young Bekians could. Ho-hi grinned and worked her way towards the outer edge of this throng.

I am here on business. I shouldn't actually dance! Oh why not? Ambi will laugh when I tell him.

The last song stretched into a long jam session, followed by an encore before the band left the stage.

The MC announced that Bam-shuxîxj himself would speak to the crowd in the keynote speech next. The crowd waited restlessly.

Who on Bek-su is Bam-shuxîxj? I've never heard of him?

Everyone around her seemed to know *exactly* who Bam-shuxîxj was. The crowd collectively gasped as a small Bekian male strode confidently onto the stage. Ho-hi couldn't see his features too clearly but he had very short ears, even for a third-generation Bekian. He also looked particularly short and slight.

I know the type. Small and bitter! A pain!

Most strange of all were his clothes. He wore a sort of triangular black hat, which wrapped around his ears with one point projecting over his snout. He wore a blue suit, military in style, and had a black-edged armband with a symbol, which Hi-hi couldn't quite make out, coloured black in the centre.

Very odd!

He raised his paws and silenced the crowd.

"Friends," he began. "It's an honour to finally come to E-îx-eej, the last bastion of conservatism, to deliver our message! The WLP's ideas for freedom and progress cannot for much longer be kept out of this great town, now that the biomium walls have come down!"

His voice rose to a crescendo at the end of the last sentence and the crowd went wild. He had to raise his paws again to silence them.

Who is this runt?

Though aware she was one of the elite on Bek-su and had no particular axe to grind, Ho-hi felt nevertheless appalled by his polemic. He began with a long discourse on the deterioration of society on Bek-su. Each statement seemed oxymoronic to Ho-hi, contradicting itself and canceling out any meaning. He was, however, fascinating to watch.

He dipped his head for a moment, deep in thought, before continuing.

"Friends. Bek-su has plenty of mineral wealth. We have water and minerals, more than we need. And we have tools to extract these minerals. But each time we progress by inventing some new, sophisticated tool, we find that it's instantly outlawed by the ruling elite! Reactionary Conservatives, each and every one of them! They maintain our existence here on Bek-su as a form of servitude. They poison our minds with ideas about religion and morality, which keep us in servitude. I say that the Workers are the ones who make this planet what it is. Oh yes, we know that we were brought here by Ischians, those we call Sky-Gods. And we are grateful. But now it is time for us to create an identity for ourselves. To take what we have worked for and make it ours!"

The crowd applauded enthusiastically.

"Complaisance is not an option! It leads to a kind of liberal decadence! Oh yes. This is what I mean when I write about the decadence that not only permeates our society but even the ranks of followers around you. Drugs, prostitution, artisan networks who have no knowledge or interest in work. Yes. We have all seen them and even here, in E-îx-eej, in the Conservative heartland, I believe there is *such* a community. And the most decadent and insidious element of all? The religious! I will come to them later."

She saw much nodding from the crowd.

"Do you know the reason for these... problems? This deterioration in our true state. I will tell you. Have you not noticed how each generation of us lives shorter lives? Yes, I see that you have. We know who's doing this to us. It's those we call the Sky-Gods. They are doing this to us: it's genetic-engineering and it is Evil! I tell you it is *is Evil*!" Pleased with the way he had worked them up, he then calmed the crowd with a gesture of his hands.

"Calm yourselves friends. All is not lost. Let us, the Workers accept what, and who, we have become and make a stand. Let us cast out those we once thought of as the elite, those gangly individuals with long, furry ears and a superior-to-thou attitude. Theirs is the greatest decadence and it pollutes our society."

Ho-hi felt the suspicion of those around her. The hairs on her neck stood up.

After clarifying, at some length, just how to identify the elite's impure form of thought, he reached the climax of his speech.

"Friends. If we are to become a great people, a planet of beings proud of their heritage, we must pull together. And I don't just mean the working males. I mean the old, the young and the females too. Although we do not believe in the rule of females, another insidious tradition of the elite, we do believe in equality. Females too will find a place in our New World. And I tell you something else! I cannot tell you where, or when, but I *can* tell you that there are new lands to conquer. There will be much mineral wealth and food for all. No longer will there be those scraping an existence on the very edge of society, forced to live in places where nothing grows and there is no clean water. *All* will be provided for. We will have new lands to settle and new communities to build! Where will this be? I cannot tell you yet. But follow us and soon you will learn this secret. So 'how should we live?' I hear you ask. Do you see the robots that serve us every day? Are they not content? They do not feel, do not cry and do not hurt others. They feel no pain! Be like them. Feel nothing. Do not give in to the appetites of the body. Obey only those who are your natural leaders. And now we come to those who deserve our most careful consideration. I told you I would come to them specifically. We have discussed how we are being manipulated – I cannot bring myself to name the science that they use against us because it is too vile – by those the elite are in league with. You know who I mean. Yes. Those up there."

He jabbed his finger at the sky.

"Religion! Ha! Tell me of religion and I will tell you a fairy-story for young Ischians. I tell you the elite are the real slaves around here. Their obsequious allegiance to the so-called Sky-Gods, and their false ideas are a kind of servitude. If there are demons, and I do not say there are..."

He paced up and down the stage, giving the crowd time to feel included in his deepest considerations.

"... *the elite* are the *demons*! But the most evil ones are these so-called Sky-Gods. Do you remember how, at first, they were keen to have us worship Vîu? How they tried so very hard to stop us worshipping them as gods? Many of you won't because our lives are so short now but some of your grandparents might, if they are still alive. They didn't try very hard, or for very long did they? Soon they were only too happy to accept the elite's worship of them as gods, as *the Gods*. They are false. Why do we not have better weapons to defend ourselves? Because *they* tell the elite to ban them. They are scared. How can a god be scared? They make our lives shorter and shorter. Why do they do this? Because they are scared of *us*. And anyway, why would a god do such a terrible thing? It is not right."

Very clever that bit. Covering all bases, taking in the religious and the non-religious.

"I tell you, in my opinion, there are *no* gods. *But whether you believe in them or not, we* know the way forward and it is not through religion, but hard work. Put your faith in us and we will take you there!"

The crowd rippled like a choppy sea now.

"But it won't be easy! Those so-called *Sky-Gods*, who are really vagrants, sneaking around as they do in invisible ships, will try to stop us. Our struggle must continue and it will reach a point, not very far off, when it must become an armed struggle. I see that now. We cannot avoid it. It will come to that and we must be ready."

He drew himself up to his full, if not significant, height for his final blast of vitriol. "Friends! Arm yourselves! The day for battle, and victory, is near!"

The crowd erupted into a thunderous storm of applause and shouting. Young Ischians were thrown in the air, along with streamers and anything else the frenzied crowd could find. Hands pushed at Ho-hi and she felt a thump on her back.

Disgusted, and scared, Ho-hi peeled away from the throng and headed towards where she remembered the gate to be. She noticed a white banner above a tent with a black ring on it.

That's the symbol on his sleeve!

As she passed the stall under the banner she saw out of the corner of her eye, something blue and shiny, passed from one paw to another in the shadows. It would not be her last glimpse of a laser before she left the rally.

***

Ho-hi hurried into town to reach her brother's house before nightfall, scared for her life.

"Ho-hi! What's the matter? You look like you have seen a ghost!"

"I think I have. Or something like it."

"You are earlier than we expected. Just putting the kids to bed. Take a seat and En-hu will get you something to drink. En-hu!"

The drink calmed her down and Ho-hi waited until they had finished dinner before explaining her state.

"I just went to that rally outside town, the Workers' one."

"Oh them. Yeah. We hear a lot of rumours but I don't think they will amount to much," her brother replied.

"I don't know. I am not so sure. The main speaker, Bam-shuxîxj, was pretty convincing. I abhor his ideas but a lot of people seemed persuaded by him. He has a power over a crowd. I think he's dangerous."

"Oh him. Yes we have heard he is arming people, militia, in some of the more backward towns."

"Kri! Don't say 'backward.' If we are ignorant, we become like them and then they really will *gain* ground."

"Sorry! Well if you are interested, there *is* a rumour that it has something to do with aliens, you know those 'humans' or whatever they're called. Some say that there is a … colonisation of their planet being planned by a break away section of Sky-Gods and that the ground-troops will be provided by Bam-shuxîxj."

Ho-hi didn't know much about the humans. Ambi-xjhu had told her they were a very stubborn race. Apparently the worm-hole that Ischian scientists had created to Earth's past terminated at a date 1.2 K-years in the past. Excited at this discovery, the scientists made an attempt to induce the humans to look for the True God, father or mother of Vîu. But the humans had convinced themselves that the scientists were gods and worshipped the image of Vîu. They could not be dissuaded from this and so were abandoned. So, as had been the original plan, the race of Bekians were created to look for the True God. Now that seemed to have failed too.

"My Vîu! Do you think that's possible?"

"Well, if you want my opinion, I don't think it's very likely. What able-bodied support has Bam-shuxîxj got? One-hundred thousand, a million at most. I hear the population on Ear^h is in the trillions. Even if you had all the Bekian males between 800 and 2400 years old, that would be still only about two million."

"No, you are right. It could never work."

"Mind you. I hear that Ear^h is dying anyway. And the population is divided; rebels and some organised states. It might well be worth just extracting the mineral wealth. The planet has enormous mineral wealth. They say that iron is one of the most common. Imagine that! Here only the very richest can afford bracelets made of iron! We could mine it and let the planet die."

"Kri! I can't believe you are saying that! You are sounding just like one of these … revolutionaries."

"Well. You have to admit. Things are getting pretty bad."

Ho-hi pushed the remainder of her food around the plate with her knife. "Do you still believe in the Gods, Kri?"

"With what you hear these days, factions within them, and the restrictions they place on us, it's hard to know what to believe."

***

After she had checked on Avonaico's progress on returning to the village, Jay immediately embarked on her programme of teaching hygiene to the Naxa women.

Jay had been walking back from one of her hygiene lessons a few days after Stone's visit to Enkoodabaooh when she came upon Stone walking around the village. He became lost in thought. Her blue eyes gazed at him steadily from beneath her increasingly thick mane of dark hair.

"Your hair's getting long, Stone. You can hardly see it was a stripe any more. It's just longer down the middle. But you look well-shaved! Ha!"

"Yeah. I stopped shaving. I don't need to any more. Weird innit? I can't explain it."

"Really? That's strange."

"Yeah. Same for Dee. Almost like we're getting younger! Ha! Have you been out to the ship lately?"

"No. The women want me to go. Shihu went yesterday but I'm just too busy here, hm."

"I'm going tomorrow. Dee wants my opinion on something. I think they're making pretty good progress."

There had still been no sign of a hunting party sent to the great plain and there would be no dried mammoth left within a day or two, perhaps fortunate because everybody had grown sick of the taste of it. Nevertheless, food had become short so everyone only took a small pack with them, to the ship. It contained only a large water bag, some stale bread wrapped in damp linen and sixteen thin strips of salty, dried fish. He had strapped his wooden shovel to the pack's side.

"Hey Stone!" shouted Dee, as he caught up.

"Hey."

"What's up?"

"Nothin' much. Just told Jay about our … er … un-growth," Stone said stroking his smooth chin.

"Oh yeah. Weird, innit. I wonder if she has noticed anything … ."

"Like what?"

"I dunno … ."

"How's it going with her? We haven't talked for a while have we?"

"No. Been too busy. You mean in bed?"

"Well, that too, but in general?"

"Yeah. It's fine. I think sometimes some of her ideas go over my head but we get on fine," Dee replied. "Great in bed though! Ha! She's really something.' Really hungry for it, know what I mean?"

"Heh! Yeah. Shihu is … . Well … . Oh you know what I mean."

"Nope. I guess for the first time ever you are a bit shy, aren't you Stone? *Aren't* you?" Dee pointed his finger accusingly at his friend, laughing.

"Maybe. I just wonder what'll happen if we do leave. We can't take her … . I just don't know what to do … . She makes me feel … ."

"Yes?"

"*Humble.*"

"Oh Stoney!"

"Shut up!"

"Anyway, you should have thought of that before."

"Thanks! How *is* Jay? You know I thought I was the leader around here but now I realise that it's Jay who is really controlling everything. She's amazing!" Stone chuckled.

"Careful. She's not for sale!" Dee looked darkly at Stone.

"*Sale*? I never heard you use that term before." Stone pondered this for a few minutes and then continued:

"One of the few things we both stood for … . I mean what we stood against was the New Feminism; that women should see themselves as products. Are you saying you have bought into it? Become cosy?"

"Not cosy, no but maybe. There's a lot you don't know about me Stone."

"Or is it … ." Stone daren't finish the thought. He shook his head.

Did he mean making money from her? Not Dee, surely!

It was too awful a thought to contemplate, even for Stone.

They walked along the trail, making use of any shade they could find as the fierce sun climbed higher in the sky.

"Any power in that thing?" Stone said, pointing to the headband hanging around Dee's neck.

"Naah! I'm taking it out to the ship, hoping to charge it. Those batteries drained long ago. You know, it worries me … . The reactor torus in the ship; we're lucky it wasn't damaged in the landing. It's designed to last for months and in almost any conditions. It has its own coolant supply but I seem to remember reading somewhere that they do loose some of the heat through the air-con system and some through the skin of the ship. Trouble is, I can't remember where. Obviously the air-con don't work anymore but we need the reactor to cool through the skin. I just don't remember where. If we don't dig it out soon it may just melt-down. I have never heard of one doing that just by being left, but you never know. It's bloody hot out there."

"How come you never told me this before?"

"I dunno. Didn't think of it I guess. It's been kinda nagging at my mind for a while but I wasn't sure what it was. Half-formed thought, if you like. And another thing. I dunno if there will be enough fuel in the engines to get us off. I do know that they won't develop full power. They're gonna be damaged, that's for sure, and although they are basically just pulse jets, we won't be able to get them generating more than basic raw power. The second stage injectors won't work, or at least the timing is probably screwed, and I doubt the engine-flow regulators are still working properly."

"Oh great! If we don't have any fuel for them we're really screwed!"

"Well I dunno Stone! I'm just saying..! Anyway we can probably make fuel for that. Any alcohol would probably do it, even Enky's white stuff."

"Ha! I found out what it's made of. You can definitely have it for fuel. I ain't drinking it again."

"What's in it then?"

"Never mind. Tell you later. So what is the biggest problem then? I mean, with the engines?"

"Like I say, they are just pulse jets … ."

"Don't mean nuffin' to *me*."

"Well, they are simplicity itself but the problem is going to be power. As you know, normally you can rotate the pods to vertical, we don't even know if we can get that to work, but assuming we can, the problem then is that they won't generate enough power for us to take off. These middle-of-the-range cruisers are great for just hopping around but they are not military grade; there's no inbuilt power margins. Full power is only just enough for most moons and planets of say, up to 0.5G. They aren't designed for a takeoff from a 1G planet."

"Great. So what we gonna do then?"

"Well. What I'm starting to think is that we cut a slope in the dune, down to the channel between the dunes, a shallow slope. Then we turn the pods to … maybe forty-five degrees, which will only need about seventy percent of the power. Of course it will take about half a mile to takeoff but it's much more likely to work. The danger if we go for vertical takeoff is that we will shake the thing to bits and still fail to get anywhere. We probably don't have much fuel left so we don't want to waste any more."

"Half a *mile*?"

"Yeah. That's what I wanted to show you today. I want your opinion on whether you think you can do it. There's enough space but at the edge of the valley is that steep rock face. And it goes up for … what? Five hundred feet?"

"Yeah and we're gonna be pulp if we hit *that*. Won't the friction of the sand be too great?"

"Not really, dude. You can even surf down sand dunes if you have a board. It acts like water when its fine and really dry, like this stuff. As long as we don't do it early morning when it's dewy, or soon after rain, we should be fine."

"Okay. We'll take a look. You know those women dig like demons. It makes me ashamed. An hour and I'm exhausted."

"Yeah. Me too. You know some of the women are sleeping at the ship now?"

"No! Since when?" Stone asked.

"I dunno. I was out there last night. I gave them the usual slide show which they loved and then I left with most of the women and men. But some stayed behind including Avonaico. He said it would be fine. They know how to lock the hatch if necessary, but mostly the men sleep outside and the women inside. I don't think they touch anything."

"First I heard of it!" Stone said.

"Well it means they get more digging done … ."

"That's true. I guess as long as they don't touch anything."

That night, Stone could not sleep. Something tugged at the corner of his mind. He left Shihu to sleep on her palate while he leaned against a post on the porch to feel the breeze. Sleep had begun to take him when another vision flashed before his eyes:

Strange dog-like aliens were attacking a rebek camp. Stone had been fighting with a female rebel called Ryan. The battle seemed lost and Ryan yelled for him to search in the dirt.

"What am I searching for?" he yelled.

"A door."

He scrabbled in the dirt and found something red; a red chord. He pulled it and a door opened, revealing steps down to a tunnel. But as he descended the stairs, the vision evaporated and he remembered where he was.

"What the fuck was that!" he said to himself. "Me in a battle? I don't like it." He felt cold. "Not long until dawn." He stood up and went back inside the hut to sleep.

***

When the three visitor next approached their ship with Chief Cheveya and some of his tribesmen, Stone saw something unexpected, a mass of jumbled footprints in a ring around the ship. Apparently, something unusual had happened during the night. Next to the ship, Stone saw the remains of dead Itchik warriors. When Dee opened the hatch, ten tribesmen and some women tumbled out, talking excitedly. The only word Stone could make out at first was 'Itchik.'

The men talked quickly to Cheveya, who translated for the visitors:

"Itchik attacked during the night." The Chief shook his head. "Digging must stop while I think what to do."

His men followed Cheveya as he started back towards the village.

"Wait!" Stone shouted. He rubbed his head in consternation. "Chief Cheveya!"

"Yes Stone?"

"I have an idea. Enkoodabaooh told me the Gjanga used similar icons as you do, to guard sacred sites. Why don't we put the Itchik remains on sticks and place them around the ship. Enkoodabaooh told me this stopped tribes approaching the crashed alien ship."

"Yes. That is true but the ship is not sacred to us. It would be sacrilege for us to do this thing."

"But not for me. I don't believe in God. This might even be my last act as an atheist. You never know."

"I cannot allow it Stone. You would be damning your spirit forever. It would never escape the Earth."

"Surely that is my choice."

Cheveya looked undecided. Stone saw his chance.

"I will put them on the sticks myself. Your men don't have to do anything. And when we leave, I will take them down."

"No Stone. *I* won't allow it," The strong, assertive, female voice which spoke from behind him, belonged to Jay. "It's barbaric." She spoke quickly in English so none of the tribesmen could understand. "Are we going to lower ourselves even further than the Naxa?"

"It's my choice. Look Jay, I said I'd get us out of here and I *will*! Let's not talk morals now. We can argue about them all you like when we are out in space, going home, but now, just let me make this difficult decision, on my *own*!"

Jay, unhappy, swore. "Shit!" She crossed her arms and huffed loudly.

Cheveya winked at Stone. "We will do this for you Stone. Tomorrow Avonaico will bring back the bones, painted white, as is the custom of the Naxa. He will bring spears too. The Chief explained the plan to one of the tribesmen who joined the party heading out for the village."

Stone kept to his word the next day and personally placed every bleached Itchik skull available on a spear and planted these evenly around the damaged ship. In the gaps, he placed the rest of the spears and tied the pathetic white bones that were left, mostly femurs, in bundles, to the top of these. Some of the Naxa said little prayers to the New Gods or the Mysterious One Above while they watched.

Dee said a little prayer to himself for his friend.

"You are cursed now Stone!" he said, joking.

"Shut up! Now show me what you wanted to show me yesterday."

Dee took him to the nose of the ship and pointed along the length of the tall dune, to the hazy form of the hills along the edge of the wide valley.

"I reckon it's about a mile to the cliffs. I'm going to pace it out today. Now if we cut a slope down to the base of the dunes there, I think there's enough space between them. The pods shouldn't snag on the dunes."

"Yeah! *Shouldn't*! You realise I can't steer this thing on sand Dee? It has steerable skids under the hull which will help but these dunes aren't straight. Look at that one, about four hundred yards along this dune." He pointed to it.

"Yeah. I see it. Well we will have to just smooth off the corner or something. It's the only way Stone. I just know vertical-takeoff won't work!"

"Okay! Okay! I hear you. We'll work something out. Okay, so a ramp. Yeah. I can see that. Then, assuming we get to takeoff speed, there is the cliff. Like you say, about five-hundred feet high. Hmm. Of course I could turn and try and go *along* the valley … . That's just a decision I will have to take at the last minute. It depends on how she's behaving … ."

"She! Ha! Ha! Stone, you should hear yourself!"

"Listen, if you really need something special from any machine, you have to talk to it, treat it special. You should know *that*!"

"Okay Stone. Okay! It's you whose gotta fly it."

"Her."

"Her."

"Okay lets pace it out."

They spent the morning exploring their takeoff route right up to the almost-sheer cliff at the end. Reddish-brown in colour, it only had scree and stumps of tough weeds in places to break up its forbidding façade.

"Fitting grave-stone." Stone said, under his breath.

"Really, Stone. You are quite eloquent at times."

There were three kinks between the two long dunes, on the way to the cliff. The last lay beyond what they hoped would be the takeoff point but they couldn't take risks.

They explained the plan to Cheveya.

"It will be much work Deem" the Chief replied. "I am not sure if we can do it. Are you sure it will work?"

"Yes," replied Dee.

"We will try."

***

At last the hunters returned from the plains. Food had been getting scarce. The whole tribe gathered to hear the hunters' tale.

"We traveled almost as far as the Blue Mountains. I have never gone so far before," said the oldest of the men. "We saw nothing until three days ago. Then, far out to the south we saw a small herd of moosto. Sixteen mothers with their calves, one older bull and four young ones. We debated what to do. We knew we couldn't kill the old male. He might be the only one able to breed next year. We didn't want to kill any of the females because they were still suckling the calves. And we did not want to kill any of the young bulls! It was such a small herd. Whatever we killed could end the life of the herd."

"I see," said Cheveya. "It is very sad, and a hard choice for a Naxa hunter. What did you decide?"

"We took the two smallest bulls and one old female without calf."

"Um. It's a good choice. We will eat well for the next two moons. And then it will be autumn and there will be much more to eat. The deer will pass through the forest on their way south and later there will be the salmon. It is good."

Cheveya seemed content, but Stone noticed the great sadness in his eyes.

"When the ship flies, Cheveya, we will search for the great herds and tell you where to look. It will be our present to you."

"That would be a very good thing, Stone. The Naxa would even start on a great journey if we could find big herd of moosto."

"I am sure they are there, somewhere."

"Stone. You cheer a warrior's heart. Let us drink to it!"

Stone, intoxicated with the tribe's mood of celebration and the hope of flying again, became very drunk that night. Before he had fallen asleep, uppermost in his mind had been the mission to the alien ship.

We must go soon but I don't want to burden Cheveya with another difficulty yet.

***

Another Red-Earth Moon Ceremony passed before Stone mentioned his intention to Cheveya.

The Naxa Chief listened solemnly, before speaking.

"This is madness Stone. I have heard of this place. So deep inside Gjanga territory, all warriors would die. None would return."

"But Enkoodabaooh says it's possible."

"Enkoodabaooh says many things, some that are possible and some that are not. Some we can only dream of."

Cheveya sat thinking for a while before continuing:

"If Enkoodabaooh says it's there, then I believe him Stone … . But he *also* says it's very dangerous. Are you sure you need this 'navigation'?"

"Without it we cannot find out way home. It's like trying to find your way home without being able to see the sun. But in space, there are many thousands of suns so it's even harder."

"Ah yes, that would be very difficult. But men will die on such a mission. I must think about it. Some of the young bucks would like something to bring them glory. Would this be such a thing?"

"Yes. I think so."

"Would there be valuable goods that they could bring back to woo young wives with?"

"I think so, but I can't promise this. The ship has been there twenty summers and perhaps the Gjanga have taken everything."

"I will think on it and let you know my decision in three days-time. If I do permit this, it would be best in fourteen days-time, when the moon is dark."

"Ah yes. I agree."

"Deep within Gjanga territory, it would indeed be a glorious mission. But after you've gone, the Gjanga might be enraged enough to attack us many times."

* * *

Stone knelt on the ship's hull, watching the left, rear pod intently. Suddenly a whirring noise came from inside the supporting pylon. With a judder, the pylon started to rotate. First just a few inches, and then with a sickening sound of scraping selibdenum, it jolted up a further foot before stopping, the pod rocking up and down violently. The whirring sound continued.

"Stop!" Stone yelled. Moments later, Dee appeared on the dune above the pod.

"What happened?"

"Well. It shifted, but not by much more than a foot. It's stuck I think. I could hear the motor but it just stopped; *really* jerking around."

"Shit!"

"Jammed somewhere I guess."

"Yeah. Not surprised. Well I will get the tools and take a look. You staying?"

"Yeah. I wasn't coming out today but I fancied the walk."

While teams of Naxa women continued digging out the belly of the ship, Dee and Stone set to work underneath a linen sheet, draped over the pod-pylon.

"Hand me that torch Stone, Dee said from inside the pylon. Did you speak to Cheveya then last night? About the alien ship?"

"Yep."

"Whadeesay?"

"Well, he wasn't keen. Says he has to think about it. Says he will tell me his decision in three days-time."

"Oh. Do you reckon he will go for it?"

"Don't know Dee. Sounds tricky. Apart from the sheer mortality rate of such a mission, he is really worried about angering the Gjanga. So far inside their territory, it would be seen as a real insult."

"Oh."

"So Dee … . Tell me how all this works. I mean the … pulse jets and fusion engines. Normally I wouldn't be interested of course – I never listened in class – but anything might help me when we try to get this baby off the ground."

"Well, what do you wanna know?"

"Well, like why can't we use the fusion engines in a planetary atmosphere?"

"Ah well, that's fairly simple; basically the torus creates a plasma ball, which releases a pulse into the expansion chamber. This is where the main explosion happens. It's only a few feet from the tail-pipes so if there is any inconsistency in the atmosphere, say a concentration of dust or ammonia, it can cause the explosion to be inconsistent and blow back, destroying the ship and all in it."

"Oh. Not good."

"No. In space things are pretty smooth so you don't have to worry about it. But in the early days quite a few ships were lost this way, even in thin atmospheres."

"Okay. And the pulse jets. How do they work?"

"Well. You've seen the long intake all around the nose, under the main deck?"

"Yep."

"That leads in to a long set of tunnels which are wrapped in a water jacket which contains superheated steam from the fusion reactor when it's not causing those big explosions."

"Oh, okay. Like when we are in an atmosphere?"

"Yep. You see the problem, is that pulse jets don't generate much thrust at low speed so just as they are they are no good for takeoff. Now on this ship, the superheated water not only heats the intake tubes, but it also drives turbines which suck in the air and force it out through these pylons into the pods. If you look in here you can see the ducting for the air."

Stone reluctantly stuck his head up inside the access hatch and peered at the area lit by Dee's torch beam.

"Oh yeah."

"A second set of turbines, compresses the air, or atmosphere, even further ready for detonation. The more compressed the air, the bigger the explosion, the more thrust."

"Um, hm. I get that."

"Right. Well, all a pulse jet is, is basically another expansion chamber, but the only expansion is backwards. A spark ignites the fuel initially and then fast pulses of fuel ignite the incoming, hot and compressed air, and force it out the back. Well some of it goes forward, actually, and that's why they are no good on their own for takeoff. No thrust. But at higher speeds, the incoming air pushes the exhaust out of the back."

"Cool. And how about the intakes on the front of the pods?"

"They are for cruising. If you really want to save money and go for the super-economy version, you don't bother with the turbines and main intakes, you just take the air in here, explode it and the exhaust drives the ship forward. No good for takeoff or for high speeds, but super cheap. Like I say, pulse jets are just about the simplest and cheapest engines known to man. They might as well be called the Acca-economy engine."

"Ha! Really. That cheap? You don't still shop *there*? Everything at Acca is knock-down."

"I do like their version of Snookie bars. It's more creamy than the authentic ones."

"I thought I saw one of those wrappers in the refuse tray a while back in the flat; one of your friends?'"

"Like I say … you don't know everything about me Stone."

Stone heard Dee grunting as he heaved on something inside the pylon.

"I think I see the problem. One of the hinge-struts has buckled. We're gonna have to take it out and straighten it."

"Can you do it?"

"Huh. Not gonna be easy. Take best part of today just to get it out I reckon. Get me some wire-cutters. There's a lead here, three wires together. I don't know what they're for but I can't even see where they go so I'll have to cut and reconnect them later."

Stone returned with the wire-cutters.

"How's it going with Shihu, Stone?"

"Oh, you know … . Fine."

"When are you going to make your mind up about her? Jay tells me some of the women are beginning to talk … ."

"Yeah. I've been thinking a lot about it. The trouble is I just don't think we can take her with us … ."

"That's just an excuse. You haven't decided about her, have you?"

Stone took a while to think before answering. "I thought I had Dee but every time I think about leaving, it gets really complicated. Nobody has ever tried taking somebody forward in time before. We don't even know what will happen to *us* if we do."

"Well, there are the beacons. I reckon it's a pretty safe bet the Anubians have gone forward in time and survived. If not, then where are they all?"

"Yeah. I s'pose … . But somebody from the past, in the future … . Can it be done? All the theoreticians would seem to be saying *no*."

"Because it will change the past and therefore change the future?"

"Yeah."

"Christ Stone, we have already changed the past enough I reckon."

"Still. I am pretty fond of her and I wouldn't want to risk her life. You know they're pretty good people, these Naxa."

"Yeah. I know what you mean. Listen Stone, I been thinking about this whole time-travel paradox thing and, well... remember how Enkoodabaooh said the Holy Dogs, or whatever he called them, took some of the girls on, maybe to breed, we don't know … ."

"Yeah?"

"Well. Did Enkoodabaooh say they came back? I don't think so. I'm thinking that the Anubians took the girls with them."

"You think so?"

"Maybe... I tell you, there is only one person who will know ... ."

"Who?"

"The great shaman himself, Enkoodabaooh."

"Yeah! Maybe you're right. You can ask him Dee."

"*Me*?"

"Yeah. If anybody around here can understand any kind of theoretical science, and talk philosophy, it's you."

"Shit! Okay Stone, if you want ... ."

***

Three days later, Dee, Jay and Stone were back at the ship. The strut had been straightened and reinstalled. Now they were ready to test the pylon again.

"Okay Stone. Signal as soon as it jams, if it does!" shouted Dee and went to the flight deck. They had placed one of the warriors, on a digging break, between the flight deck and the rear pylon so that Stone could signal him and he could relay it to Dee if necessary. He looked full of importance, to be carrying out such a task.

Stone leaned close to the pylon and heard the whirring of the servo inside the seribdenum skin. Suddenly, the whining increased and the bent pylon began to rotate. It jerked a few times and then continued to rotate smoothly until the pod facing vertically. The whirring stopped. Stone held his thumb up and the warrior made the same signal to Dee, solemnly.

"Okay, down!" shouted Stone, pointing down to the ground.

The Naxa man did the same, shouting, "Ok'ay', do'an!" He looked very pleased with himself and grinned.

The whirring started again the pod rotated smoothly back to the horizontal.

"Works!" shouted Stone, laughing

"Wo'aks!" repeated the warrior.

Dee came running back from the flight deck. "Okay? Did it rotate all the way?"

"Yep. No problems!"

"Cool. What say we try and engine-start?"

"What, now?"

"Yeah. Now we're on a roll … and it's a good time to do it, before the skids are completely exposed. Right now, we can run it up to full power without worrying about it shifting on the sand. After it's completely dug out it gets more tricky."

"But won't the torus need time to get heated up; it's just been on tick-over for weeks. Months in fact."

Dee shook his head. "Don't need it. Just run the pulse jets on their own using the pod front intakes."

"Okay. If you say so."

"Clear everybody outta the way Stone!" Dee shouted over his shoulder, striding confidently to the entrance hatch.

Jay and Stone cleared all the digging crews away to positions on the two dunes either side of theirs, level with the nose of the ship. The crews were only too glad for a break and keenly interested, once he had explained what would happen.

"Okay Dee," he said poking his head onto the flight deck. "Ready when you are. Where should I be?"

"Um. Stand with the others, on the left dune. Keep an eye on that engine. Get everybody to lay down so only their heads are exposed. Duck if anything happens."

Stone skidded down into the trough of the dunes, and climbed up to where some of the tribe were waiting. He told them to get down and signaled for the crowd on the other dune to do the same. Then they waited.

Stone heard a mechanical noise from the pod.

Intakes opening. Ah, ignition.

A red flame shot from the front of the pod and then a bluish one from the rear. Then with a high-pitched burble, the engine burst into life.

Wow! They work! Shi ... !

Stone ducked. A blinding flash of yellow-red light filled the sky and an instant later a large explosion rent the air with a 'crack.'

Moments later, Stone lifted his head, only to see something metallic spinning, high in the sky above him. It fell, still spinning and sliced into the sand like a giant knife, only a few feet in front of him. The 'clang' of its impact was swiftly followed by then Dee's voice:

"Stone! Stone! Are you alright?" Dee yelled.

Stone stood up.

"Phew! That was close!" Stone said, under his breath. He gave the thumbs up to Dee and grinned.

Dee stood next to the ship's nose, holding a red fire-extinguisher. Flames and black smoke wreathed the left pod. Just in front of Stone lay the metal panel.

Could have been my gravestone!

Dee walked slowly towards the burning engine and activated the fire-extinguisher. Stone and Jay joined him. Slowly Dee brought the flames under control. One last blue tongue licked around the edge of a missing panel and then went out.

"Shit!" said Stone again.

"Fuck!" said Dee.

"Is it okay?" Jay asked.

"Looks bad," Stone said.

"Looks worse than it is. Too bad the designers didn't see fit to equip it with proper engine-extinguishers. Cheap-skates! Wait a moment!" He went back to the flight deck and shut off the fuel valves and closed the intakes.

"Safe now," he said returning. "Let's see the damage."

Jay went to organize the workers while Dee and Stone peered into the missing panel.

"Uh huh! Hm. Hold on to my legs Stone."

"What?"

Dee tore his T-shirt into strips and wrapped them around his hands. Holding on to the edges of the cavity in the engine casing he stuck his head inside and jumped. Stone held on to his legs. Dee's voice echoed from inside.

"A-ha. Not too bad."

"Well?"

"Pull me down."

Stone dragged Dee out and lowered him by his legs to the sand.

"Just lost a section of the main casing for the expansion chamber. It was a cheap casting and blown to pieces. It's not a big problem. We just need to replace it."

"With what?"

"Oh anything. Most of the inside of the ship is seribdenum though. We can't use that because it will melt. We need something iron-based. Or something with a high-melting temperature anyway. Mind you Enki can't make anything that big. We'll have to scavenge it from the alien ship."

"Hm. If we get there, that is."

"Hm. We're done here!"

"You don't sound too *disappointed*?"

"Well, we achieved quite a lot."

"But what about the bend in the pylon?"

"Yeah. To be honest, not much we can do about it. Actually it will have to be trimmed out Stone, but the pylon itself doesn't give any lift so it's just the torque that will be different. It will probably feel a bit weird, but if we try and straighten all that lot, with the mechanisms inside *and* the ducting we'll probably make it worse."

"Okay! Whatever you say."

"A job well done I think. We have to straighten the front wing-let and then we can try another engine start.

You need to get Enki working on brewing a lot more alcohol. Ha!"

"How much?"

"Well as much as you can. Anything you can light with a spark. It's not used as fuel, just to ignite the air initially but last time I checked, we only had two hundred gallons. That's plenty for the usual places people visit on cruises, nice moons or planets with weak atmospheres, but not something with Earth-type gravity. I never figured on this. Two-hundred gallons might get us off the ground but won't get us up to a safe altitude for the fusion drive."

"Okay. I reckon these guys will drink more than we save but I'll give it a go. I guess any fermented fruit or veg should do it. So did you ask Enkoodabaooh?" Stone asked Dee.

"Oh yeah. Well. He told me that the Anubians took almost all the girls with them and most Naxa believe that they are gone forever … ."

"Go on … ."

"Well Enkoodabaooh doesn't seem so sure."

"Why?"

"Well I could see by the look in those old eyes of his that he held something back. I kept pressing him and he laughed but eventually he told me something very interesting."

"*And* … ."

"Well he said that two strange things happened after he thought the Anubians had left."

"Okay." Stone's eyes were closed while he savoured the effect of the chum.

"He said that one of the girls, Charisa, was somebody he was very fond of. He wanted to marry her and he felt very sad when she went. Weeks later they found the body of an old woman near the canyon. Her body had been battered as if from a big fight and yet there were no signs of a struggle on the ground. Also, even though she had been there for a few days, no animals had eaten the body.

She had the distinctive marks on her tunic of a Naxa woman so they brought her to the village but nobody recognised her."

"Oh."

"Nobody except Enkoodabaooh, that is. He says he looked closely at the face because it seemed familiar. He thought it was Charisa but as she would have looked as an old woman!"

"Wow! That *is* weird. Probably just imagining it. And the other?"

"Well, even stranger. Years later they started hearing rumours about a woman who had been traveling from tribe to tribe, moving back towards the Naxa from far away. Stories were told of how she said she'd been on a ship above the Earth and it had been flying away when she had been pulled from the ship … ." Dee paused to let the image sink in.

"Pulled … ."

"Yeah, *pulled*! And then, somehow, she had found herself alive far north of here, in the snow. She had spent the rest of her life traveling back to her tribe, whom she called the Naxa."

"And what happened?"

"Well, that's the sad thing. Apparently she died just before reaching here. She had been with a tribe who the Itchik were in contact with, and a tradesman brought the story here."

"And Enkoodabaooh believes it?"

"Well her name was Pakwa. And you know what? Pakwa was the name of one of the other girls who was taken!"

"Shit!" Stone's eyes were open now and he stared at his friend's face, looking for signs of a joke; there were none. "Makes you think, dunnit?"

"Yeah. Kinda."

"And … that means it might be possible to take somebody forward in time. So you *could* take Shihu!"

"But those other two girls?"

"Well, it was only two. We don't know about the others and one of those two survived."

"Hm. I need to think about this, Dee."

"Okay." After a pause, during which he rolled another cigarette, Dee continued, "What's Cheveya's decision?"

"We go. The new moon. In about ten days' time. So what're we *after*?"

"Well, we need some of that stuff the aliens use instead of seribdenum. They call it biomium, don't they? We need some of that … "

"But how will we fix it. We have no welding stuff, and anyway it's made out of vegetable matter, innit?"

"Hmm. We can rivet it. As long as we can drill it."

"So we need to make a drill?"

"Yep. We don't have one."

"And the riveting?"

"We can make the rivets, using Enkoodabaooh's little furnace."

"Okay. What else?"

"Well, mainly just the navigation stuff. God *knows* what that'll look like. We'll figure it out later."

"How do you reckon it will work?"

"Well, like most navigation gear I guess. Probably uses giros and some kind of grid for inter-stellar travel. I hear that they're like us, they haven't really got to a full grid-layout for the whole of the universe. Couldn't really. Both our civilisations are like the early sea-farers on Earth. Just taking compass bearings and distance from some known point of origin."

"Yeah, they are *way* ahead of us though."

"In some ways, *yeah*. I reckon in terms of philosophy … and theoretical science, yeah. But technologically I don't think they're far ahead of us. They've been held back by the lack of metals in their world. Their sun, which we once called Kepler11, I believe, is too cool for metals. Their planets don't have an iron core like ours. That's why they are here. That's why they allied with the Ionians. *Think* about it. What is everybody looking for?"

"What do you mean? Here?"

"Yeah. Here. On Earth. On Io?"

"Metal. Iron, I guess."

"Exactly. *Iron*. The Anubians crave it, the Naxa build their lives around it because now they can actually make it. And the USAC and IM have only just finished a very long war for it. And you know what? Deep inside that Anubian navigation console, I bet there is a tiny iron needle. Most planets have a magnetic field and this one certainly does. If they wanted to find their way around they would need some kind of compass. And to them, that little iron needle would be worth its weight in gold."

"Well, that's an interesting theory, Dee, but I think you've got it wrong. Well, you are half right."

"Eh. Whaddaya mean?"

"I think the iron, the metal, I mean, is a symbol. I think that's not what people are really after … ."

"What are they after then? What's it a symbol for?"

"I once read a book by a philosopher, Jean-Paul Sartre, called 'Iron in the Soul'? I think people are looking for something hard in the soul, that strength. A strength of belief. I think maybe the answer for me is in *that* pyramid. I gotta go there before we leave."

"Okay. After the mission. If we survive."

"Yeah."

***

Ry^duxjhi called out, "Close door," and watched the plush seribdenum panels slide together, sealing off her view of the blonde-haired, receding Darda.

Another girly chat session over!

She threw herself on the bed, turned the thermostat up to 70 Degrees Centigrade and shouted, "Music: Terrans; Volume One, Volume Eleven," and poured a whole packet of chum into her upturned, gaping mouth. She pulled off her top two layers of clothing and kicked off her foot-ware.

I am beginning to really quite enjoy this lifestyle!

Track one, from volume eleven by the Terrans seeped out of the speakers, weakly.

"Shrnnkoch!" She swore in her native Ischian.

Forgot again! Damn thing can't tell the difference between album volume, and sound volume!

"Shrnnkoch! Volume Eleven!" This time, track one, Volume one by the band Terrans blasted out of the new sound system at full volume. She closed her eyes.

At four hundred Ischian years old, she was more or less twenty Earth-years old, the same age as Darda but she felt older. Talking about male Ischians was all very well but 'politics' interested her more.

Trying to get this girl to even say the word is hard enough! I just don't understand what she can find so fascinating about human men? And as for fashion..!

After the Terrans she put on the new album by The New Gods of Oblivion.

I'm becoming quite fond of human music. It's more melodic than Ischian music ... although I always have to turn the treble' right up to hear it clearly.

She played the album several times before pouring herself a funnel of red wine, another human product she now had a a taste for. Wine glasses, she still couldn't handle but then they weren't designed for Ischian snouts.

I really am becoming pretty decadent aren't I? Ha! Ha!

She downed the red liquid from the funnel in one draft.

Looking down the length of the funnel, she noticed that the red, alert light on her com unit was blinking. She called out, "Messages, play!" in her best Amero-English.

"Delivery: parcel from Bek-su, first class," the unit replied.

* * *

6. Charm

Since the first Bekian agents had contacted the Ionian humans, they had shared their technology in exchange for rare minerals. Soon, a regular trade route between Bek-su and Ionian Militia territory had been established, which also reinforced an allegiance. With time, that had extended to rebel territory on earth, even before the USAC launched their offensive to take back control of the wasted planet. This re-colonisation only partially succeeded but the uneasy truce that now existed had been largely fueled by the balance between the USAC's appetite for Ischian technology and the rebel's need for water.

Ry^duxjhi hurried to the collection office and returned with the parcel wrapped heavily in tape.

Hmm. Interesting. There is only one thing ... .

She felt filled with nervous anticipation when she saw the heavy blue tape; it had to be a parcel from her contact.

On her bed she used her claws to rip open the parcel.

"Not very polite, but ... ."

In the box, each on a flat panel of black cloth, were three collars made of gold. A note had been wrapped around the top one. A message scrawled on the note:

'Only wear this one. It will give
you a pleasant sensation. Find a
suitable subject who will enjoy it
and give the second to them. The
bottom collar is for special use.
Await further instructions. On no
account use this, or wear it, before
receiving instructions.'

'Subject,' Ry^duxjhi knew, was code for the human she would be expected to befriend and use: in her case Darda.

"Well. What a mystery!"

She turned the collar around in her paws. It had been shaped like a torque; thicker at the front and with a small gap at the back which could be widened to admit a neck by pulling the two 'arms' apart. She slipped it around her neck.

At first she noticed nothing, but gradually a warm, calm and relaxing feeling washed over her. The effect wasn't as strong as a drug that would make you lethargic, but nevertheless it felt pleasant.

I know just the place to try it.

***

Ry^duxjhi turned up to the party, Darda had invited her to, wearing her best female-dress. It wasn't like human female-dress because it consisted of a thickly lined and heated jump-suit but nevertheless it had been decorated with pretty colours and delicate patterns. Ishian females were very sensitive to colour and shape on the small scale but not yet influenced by human female fashion as far as the cut was concerned. To top off her outfit, she wore the gold collar.

"First time I have seen you wearing jewellery, Ry!" Darda shouted over the loud, post-rake music.

"Hi Darda. They are all the rage on Bek-su!"

Careful. Not too keen.

Ry^duxjhi was careful to appear reluctant to let anyone even touch the collar.

"Is it a gift from an admirer, Ry?" Darda asked, her curiosity finally getting the better of her patience.

"You mean a male Ischian? You must be joking! Out here? The only males worth dating are back on Bek-su. And even *then*, not many are worth the bother!"

"Well who is it *from* then? It *clearly* means something to you."

"It's not a gift actually. I ordered it. You see it has a special quality."

"Uh huh. What's that then?"

"Oh well. Go on try it! Tell me how it feels."

Ry^duxjhi spread the collar ends and placed it around Darda's delicate neck. For just an instant she had the urge to crush the creature between her paws.

"I don't feel anything!" Darda exclaimed, dancing.

"Wait."

"Hey! Yes! I feel something! Oo. It feels nice. It feels like I'm being massaged … like a really good head-massage. Wow! How does it work?"

"Oh I don't know, Darda. Science is not my strong-point."

"Could I get one?"

"Well let's see, shall we? Maybe if you are really good to me I can order you one."

"Ha! Ha! Okay."

They hugged.

***

Avonaico, Dee and Stone were the first to leave on the expedition to find the wrecked alien spaceship. Before they left, Shihu and the three visitors had eaten a meal together in a clearing. This was the spot designated for training and two warriors had been practicing with spears and bows nearby.

"How's the brewing business?" Dee asked Stone.

"Well, I delegated!" answered Stone. "Enki wasn't really interested so I put this young village kid, who fancies himself as an apprentice shaman, onto it. I can tell you he was bloody enthusiastic about building the pressing vats, once I showed him how. We put all sorts in there; old vegetables and fruit skins and some water of course. Pressed it down a treat. 'Course we really need a still to get anything more than about five percent alcohol but it'll have to do."

"How much you got?"

"Not much. I think he's been drinking a good deal of it, him and his mates, but we have about twenty gallons. We only really started storing it yesterday. We should have about two hundred gallons by the time of the launch. That should make four hundred in total."

"Not much, but it'll have to do, dude."

"Oh! I forgot to tell you Stone!" Jay burst out. "We got the shower working in the ship!" Stone almost choked. "Clipped my nails and polished them, just for a laugh. I showed Shihu how to use the shower and she loved it, didn't you Shihu?"

"Showe'ah great!" said Shihu, breaking out in a big grin.

"Typical *women*!" Stone quipped. "While *we* are going to risk our lives, *you two* are worrying about your appearance!"

"Hey!" Jay retorted. "You may be the mules that are going to fetch the parts but it's me who has been working things out so we can get away from here!"

"Wow! I didn't expect that!" Stone replied, laughing.

***

Dee carried screwdrivers, an old, adjustgable wrench and a small sockets set with him when he left the village with Avonaico and Stone. Ten men were to follow them, including two large warriors, to carry the console. One of the men was Shihu's father, Makya.

It wasn't yet dark. Avonaico planned for them to reach their border, near the Red Hill, at dusk. Without a moon, shapes would be indistinct and hard to see. But Dee and Stone were not as fit as the tribesmen. They would not be able to keep up if they jogged all the way with the others. Avonaico's plan was to head off directly north, slightly away from their true destination and hope that, if they were seen, the Gjanga would go looking in the wrong place.

Chief Cheveya had turned up to wish them well. He shook hands with them and clasped them to him, each in turn.

"Do not forget your promise to find the big herds if you return Stone," he said. "Now we know the real reason for his permission."

Blacked up with charcoal, the three headed for the Red Hill. They crossed the open space to the Red Hill quickly, jogging, and then turned to the left and waded through rough grass to a point on the opposite side of the hill. Only Avonaico sensed when they were actually at his tribe's border. He stopped and held up his arm in the gloom. They stood silently while he listened. Away to the east they could see two small, flickering points of red light on the horizon; camp fires. They could hear crickets and other creatures in the night. Avonaico seemed satisfied.

He led off again at a very slow jog and the others fell in behind him, trying to keep their breathing slow and even.

Occasionally, Stone stumbled, barely being able to see the outline of trees just before the branches hit his face but their path had been well chosen and they made good progress. After what seemed an eternity, when Stone's breathing ripped at his lungs, a hand on his shoulder stopped him and pulled him firmly down into the grass.

"Rest!" Dee whispered.

Water! I just have to drink.

"You okay … . Stone."

"Huh, huh, yeah. I huh guess. You?"

"Jesus! These guys are fit! He's old enough to be our *father*!"

***

"Hear it?" Dee asked after another long spell of running.

"Crickets?"

"No. River."

"Ah. Must be the river that comes through the forest, Dee?"

"Maybe."

They crept forwards and the sound of gurgling water grew louder.

Avonaico searched for a place to climb safely into the water. He found one and lowered himself cautiously into the swift stream. "Wait," he whispered.

After a pause, he beckoned them to follow him in. Climbing the far bank Stone stopped short. A cold-white skull grinned at him from the gloom, a Gjanga border marker. Perhaps bleached of its yellow by age, or simply bleached out by the dimness, it's white, pallid horror made Stone shiver.

They walked across a grassy plain for a while until again they heard the sound of water.

"We wait here!" whispered Avonaico.

They did not wait long. Faintly, Stone heard owl-hoots. He had just been about to remark on how strange to hear a whole group of owls, all around them, when he heard a hoot from right next to him; from Avonaico. Another hoot answered the leader's. A moment later, Shihu's father, Makya, peered at Stone from the almost total blackness.

After a brief exchange between the two Naxa men, the whole group waded quietly into the small stream and followed its course upstream for a few hundred yards.

Clambering out onto the far bank, they followed the stream until they found themselves climbing the rock-strewn face of a steep hill. The water tumbled in phosphorescent, foaming rivulets next to them.

They heard the bark of a dog over the noise of the water and another answered it.

Up they went until they found a rough path next to the tumbling water. They reached a plateau and crossed it toward what seemed like an impassable cliff. Like curtains on a stage-set, the rock wall ahead of Stone suddenly seemed to move apart and a lighter soot-grey of the night-sky filled the gap. They passed through this gap, about one-hundred feet wide, and then Stone could see they were entering a long, thin valley. It looked perhaps two miles long but impossible to tell for sure in the darkness.

Trapped!

Avonaico ordered Makya and a few others to stay back and guard the gap. The rest continued on.

Stone's heart pounded now with something other than fear and exhaustion; the anticipation of a tell-tale glint of a spaceship wreck in the gloom.

His ankles were whipped by soft, wet grass, and occasionally by tough weeds, while they crossed the valley's length. At its widest, the flat bottom looked about half a mile wide.

They split into three teams to search the valley. They did not have to search for long. A man from Dee's group, which had been on the right flank, came running back to Stone's group.

He beckoned to them and Stone sent one of his men to fetch Avonaico's men, to their left. They found Dee following long, deep grooves in the earth which led towards the head of the valley.

"Must have skidded all the way along here Stone!"

"Cool. We have her now!"

The grooves were five or six feet deep and the grass had grown over the scars long ago but they were easy to follow.

"I see it!" shouted Dee as they approached the end of the valley.

***

Stone had been getting tenser as the night passed. If they weren't out by dawn it would be all over. With relief he saw the glint of something large and smooth ahead of them.

"Well?" he said to Dee, as he caught up. Dee ran his hands along the smooth length of the ship, tracing its contours.

"Beautiful. No rivets. No visible sign of welding or joints of any kind. I don't know how they *made* it!"

"Perhaps they grew it?"

"Yeah!"

"Avonaico! The torch!"

Within a few moments the warrior had lit the torch and held it for Dee to see. They went along the right side of the ship, to where Enkoodabaooh had said the hatch was.

"There!" Dee shouted, pointing to a dark, vertical slit.

Dee gripped the sliding edge of the hatch and heaved. It wouldn't budge. Avonaico handed his torch to another and took a firm grip. Two other men joined them. Together, they heaved in unison. A 'crack' accompanied the sudden giving of the derelict door, and it crunched, rather than slid, along crumbling tracks.

"Torch!" Dee called.

He had begun to clamber inside when Stone shouted, "Stop!"

"What, Stone?"

"How d'you know it won't go up in flames. There could be pools of fuel, or anything in there. Battery fluid, gas … ."

"You're right. Here!" Dee passed the torch to a tribesman and showed him how to hold it just outside the hatch, so that it lit the interior. Dee slipped inside. Stone followed him, and so, reluctantly, did Avonaico.

"Wow!" exclaimed Dee. "Look at this, man!"

"Cool. Pretty bad mess though." Bits of equipment lay tumbled randomly on top of each other. Anything that could have been moved, furnishings, panels and various other unidentified parts, had been piled thoughtlessly on the floor. There seemed little left that could be carried. Apart from the main consoles, only a single, giant seat remained intact, just behind the console. Its upholstery had been ripped off but the hard frame and swiveling base were still attached firmly to the floor. A faint, foetid odour could be smelled inside the ship.

"Pilot's seat!" said Dee.

"They couldn't remove that."

"I heard they were *big*! *Huge*, more like!"

The windscreen had become opaque with moss, which seemed to grow from the very windows themselves.

"Okay Stone. Now we get to work. You go and find that panel to replace the broken one on the engine pod. Anything about four feet square."

"Thanks!" Stone said, sarcastically.

"Here! I brought you a little present!" said Dee. "Thought we might need it! Charged it last night!" He unfastened his pack, rummaged for something and threw it to Stone.

"A headband! But wha- … ?"

"It's one of those cool ones, infra-red."

"Dee, you're a genius!" Stone put it on and clicked the 'On' switch. He gingerly crept through the hatch at the back of the flight deck, into a long, thin passageway. To his left and right were compartments, some of them obviously cabins with some kind of bunks. The bunks were about ten feet long.

He poked around inside a few of the compartments. In one, various strange canisters, green and red, about the size of musical drums, littered the floor. All were battered but still sealed. It looked as if somebody had tried, and failed, to open any of them. In another compartment there were what looked like computer components but all were broken and strewn around. There were no bodies. A flight of giant steps led up to the right but Stone kept on going.

Towards the rear of the ship, an overpowering and indescribable smell replaced the foetid odour. Stone almost wretched. The last few cabins were piled high with ordure. Something black seemed to wave nervously at Stone. He peered closer and yelled with horror as a thousand black, rubbery wings beat at his skull.

Bats!

He traversed the litter-strewn corridor back to the stairs and started to climb. Nowhere could Stone see anything that fitted the description of the replacement panel Dee needed. As he reached the top of the stairs, Stone heard a sudden cry, like a child screaming, and something brushed passed his legs, making for the steps.

There doesn't seem to be anything that ain't living in here!

The corridor on the upper desk lay on the ship's starboard side and the rooms off it were much larger.

Probably a ship's mess, and engineering quarters, or labs.

What Stone took to be the ship's mess still had many culinary items stacked in racks along the walls. Knifes and plates were similarly shaped to those of Earth but much larger. The drinking utensils, however, were not shaped like mugs but long funnels, which had flat bases.

For those long snouts, I guess!

Stone thought he had stayed long enough. He entered the last room, a room with a large port-hole, again covered with moss. Some kind of decoration had been placed on the walls, within frames, but had long since decayed to a meaningless flat amorphous, cracked pattern. He pulled idly on a panel that had come loose. He couldn't shift it, nor see how to detach it completely.

He headed back to the flight deck.

***

"Thanks for the bats, Stone. Oh and the fox!"

"Ah! That's what it was, a fox. No probs. I couldn't find anything Dee!"

"Well, try outside then! We haven't got much time!"

"How's it going with the navigation console?"

Dee had the whole length of his arm inside a section of the instrument panel and he grimaced with deep concentration.

"I think I have it! Just trying to … release it … ."

Stone put the headband on the panel near to Dee. "Here, you need this. I need the torch." He went outside and took the torch from the Naxa holding it. He walked quickly around the circumference of the ovaloid ship. In places, shrubs and trees had grown up against it so he had to clear them out of the way to get a better look. He noticed that where the paneling met the ground in many places, it had beeb sheered away in sharp, jagged fractures. The material seemed to be quite brittle.

Hopeful!

He tugged at a few large pieces but none would come away so he turned his attention to the ground either side of the ship. His heart missed a beat when he heard the sound of distant barking again.

Getting closer. Are they coming in here? Gotta find this piece. There!

By torchlight, Stone saw the piece he had sought. Perhaps a little large, still it seemed roughly rectangular and big enough.

Stone called for two men to help him carry it back to the hatch. It seemed as light as a sheet of paper; he could easily have carried it himself if not for its awkward bulk.

"We got it Dee!"

"Come here Stone!"

"How's it going?"

"See here. This panel. That dial there. See it has a few small circles etched onto the surface?"

"No. Well I can't really but I'll take your word for it."

"I think that's the one we want. It's one of only two that's removable. I'm pretty sure this is the one. The other's too big anyway. Probably some kind of weapons console."

"Okay … ."

"Trouble is, I can't get it out, I can see the releases and we managed to get them undone. Avonaico and I bashed the tags off 'cos we don't have the correct key. God knows what *that* looks like! Anyway, we slid it forward on its rails but it snags about here."

Dee slid the console out and down the sloping runners so it hung, almost by its edge, from the instrument panel. There it hung, jammed, supported at the front by only Dee's hands.

"I don't want to let go of it in case it falls off and breaks something. I dunno what's behind it. Stone, if you hold it here, and don't move it, I can take a look behind. Okay?"

"Sure. I got it."

Stone took the weight and Dee climbed up onto the dashboard formed by the top of the main panel. He peered into the darkness behind the extended panel.

A dog barked and then another, both much closer than before.

One of the men rushed up to the hatch. "Gjanga. We must go!"

"Soon!" said Dee quietly.

"Where's Avonaico, anyway?" asked Stone.

"Over there. Seems to have found something he's interested in."

At the back of the cabin, the chief's brother and two men were rocking something back and forth on its stand. Stone couldn't see what it was.

"Okay. It's just a bunch of decayed wires back here," Dee said. "They're mostly just fungus now. It's that funny green stuff the aliens are famous for. Ha! Anyway I reckon we can just pull them off."

Dee scrambled back down to the cabin floor. "Brace yourself Stone. You and me will pull it together. Use this as a lever!" He passed Stone the socket-lever and took the adjustable wrench for himself. "*Knew* they would be useful! If it won't budge, stick that in there and force it off. Don't worry if you break something. We've got no more time now! You two!" he shouted to the two biggest men. "Catch when it falls. Okay?"

Both men nodded nervously.

"Okay Stone! Now!"

Both men pulled with all their might on the panel but something held it firmly. First Dee, and then Stone, tried the levers. Only when they tried together and with one last, almighty heave, assisted by another man gripping the top of the console, did it finally spring loose. It fell into the waiting arms.

"Phew! Right let's go!" exclaimed Dee.

Both the big men carried the console, which trailed green wires, outside. Dee hastily looped some the wires and stuffed them inside the innards at the back of the panel. As the men gained pace, he simply ripped off the remaining trailing wires. Stone followed behind with the two men who were carrying the panel. Avonaico and his men came out last, carrying something heavy and cumbersome.

"Whatever it is, he got it!" shouted Stone.

"Boy, I wish I could have flown that baby. Can you imagine it Stone? And we didn't even get to see the engines."

"Let's just try and stay alive."

***

Avonaico led them off at a fast, loping stride, down the middle of the valley. Almost immediately, they were set upon by dogs, which gnashed their teeth and lunging for men's legs and arms. They were impossible to hit in the dark with arrows and by the time knives were wielded against them they had already taken chunks of flesh. Quick as ghosts, they dodged in and out for quick attacks. Several men went down, screaming in pain.

Stone felt, rather than heard, something whiz by his ear. Moments later, Stone saw another and then something spat dust up by his feet as he ran.

Arrows! They don't even care if they hit the dogs!

The loosely spaced column of escaping men veered slightly to the right, towards the shoulder of land above that side of the valley entrance.

"Avonaico's making for the stream!" Dee suggested.

Stone remembered that the stream had veered to their left when they entered the valley and disappeared into marshy ground. Soon, the ground beneath their feet became soft. They trudged wearily on. The dogs weren't deterred by the marsh but the incoming arrow-fire ceased.

Avonaico's expertly wielded spear took down two of the dogs. Another Naxa took down a third. Some of the dogs backed off, snarling, but the biggest ones continued to harry the men.

"Look," shouted a man ahead of Stone. He pointed to the cliffs far to their left.

Little flickers of yellow were moving along the ridge, away from the valley entrance and minutes later, more appeared on the opposite side.

"Makya must be dead!" shouted Dee.

The implications of Dee's comments sunk in.

The entrance is closed!

The two men carrying the panel, put it down, exhausted. Stone and Dee stopped, drained the last water from their pouches and threw them away. Others did the same.

Avonaico launched his spear at a black dog, the biggest. It yelped as the spear pierced its head. It fell, inert. The last two dogs backed off to a safe distance, fearful of attacking without their leader. Men's voices could be heard shouting in the distance and all the while, the little yellow flames spread along the rim of the valley. Occasionally, Stone saw the tiny black silhouette of a man carrying one of the distant torches. He shuddered to think what would happen to them if they were captured. Now, he wasn't so sure that the mission had been a good idea.

Avonaico gathered the remaining men around him to explain what they would do next. Stone couldn't catch what the leader said but the group divided in two. One of the tribesmen gestured that Dee should go to the left with the two big men and the console. Stone would go with him and the big warrior who carried the panel, now strapped to his back. The big man could run at a better pace now, although blood poured from his shoulders and thighs where it chafed against him. The rest of the men, led by Avonaico, would try to scale the cliff and pass between the watchers. From there they would go around to the entrance and launch a coordinated attack. Stone caught the meaning of the last instruction.

"Wait for the wolf-howl! Then you come!"

Avonaico's party left and the remaining dogs followed them. Stone's team led off. Before long they were out of the marshy ground and coming under arrow-fire again.

"How the hell do they see us in the dark?" shouted Dee. They turned around and retraced their steps to the marsh. The men rested for a moment.

"We're not going to get out of this Stone! Why the hell didn't we just bargain for the *stuff*?"

"Can you imagine explaining to the traders; oh, we just want a navigation console please!"

"But we could have bargained directly with the Gjanga?"

"No way! Apparently, tribes won't allow a grown male from any bordering tribe, alive, on their territory."

"I might have known. We've got ourselves into a right trap!"

"Yeah. It's bad."

"Listen Stone, when we get to that pass up there, we might not both get through. I'm trusting you to take care of Jay and get her out, okay?"

"Sure. I don't trust you with Shihu though."

An arrow suddenly flew out of the darkness, gashing Dee's leg as it sped past. Stone whipped around, just in time to see a Gjanga face retreating into the gloom:

"Damn. He's gone!"

"Aah! Stone," Dee screamed. He clutched his leg. Stone grabbed it and inspected the wound.

"Not too bad. You're lucky. Here!" Stone ripped off part of his tunic and bound the wound. "I don't think we have time to do it properly!" One of the other warriors looked at them askance.

"Ha! Looks like we're off," Dee announced.

Again they tried to move forward. Some of the Gjanga had moved to head off the threat from Avonaico's men on their flank. Stone could see, out of the corner of his eye, two of the little flames on the ridge converging slowly.

Good luck Avonaico, mate!

The men around Stone rushed forward, and over the stony ground, arrows and spears coming out of the dark like whispering death. Stone ducked just in time as a spear appeared to his right. It sailed over his head with a whooping sound as it flexed along its shaft in the air. Dee screamed in agony as an arrow went through his arm above his elbow. He stooped for a moment and then continued on, just managing keeping up. Stone came alongside him and put his arm around his friend's shoulders.

"Not again, Dee! You ain't having much luck with arrows!"

"Fuck! If I could see 'im, I would kill 'im."

"At least it wasn't your leg!"

"*Stone?*"

"Sorry … ."

Now they veered to the left, away from the Gjanga and came into a stand of trees. The leader halted them.

The Naxa warriors whispered to each other. All strained their ears for the sound of a wolf's howl. They waited, but it didn't come.

"Not long till dawn," Dee whispered, between groans.

"How's your arm?"

"Bleeding!"

"Here." Stone broke the shaft, pulled it out and bound the arm tightly above the wound, with a torn off strip of his loin-cloth.

"If I get hit again, you'll be naked!" Dee muttered, through clenched teeth.

"Nope. We'll use *your* loin-cloth then!"

"Jeez. I wish Avonaico would make that call! What's keeping him?"

They waited and the first faint, patch of morning rose started to seep into the sky above the lowest of the hills.

"It's now or never," said Stone. "Let's … ."

The distinct sound of a wolf howl, in the distance, interrupted him. One of the men in front of Stone answered. The two big men picked up the console. They launched themselves from the trees and into the clearing, between them and the valley entrance.

"This is gonna be tough!" shouted Dee.

The other men closed in around them until they were a tight, bristling pack of spears and drawn-arrows.

"I can see one," said Dee, firing at something moving on the cliffs above them. The arrow clanged onto bare rock.

"Baika!" rang out from above them. Avonaico suddenly leaped down from rocks above the enemy, and battle commenced. Two of the Gjanga engaged him but he fought fiercely, his blood-lust up.

"Now!" shouted somebody and Stone's group spurted to top speed as they tried to get through the gap. Arrows and spears rained down on them.

Other Naxa warriors appeared on the rocks, to eitherside, and the pack rushed desperately for the gap. The warriors continued shouting, "Baika!" in what seemed like one, long blood-curdling war-cry. Stone and Dee howled with them. They knew the war-cry meant 'Death!'

Stone felt panic, like a cold beast, rising in his throat, climbing from the very pit of his soul. He could only swallow to control it. He closed his eyes as two spears passed each other, like the blades of scissors, inches in front of him. For just an instant, he thought he must have been cut in half, but his legs carried on working and he opened his eyes again. He felt something thud into his back, and to his horror, saw something protruding from his chest.

An arrow head!

He felt no pain and wanted to joke with Dee but no sound would come from his throat. He had been winded by the blow. He followed, in what seemed like a dream, the remaining small group of men. They were making for the stream where it disappeared over the edge of the shelf and plunged, foaming down into the valley.

If I can just get there ... . Safety ... I ... .

Stone's thoughts were becoming incoherent.

Just before the lip, one of the two men caring the console started to fall. Stone found himself lunging to grab the precious object before it hit the ground. He made it and tried to call Dee for help but still no sound would come from his mouth. They left the warrior on the ground while Stone struggled to hold up his part of the alien console. After what seemed an age, Stone felt somebody lift the unbearable weight from his shoulder. He screamed in agony as the same person snapped the arrow shaft behind his back and threw it aside. He recognised the tattooed arm as that of Avonaico.

Stone found himself half stumbling, half-falling down the steep slope. He had just enough strength to stay on his

182

feet until they reached the bottom. Then he collapsed on the first short grass of the plain.

"Stone! Stone! Wake up! We gotta move!" His friend shook him violently. "Avonaico says we can't wait. Can you walk?"

Stone opened his eyes. For a lovely, brief moment, he could see the sun rising in its hazy red halo on the horizon to the east and a bird circling far above him. It seemed such a peaceful sight, he just wanted to lay there forever. But something stirred him from deep within and he made himself sit up. Then, unsteadily, he stood.

"Pull the arrow out, Dee,"

"I *can't*, Stone. You'll bleed to death. I don't *want* to!"

"O-oh shi-i-it!" With one sudden wrench, Stone drew the arrow from his own chest. He shuddered as its rough shaft pulled aside flesh and organs on its way out of him. He stared for a moment at the ragged hole as a little spurt of blood became a strong trickle and flowed down his chest. He passed out but moments later he came to.

"Get up Stone!" Dee pleaded. The arms of a warrior and his friend hauled Stone to his feet.

The pain washed over him in great waves. "Shit!" he said again and stamped his foot in anger.

"You okay?"

"Yeah. I think I can *walk* now. Let's go."

"Man, if your dad could see you … !"

"What?"

"He'd be so proud … ."

"Not as proud as he would be impressed that you're not angry with me!"

"What for?"

"For getting us into this. I failed."

"Where the hell *have* you been for the last five minutes? Not *failed*. You made a *mistake*. I never heard you talking defeatist like this before. Come on! We gotta go! Avonaico says we're gonna head straight for the stream but we're probably gonna get cut-off. Prepare for a fight, he says!"

"Like we haven't been already? Okay. Let's go."

Stone stumbled along, held up by Dee, at the back of the line of men while they headed due west, out onto the plain. The grass quickly became taller here, just as Stone had remembered it from the night before. Fed by the water from the stream, the ground lay thick with wild-flowers and shrubs which he didn't recognise.

The grass gave them some shelter from the occasional arrow which arced high overhead, fired by the Gjanga skirting the hill to their right.

Avonaico dropped back to check on his men.

"How many left," Stone rasped to Dee.

"Six … including us."

"Run for the stream when I say," said Avonaico as he fell in beside them. "Can he run?" he asked Dee.

"Yes I can!" said Stone. He looked defiantly at the Naxa warrior. He saw the glint of something, calm confidence, in Avonaico's eyes, which gave him hope.

Stone stumbled on, held up under the arm of his friend. Both had wounds which were bleeding profusely. A red mist passed over Stone's vision so that he thought he would pass out.

"Stop!" said Avonaico. They had just passed into a small copse of short trees, barely more than bushes. Stone noted with detached fascination the fruit on the branch nearest him. It amazed him that the leaves and the fruit were both red. He reached out to pluck one of the fruits, but for some reason his hand couldn't reach it. He tried to focus on the luscious feast but his vision blurred it.

"See ahead!" Avonaico said. Then he said a word neither Dee nor Stone recognised, "… covers the river at dawn. They will not see us!"

Some of the men laughed.

"They are crazy!" muttered Dee. "We're gonna run for it any moment Stone but as far as I can see the Gjanga are pretty much all around us."

"Okay," said Stone weakly. He felt, rather than heard, the men tensing and then he heard the dreaded sound of dogs again.

Those bloody dogs!

"Now! Run for home!" The cry went up from all the men together.

"Here we go!" shouted Dee. He hauled Stone to his feet.

Off they went, trying to keep up with the men in front who were largely unwounded. Stone could only see one man trailed behind them, dragging his leg and clutching his chest.

Not gonna make it.

They ran on. Arrows rained down on them and Stone glimpsed a white dog snapping at his heals. It reminded him of the white skull he had seen the night before. Twice it got its jaws around his shins so he kicked it hard in the face, making it release its grip. Each time, it tore off a chunk of his flesh.

"Half way Stone!"

"I can't make it Dee!"

"Yes you *can*! Stop that defeatist bullshit!"

"Ha! Ha! I can't!"

"Shit! Now I can see what the big man has been talking about. Mist! Stone. There's mist over the stream. If we can just … ."

But at that moment Stone's legs finally gave way and he fell flat on his face in the long grass.

"Just leave me here," he said quietly to no one at all. "Hey!" he said, annoyed, when two strong pairs of arms hoisted him up and dragged him over the grass. He looked up and saw a familiar face grinning at him. "Makya! I didn't know you were still *alive*?" he said but the warrior didn't hear him. They leaped into stream, whoe banks were thick with reeds. Stone couldn't see any other men. They seemed to be alone. Even the dog had gone.

Maybe I killed it!

One last arrow sliced the water between Stone's legs and then he found himself floating, face down. He kicked with his legs and flapped his arms until he began gently floating downstream on his back.

"Dee! Where are you? Makya!" His voice seemed smothered by the close, damp mist around him. But he heard one faint call somewhere, as if far away. "Stone! Kick for the far bank!"

"What?"

God I'm tired. I could sleep forever. No, I mustn't! What did he say? Kick?

He kicked his legs. If he could have seen himself, he would have seen that he was slowly being turned around in circles by the action of the flowing stream and his legs. But Stone's luck was in that day and he slowly drifted towards the far bank. Finally he felt his head bump against something soft, something which smelled nice and then he fell asleep. Images of home, his father and mother millions of miles apart, his brother on a hover-board, drifted though his mind. Then he saw another face which he recognised but couldn't place. Gradually it solidified into the smiling face of Shihu but just as he thought their lips would touch, her face turned into that of Dee.

Something familiar, a voice, wrenched him out of his beautiful dream.

"Stone! We found you! You're alive. You old bastard!"

Somebody dragged him onto the firm ground and then slapped his face.

"Hey! What the fu-..!" he said, opening his eyes.

"You're safe now, Stone." Dee's familiar round face, edged with dark hair, peered at him. Those familiar brown eyes danced with delight at the sight of his friend alive.

"Oh. It's you. I was dreaming."

"Dreaming! We thought you were dead. It's been chaos. Makya and I tried to hang on to you while we swam for the far shore but I lost my grip for a moment against the current and then so did Makya. I heard your voice in the mist but then you were gone."

Stone saw other faces, upside down, lining up next to Dee's, Makya and then Avonaico. They lifted him on to a litter and set off, away from the stream.

"How many's left, Dee?"

"Five."

"Shit. I feel really bad. All those men died! And for what?"

"Don't worry. We still have the gear. The panel got lost but it floated away and we just found it. Lucky the bend in the river at this point brings things to this shore."

"Yeah. We're lucky today. And the console?"

"Yeah. Not so good. It got dropped a few times. One of the big guys ended up swimming with it on his shoulder. It's alien though. Let's hope they build things tough. Avonaico managed to get his thing across and you'll never guess what it is? I caught a glimpse of it."

"No, what is it?"

"Some kind of laser gun or something. Not exactly sure but some kind of weapon."

"Shit! That guy has an instinct for violence."

"Yeah!"

As the sun rose above Stone's forehead, they turned south. Stone wondered why they had been suddenly so safe.

"Dee?"

"Yep. What is it, dude?"

"What happened at the river? I mean, why did all the fighting stop? How come we're safe now?"

"Well. 'Cos that was the Gjanga border if you remember. And I guess they didn't want to follow us into the mist *and* enemy territory."

"So whose land is this?"

"I dunno exactly; somebody told me the name of the tribe but apparently the leader is a relative of Avonaico's, and as long as we don't touch anything we'll be okay. Anyway this is where the plains begin and apparently they are normally out there, hunting somewhere. They travel around a lot."

"Oh. Cool."

"How do you feel?"

"Shit! Wake me when we get to the village."

***

Kek-suîxjh had rented a hotel room to look at the Project Arcadia documents. He couldn't think of anywhere safer. He read through the wad of field notes and then turned his attention to the maps in awe. He laid two large and faded sheets out on the bed next to each other. Each showed half of the dig site.

As he recalled, the dig had been in the Nemyrîx Mountains, in the southern hemisphere of Isch-su. Nobody had thought to look there for early signs of Ischian civilisation before; the mountains were surrounded by arid desert. However, the archaeologist, Dr. Piloxxrîxjh had believed the area once to be fertile. Later, industrial consumption of plants and trees had led to its desertification. On the leeward side of the tallest mountain, about two-thirds of the way up, he had found a narrow plateau. On it, preserved in the dry soil, were tombs containing mummies. These early Ischians were buried with their finest woven baskets and other items, woven from the tough fibres of local shrubs and weeds. These early Ischians had worshipped an early form of Vîu and Kek-suîxjh could just make out her long ears and familiar snout on some of the headstones in photos of the dig. Her dress had been picked out in delicate shades of blue, a plant pigment which still clung to the crude but beautiful friezes, even after millennia.

Looking at the map, Kek-suîxjh could see four of the tombs highlighted in red but it would be some days before he could work out why this was. Their formation tugged at his subconscious, like a child pulling on the hem of an adult, too busy to listen. He passed over this many times, digging deep into the expedition notes for hidden meaning. Finally, he noticed, in the Doctor's own personal notebook, the words Vîu and Vîentxa underlined in many cases. There were many myths and legends which spoke of the first Ischians coming from Vîentxa and even that Vîu herself had sailed from there in a great ship shaped like a K'ynnuia. But there were just as many legends speaking of other origins.

However, this village, or indeed religious sanctuary complex, as it probably was, pre-dated all other known civilisations by many thousands of Ischian years. When Kek-suîxjh looked at the maps more closely still, he could just make out that one of the tombs had been circled twice whereas the others had been circled only once. The two concentric circles were neatly bisected by a straight line which pointed straight to the mountains summit. Looking at the orientation of the map and knowing a little about astronomy, Kek-suîxjh realised that the line could also be pointing to the star KL42501.

Astonishing!

The star KL42501 was the brightest star in a constellation of four very bright stars, which exactly matched the layout of the four tombs. It was a revelation. The constellation KL42501 had only been recently discovered and only then with the latest and most sophisticated telescope.

So this is the knowledge which cost the Doctor and his whole team their lives! Maybe there really is a home planet for Vîu after all. I have to go there!

***

Darda stepped through the scanner and strode as confidently as she could towards the customs desk at the Moon's Tranquility Port. Her heart thumped in her chest. She felt a bead of sweat starting down her temple. When her headband registered her ID with the Officer and he waved her through, she felt like somebody who had stepped out of a plane crash and been the only survivor. She was one of the very first and only IM women to get full Moon citizenship and she didn't have a clue how Ry^duxjhi had managed to orchestrate it.

She took a deep breath and searched the crowd for a particular face.

God I hope he's here. After all this, what if he isn't? What if he doesn't love me after all?

She looked for the sign which said 'Immigration' but felt panic rise in her throat when she couldn't find the familiar blue sign.

Wait a minute! This is the Moon.

She started to read the signs on the walls and holo-signs *hanging in space.*

There! Ha! Silly me! The sign's green here.

The sign pointed to a corridor that ran out of the open customs plaza. Darda turned left and followed the passage. From the plaza, the corridor ran along the side of the transparent, seribdenum wall that kept arriving passengers apart from those waiting. She looked through the partition for a face

There!

She smiled, and the face smiled back.

"Adam … . Hi!" she mouthed. He smiled and she waved.

Not long now!

Her heart thumped even harder.

***

191

7. Transmissions

"Please sit down," the Immigration Officer said, indicating a worn, brown chair in front of the desk, stacked with important-looking documents. Darda tried to read the woman's name on her name-badge, but the writing was too small and the woman kept moving this way and that, checking facts on white plastics laid out in front of her.

"You look like the woman in the image; attractive, blonde … . Now. Let's just check the basics to start off with; Full name?"

"Darda Anne Ortega."

"Ah yes. The grand-daughter of Chairman Ortega. It's somehow appropriate that my very first immigration case from Io, I mean the former Ionian Militia Territories, should be the Chairman's grand-daughter." She smiled but Darda saw a hint of suspicion in the older woman's eyes. "Age?"

"Twenty-four."

"And you have a First Class Degree in Law?"

"Yes."

"Very good!"

"And you've just been offered a position at Hette & Partober, here in Tranquility."

"Yes."

"Excellent. That's an *excellent* company to work for. You're very lucky."

"Thank you."

"Without that, you would have a difficult start here. And in fact I don't think your citizenship would have been approved."

"Oh." Darda frowned. The woman clearly wanted to demonstrate her power.

"Now if we can get down to the particulars of your residency here; you will be residing at 421 Duke Street."

"Yes, with my partner Adam … ."

"Yes, yes. I am coming to that. And your partner, who you hope eventually will become your husband … ?" She looked at Darda for confirmation.

"Yes."

"Is Adam Enquine, son of Gary Enquine, the Governor, no less, of USAC West Coast?"

"Yes. That's correct."

"Well, well … . Very illustrious connections. Ha! Ha! I am really honoured to be talking to such a distinguished *young* lady!"

The woman seemed well-educated and curious. Darda thought her spiteful, but also condescending and suspicious, perhaps because she was slightly envious. She lay one white plastic, face down over the rest, and placed her hand firmly on it.

"Well Miss Ortega. I am happy to say that all is in order. I am very honoured to welcome you as a new citizen of the Moon. We hope, and indeed I hope, that you will have a very happy life here."

She came around the desk to shake hands with Darda, who stood unsteadily and took the woman's dry hand in her own, slightly moist, one.

"Thank you."

She turned, picked up her brown, designer leather bag, and firmly opened the door to leave the office.

"Your bags will be waiting for you at the Arrivals Lounge! Don't forget your ID!" the woman called after her.

Darda felt slightly dizzy. She had to check herself to be sure she had remembered everything she should be carrying and walking in a straight line.

She reached the railings, just before the Lounge, and a strong hand grasped her arm.

"Darling! At last. I missed you so much!"

***

Almost as soon as Kek-suîxjh had made the decision to go to star KL42501, he knew he would have to contact Ambi-xjhu. He couldn't possibly face a very long journey, possibly lasting the remainder of his life, without somebody to talk to and Ambi-xjhu was his last real friend. He also needed advice from his student on a practical matter.

Of course, with Xi-yrîx arrested, the whole ham-photoncom network had gone to ground and it would not be easy to find a way to contact his young student. Being old in a University did have its advantages however and nobody show any interest when Kek-suîxjh asked for the com number of a retired lab assistant who has worked for him, many years before. He made the call immediately.

"Hello?" a hesitant voice answered.

"Is that Mna?"

"Yes … why?"

"This is Kek-suîxjh. Do you remember me?"

"Kek-suîxjh? Kek-suîxjh? Ah yes. Kek-suîxjh! Is that you?"

"Yes."

"I get so few calls these days … . How are you?"

"Hm. Well, things are not so good but I am well. I need to ask you a big favour?"

"Of course. If it's anything I can do … yes! What can I do for you?"

"It's a bit sensitive … . It could be dangerous for you … . Do you still have any contact with ham-photoncommers?"

"Um. I see. Err, no I don't, but would you like to meet me for a drink perhaps?"

Kek-suîxjh almost gave up then but something in the old technician's voice made him curious.

"Okay? When?"

"The night after tomorrow. Not too late though. I get tired easily these days. The Mad Green Funnel. Do you know the bar? It's near the campus."

"I think so. Yes."

In the bar, the conversation quickly turn to photoncoms. Then a tall Ischian with abundant facial hair sat down uninvited, next to Kek-suîxjh. He stuck his open paw out towards Kek-suîxjh.

"One of my friends Kek-suîxjh," said the technician. "You don't need to know his name. Tell him what you want."

"I need to contact one of the Colonists," Kek-suîxjh said quietly.

"Aha. You realise there have been three more arrests this week?" asked the stranger.

"Yes. One of them was my friend Xi-yrîx."

"*Sh*! Okay, so now I know you are serious, but this is a very dangerous business these days. Please do not mention any more names and I don't want to know yours either."

After some good-natured bargaining, Kek-suîxjh handed over the required number of i-tan and whispered the message in the Ischian's ear. Kek-suîxjh thought the stranger didn't charge as much as he could have and might be in it for the thrill.

Kek-suîxjh's message to Ambi-xjhu had been a simple one. The young Ischian had explained in an earlier message that the Colonists had to invent a new form of navigation because of the vast distances they had covered. Constellations they had never seen before became local and the old ones disappeared. Their new system fixed the starting point of a line at the theoretical origin of the universe, and the line passed through the star around which Isch-su orbited, Orî.

Ischians were sticklers for detail with calendars and the Colonists more sticklers than most. The period, or Astral year of Ito, the time it took to travel around its sun was 3.1 days but Ischians, who had evolved on Isch-su, with a period of 22 days, felt this too short for organizing one's life. They had resolved this problem by creating a calendar year equal to 310 'short years' which came to 961 days.

The line continued on as one axis, space around it divided into 961 degrees with 0 pointing towards the nearest star to Orî, Inîa. The line from the theoretical origin of the Universe to Orî, is divided into 961 gradations either side, each gradation being 1000 Ischian light years. Perpendicular to each gradation lay another imaginary line for each degree, for a distance of 742 gradations away from the base line through Orî. Thus the location of any star, anywhere, could be fixed with three numbers. Orî lay at the point 0,0,0.

Although Kek-suîxjh thought he would probably be the only inhabitant of Ito trying to use the new system, he had worked out that KL42501 lay at +1.2227,317,44. For the next few years he would be somewhere along a line between Ito and KL42501. This constituted the first part of his message to his former student.

The second part was to tell his student about the purchase of the four PBSs. Ambi-xjhu had also told Kek-suîxjh in an earlier message that the Ischians had laid beacons at the beginning and end of each worm-hole they had used on their long trip to the new colony. This allowed them to send quantised-photon messages, contained in laser carrier waves, all the way back to Ito. The PBSs were a military version of these beacons but slightly more sophisticated in that they could track a moving ship. The K-17, an outdated ex-military space-ship, could nevertheless carry PBSs. Kek-suîxjh only had to drop off a PBS every few light years or so and Ambi-xjhu could relay messages to him from the nearest Colonist beacon to Ito.

Kek-suîxjh could only hope Ambi-xjhu would get the complete message. He had no time left to check.

***

When Stone woke, he felt as if somebody had parked a hover-car on top of him. The only things he could move were his eye-lids and mouth but his mouth felt so dry he wondered if somebody had dessicated it with salt. He moved his lips but he could do little more than make mumbling sounds. Stone could only remember fragments of the events as the men had arrived back in the village. He remembered Jay shouting instructions to Shihu, who appeared to be next-in-command, and the young Naxa woman started to clean Dee's wounds.

Jay leaned over stone and offered a bowl of water up to his lips.

"Fank oo," He rasped

"I don't know how but the arrow seems to have missed anything vital." Jay said to Stone.

"Yeah. My bwrain's uff 'ere." He'd pointed like a drunk at his head.

"In your case, that's not so vital."

He remembered grinning.

***

"Mwarhmmer!" Stone said as loud as he could. His head pounded, and he swore silently to himself.

"What do you want da'ahling?" said a familiar voice.

"Mimu!" he said. Shihu leaned over and kissed him.

"You've been asleep for a whole day! You'ahe the last one he'ah!"

"Wmmarmber!" he said again.

"What?" He licked his lips.

"Oh. Wait." She fetched some cool water and poured it slowly between his lips. He smiled gratefully and fell asleep again.

Again, when he woke, his head still pounded but this time he could speak more clearly and managed to drink four small bowls of water with Shihu's assistance. She called Jay to take a look at Stone.

"We changed your dressing quite a few times, Stone. You lost quite a bit of blood but it's stopped now. I think you'll be okay. It was even luckier for you that you fell in a river. That probably helped stave off any infection until I could get to it."

"I didn't *fall* in the water. I was dropped!"

"Oh. Okay."

"Anyway it was probably the last *chum* I smoked. The dealer, who's a mate of mine, told me it had lots of medical stuff mixed in, including antibiotics!"

"Oh."

"Are the parts for the ship okay?"

"Uh huh. Dee is looking over the console right now. His arm's not too bad. I put it in a sling and he's pretty much able to do most things. You were the most seriously hurt. You need a lot more rest."

Knowing that Dee was already at work on the console spurred Stone on and the next time he woke he insisted on being carried on a litter to see how the work progressed.

"Hey Stone!" Dee rushed towards him and grabbed his hand.

"Ow! Careful."

"Oops! Sorry."

"So how's it looking?"

"Well. It's not as bad as I thought. First of all, the console is a sealed unit. That means no birds or insects could get in and make nests … or eat anything. Provided it didn't get too damp it might be okay. And see this?" Dee held up a length of the green wire which become encrusted with some kind of fungus. "This is the external wiring and, as we know, alien wiring *does* tend to be organic and somehow something local here seems to like growing on it so it has just become frayed and almost useless. Luckily I have managed to pull a short length out that's pretty much pristine. Anyway, there's no way to tell if it will work until we try. We just have to run some juice through it."

"Um. Okay!"

"Course, I don't know what voltage or current they use and that's going to be a bit of a problem. There are markings on some of the components, but I can't read them. I was wondering ... ."

"Yes?"

"Well, do you think Enki speaks any of the lingo? I mean just a few words would help. Jay is pretty good at languages so she might be able to pick up something. And if he can write even a few letters that would help even more."

"Well, ask him!"

"Okay. Yeah. I'll go with Jay tomorrow."

"How about the panel?"

"Ah, not so much luck there, man. It's some kind of polymer, so far as I can tell. Light as a feather but, harder than steel. There's nothing hard enough here to drill it with, even if we could make a drill."

"Shit! What'll we do then?"

"Well, I think we can strap it on."

"Strap it?"

"Yep. We can use strips of iron as straps. It won't seal of course but I thought of that. We can pack clay around it and bake it on in the sun."

"That's crazy! The first time we fire the engines up it will just disintegrate!"

"Yeah! True, but it doesn't matter. We only need full power for the takeoff. Just once. After that it doesn't matter if it's inefficient."

Stone raised his eyebrows. "Oka-y! If you say so!"

"It'll be fine Stone."

"You know, I feel so bad about all this. It's really my fault. Now, we really *have* to find this heard of Bison for the Naxa."

"I know. I think it'll be okay. Once we are airborne, we can probably cruise around for quite a while before we need to go into orbit. Anyway, if you remember, this baby is fitted with pretty sophisticated viewing gear. We can zero in on something as small as a bird from near the stratosphere. At that height we can run the main engines, at reduced power."

"Cool. I've thought how we can take up Cheveya as well."

"Are you kidding?"

"Nope. It should be fine. If he wants to risk the takeoff … . We owe him Dee! Big time! Besides which, it's no good us finding a herd in Montana and then just dropping him a note. We need to make sure it's somewhere he can take the tribe."

"Okay. How then?"

"Simple. But crazy!" Stone grinned. "We just lower him on a rope. Glide down by the river, lower him on the rope and then let him drop into the water. We don't need to land. We should be able to manage to slow down for a minute or two?"

"Yeah. I guess. It's a pretty mad idea!"

***

Keeping his word, Dee organised a visit to the pyramid as soon as Stone could comfortably walk. They took a light ladder with them.

Stone climbed up onto the pyramid base and walked to the spot where he had stared down to the mysterious, descending corridor.

"No doubt, either this was going to be blocked, a dead-end, or they were going to put some kind of ramp in here to lead up to another level. Who knows?" he speculated. "Let's go down."

Jay lowered the ladder down into the pit so that Stone could climb down. His voice echoed off the cold walls.

"Wow! It's so well made! The Naxa must have taken years on this!"

"Can you see any graphics … what do they call them … hyra … ?" said Dee

"Hieroglyphs," interjected Jay.

"Yeah, hieroglyphs!"

"Hey look at this!" Stone exclaimed.

"Anubis, hm," said Jay.

"Oh yeah!" said Stone. "Anubis! I forgot his name."

They looked at the beautifully and brightly illustrated profile of the jackal-headed god Anubis, appearing just as he normally did in Egyptian friezes. Painted dark, almost black, he carried some kind of votive offering on a platter.

"That's how the aliens got their name," said Stone. "Funny if it turns out they really are the same!"

"Nope. Just plain stone here."

When there were all down, they walked along the open-roofed corridor, something like a stone trench.

"Imagine what it would have been like if it had been finished!" said the awed Stone.

"You really are sold on this place, aren't *you,* hm?"

"Dee. You know, when I was a kid I really wanted to go to Egypt when I saw those vid pictures of the pyramids. When my dad told me we couldn't go, because it lay in rebel territory, I was so disappointed … . That's partly why I stole my first ship! Ha! Never did see 'em though. Okay, now where? We're at a junction?"

They reached a junction; where their corridor met one running transversely.

"Right, if I remember!" said Jay.

Stone turned right and recognized the corridor as the one which sloped gently down, towards the centre of the pyramid. The remaining sunlight cut a hard diagonal on the wall down to a depth of a few feet, but below that the walls were in deep shadow. Stone touched the block nearest him. It felt cool to the touch.

"Not much light gets in here!"

He walked on, into the gloom, letting his eyes adjust to the low level of light.

"Ah. Here it is! The descending passage!"

The floor in the floor of the corridor had been cut into by a rectangular opening, which sloped down at about a thirty degree angle. Stone found it possible to skirt around it, there being two feet wide ledges either side, but he took the sloping passage. Immediately his senses were assailed by bright colours on the walls.

"Wow! Paintings!"

"What are they of, Stone?"

"Well. Hard to say exactly. Not being an Egyptologist myself. This is called a cartouche isn't it, Jay?"

"Where? Let's see."

"What's this mean?" Stone asked. He pointed to a series of symbols, such as; ◇, S, o and a picture of a bird, all encased in an elongated, vertical oval.

"I have no idea, but the 'S' is actually a snake, I think," Dee replied.

Stone continued on down the corridor. "Looks like some kind of feast. There are loads of offerings, and it looks like the people making the offerings are Naxa. Look at this. See, their tunics have Naxa symbols on."

"Oh yes!" said Jay. She clicked on the headband to start recording.

"What are they offering?" said Dee. "Can't be coffee, or tobacco, or anything useful!"

"Looks like possibly sacks of something and bison parts I think. There is a complete bison. And a man wearing a bison's head! I wonder if he was Enki's predecessor? Hey look! Wow! Look at this. That looks like an Anubian. Wow! Look!"

They peered at the silhouette of a tall dark being with a jackal's head. He wore a simple loin-cloth of gold, draped with gold palm leaves.

"See, he's black! Why are they always black in art but in real life they're *not* always black?" said Dee.

"Dunno. Some people think they cover themselves in some kind of insulating layer. They might come from a really hot planet, but nobody knows. They won't talk about it. Anyway they wear heavy clothes on Io and Earth, the ones I've seen on vids, anyway."

"But he, or she, is wearing almost nothing here!" countered Jay.

"Maybe that's meant to be on their home planet then?" speculated Dee.

Stone led the way down, deeper into the pyramid. "You got that torch, Dee? Light it up. It's getting too dark to see."

Finally the corridor reached a flat section with a junction. A passage to the left led at a very steep angle down into the pyramid. Steps were cut into its surface. Another corridor led straight ahead and yet another led to the right for a few yards, and then doubled back on the corridor they had just left.

"I don't fancy that one there!" Jay said, indicating the stepped corridor with a nod.

"Nope. Straight ahead," agreed Stone. He took the lit torch and led the way ahead. Both the walls and ceiling were encrusted with brightly painted feast scenes. There were far more Naxa in the paintings than now inhabited the village and in places there were faces and tunics which seemed to be those of other tribes.

"Could this guy be Gjanga? See the yellow face?" Dee said, pointing.

"Could be. Strange to think of them as friends once, hm."

Further on, Stone spotted something high up on the wall; a long dark shape with yellow stripes. He held up the torch.

"Wow! Dee look at this. That must be an Anubian spaceship. Looks like the one we found. Just like it, in fact." Stone had to reach up on tip-toes and extend his arm to its full reach to light the shadowy shape in the gloom at the top of the frieze.

"Wow!" Dee exclaimed. "Yeah, Stone. You're right. Not much detail though. I reckon a Naxa painted that. It's got the two yellow stripes though. What's it doing? Is it carrying anything?"

"Don't look like it. Just flying."

"Oh."

"Hey, looks like the corridor comes to an end. It's a dead-end."

"Let's turn around then," said Jay.

"Just a moment," Stone protested "Let's go right to the end,"

"*You* can Stone. We'll wait here. You didn't charge this up properly," she said to Dee, indicating the headband. "It's out of juice."

"Nah! Probably the low light has drained it quicker!"

As Stone edged forward, he noticed that, whereas before it seemed often as if the Naxa in the paintings were at least in awe of the Anubians, here, even the Anubians themselves were prostrated, facing towards something painted on the end wall. Stone tremulously walked up to the wall and shone the full glare of the torch on the frieze. On a green background, inside the shape of a great, reddish-brown pyramid, stood something large, dark and man-shaped but Stone couldn't make it out. There were almost no Naxa here. Only two, very richly adorned Naxa prostrated themselves; probably the Chief and the shaman. All others were Anubians. A great deal of worshipping could be be seen but still Stone couldn't see *what* they were worshipping. He shifted the torch to the side to get a better view and noticed that the shape on the wall changed.

It's cut away! Somebody has cut it away!

Right in the centre of the painting, where there should be some almighty powerful being, Holiest of the Holy, there remained just a ragged, ugly pit in the limestone. Its jagged edges had been hacked to a depth of a few inches by something crude like an axe. Disappointed, Stone peered closely at it for any clues as to what might have been there.

He could see it had been roughly Anubian shaped and this seemed confirmed by the tips of two long ears just above the top of the defacing. The ear-tips were gold in colour. Remembering the story Cheveya had told him, how Hotoato had carved the likeness of Vinu, Stone guessed this to be the Anubian god's golden ears. Just about to turn away, he noticed something else. He thought he could just make out something above, and to one side, of the jagged hole and the golden ears. He shifted the torch around to get a better view. The two shapes, painted the very palest blue, were so faint and faded that he wasn't sure that he saw them at all for a long while. He blinked and looked again.

Yep. Definitely there! Wings!

He could see the most diaphanous wings, like those of a dragon-fly.

Perhaps there were more once!

But he could only see the tips of two. It looked like they were attached to something, a creature or small being of some kind, but the figure had been so hastily and crudely drawn that the rest had faded away. It looked almost like graffiti that had been added to the painting after the defacing.

How weird.

"Hey. Dee, Jay. Come and look at this!" He showed them the pale blue shapes. "Can you see what I am seeing?"

"I think so," said Dee.

"Wings?" said Jay, unsure.

"Yep. Wings. Some kind of winged god. But it looks like it's been drawn on later, after the main image has been destroyed." Stone pointed to the pitted stone. "I reckon *that* was Vinu, the Anubian god which Hotoato had painted. That's what annoyed them so much."

"Yep. Come on Stone."

He followed them back to the junction, deep in thought.

"Let's just check this corridor to the left and then eat something," Jay suggested. They followed her to the left and then turned right to emerge into a large rectangular chamber with a high roof.

"Burial chamber!" Dee said, seeing the large stone coffer in the centre of the room. It lay empty and its lid lay against the wall. "Probably weighs a good ten tons."

"Nobody in it though," Stone said, dismissing it.

"Okay. Nothing here really. You satisfied Stone? Let's go and eat."

"Yeah. Feeling a bit strange though. Everything seems to be bathed in golden light. And the hairs on my arms and back of my neck are standing on end. Do you feel anything?"

"Nope," said Dee.

"Nope," Jay confirmed. "Come on Stone."

They retraced their steps back to where they entered the pyramid corridors. Dee, the first one to turn the last corner, yelled:

"Hey! The ladder's gone!"

"Oh shit! Now what?" Jay exclaimed

"Don't worry!" said Stone. "It's just somebody being mischievous. Shihu will send somebody to find us when it gets dark. We're quite safe."

"I hope you're right!" answered Jay.

"Let's eat," said Stone. "You know, I feel great. I feel really safe here. I wouldn't be surprised if I know exactly who took the ladder."

"Oh?" said Jay.

"Yeah. Somebody whose name begins with 'A'"

"You think so? Him again? You don't much like him do you?"

"Just saying … ."

They ate their lunch, leaning against the cool limestone walls in the pyramid. The blue rectangle of sky above them gradually grew brighter as morning became noon.

Makya found them by the dim moonlight. He also found the ladder, which had been tossed into some bushes.

Only when back in the village did they find out that the Gjanga had been seen moving not far from the village.

"They are watching us!" said Cheveya. "I think they are planning an attack."

***

But the attack didn't come yet. As planned, Dee and Stone and Jay paid their first visit to the spaceship since the mission into Gjanga territory. Several of the warriors accompanied them, carrying the new parts. Stone walked as far as he could but had to be carried across the sand on a litter. When they arrived they saw that all the digging had been completed and a smooth ramp led down to the narrow lane prepared between the dunes.

"Good job Jay!" shouted Stone.

"Condescending bastard!" she answered.

"Hey! Kids!" interjected Dee.

"D'you know, I think you are just always gonna be a male chauvinist, Stone?" Jay retorted.

Stone disagreed, but he let it go. He felt too tired to argue. Apart from the tiring trek out to the ship, Stone hadn't slept the night before. Feeling as if a strong electric current coursed across the skin on the whole of his body, he had lain there thinking about the pyramid and the friezes. Shihu had clung to him, feeling that he would fly away at any moment.

For the first time, Stone could see under the ship. Her skin felt very hot and had to snatch his hand away quickly. After what Dee had told him about the reactor's cooling mechanism, he felt surprised that the sand underneath hadn't turned to glass.

Two of the Naxa men helped Dee bind the Anubian panel around the gap in the engine casing. They used cord for now. Iron bands, which Jay would ask Enkoodabaooh to make, would be strapped on later.

"Fits like a glove!" joked Dee.

"Phew! You're joking mate!"

"Now! Now! Don't criticise what you can't improve on."

"What's that, some kind of saying?"

"Yep. I just made it up."

"Oh. So what's next?"

"Well, not much. Let's just pull out the old nav unit and see how we can attach this one."

While they worked on the flight deck, they noticed the occasional warrior coming in for a shower. Each would come out wearing a towel, much in the fashion of a 22nd Century man. Then they would proceed to oil his hair and comb it fastidiously, while draping themselves over one of the sofas in the ship. Stone and Dee exchanged astonished glances.

"Gotta go guys!" Jay popped her head around the hatch entrance before leaving for the village in the early afternoon. "Gonna visit Enki this afternoon; order the iron bands and find out about this Anubian lingo for you. See you tomorrow."

"Oh before you go Jay … . Has there been much Itchik activity around here?"

"Oh, they've been around. We see small groups of them sometimes out on the dunes, but they're mostly just watching, I think. Your magic seems to have worked!" With that, she left.

"Oh," said Stone, after her, puzzled. "What magic, Dee?"

"I guess she means the stuff you put on the spears, those markers."

"Oh."

***

"Well, there's no way this console will fit in the gap left by the old one," Dee declared, on the flight deck. "We'll just have to make a stand for it and walk around it. Let's try wiring it up!"

"But isn't there a danger of blowing it up?" Stone retorted. "Suppose the voltage is all wrong?"

"Don't worry. I've switched off the main console bus so there's no current at the moment. I am gonna wire in a voltage pot, so we can vary the voltage and see when it comes alive. It will be a bit of trial and error but should be okay."

"Well, don't blow it! It's the only one we got and it cost so much … so many lives … ."

"Don't worry, Stone."

They worked on until the evening. Stone couldn't face going back to the village for the night so he stayed behind with a few of the men. They watched some vids, listened to music and drank some kech before shutting the hatch for the night. Stone felt uneasy. He kept wondering if the Itchik might be watching them.

Need to go soon. Or we'll never go. Too many things closing in on us.

***

Their task lightened somewhat when Dee found a plasma cube for the n-gen. Their first thoughts were of coffee. They made more cups for the Naxa men who sipped tentatively at first and then enthusiastically.

"Right! We need to get to work!" announced Stone, when all the cups were drained. "We can think of something else while we work."

Once Dee had shown them what to do, they set the Naxa men to binding the panel in place on the engine casing with the crude iron bands, which Enkoodabaooh had made.

Then Dee, Stone and Jay retired to the flight deck to study the markings on the navigation console.

"I dunno," Jay said after casting her eye quickly over the visible markings. "Enkoodabaooh showed me a few … what some words mean, and how to pronounce them. I wrote them down! Here." She took out a sheet of note paper with symbols scribbled on them and their English meanings next to them. Stone and Dee pored over them.

"Where are the numbers?" asked Stone

"He only knew a few; one, two, four, and ten."

"Well it's a start. Which are they?"

Jay pointed to a symbol. "One, pronounced 'Axha,' I think"

"Nope." said Dee

She pointed to another. "Two, pronounced 'Brxsha,' or something like that."

"Yes! I've seen that one. Wait a minute!"

Dee went to the Anubian console, coloured dark green, almost black. He scanned the knobs and dials and found what he sought. "Here and here!"

Stone looked. "Hey, cool! See, they're like a keypad. These others must be the other numbers. But there are twelve of them!"

"They have twelve fingers apparently!" said Jay.

"And why is only the 'two' marked? And that one down there?"

"Maybe it's like those old com pads. Some letters are marked for people who are blind?" suggested Jay.

"Could be. Yeah!" agreed Dee. "That would be so cool if it's the case. It would mean we would know all these keys. But still we don't know what the numbers look like." He scratched his head. "Show me the 'four.'"

Jay showed him.

"Nope. Haven't seen that. Ten?"

Again she pointed out the symbol.

"Hmm. That one, I think I've seen." He went back to the console and swung it around on the surface it rested on. He peered into the back of the unit and called out,

"Yep. Here. On a socket. I guess that must be something to do with the voltage' or amps' or something. Oh well, it's a start!"

"Two out of twelve!" said Stone, glumly. "It's not much."

"Think about those ancient Egyptologists. They had even less than this to go on and they managed to decipher the codes."

"Yeah, it took them years!" countered Stone.

"Well, we won't get anywhere if we don't try!" Jay countered.

"Yes boss!" said Dee

"*Yes* Captain!" said Stone, only slightly sarcastically.

"I hoped we'd get a clue about the voltage," said Dee. "Oh well, I've wired in two rheostats which I cobbled together from the old unit so we're gonna try that. We can vary the voltage and amperage at the same time. I've turned them down to 0.1 volts and 0.1 amps. I'm going to turn on the main bus. Let's see if there's any life!" He pulled a switch but saw no sign of life from the shiny black-green console. Dee put his ear against the top surface. "I think I can hear a faint hum. Not sure. Let's turn the voltage up! 0.5 volts."

Stone he saw no reaction so Dee tried, first 1 volt and then, 2 volts. He kept the current constant at 0.1 amps.

"Still nothing," said Stone.

"Okay. I am going to start varying them both at the same time. Otherwise we'll be here all day!"

"Okay but be careful. Stop as soon as I yell."

"Will do." Dee continued to increase the voltage in tiny increments and each time he did, he swept the amperage pot smoothly and slowly round to test various amperages. He reached 3 volts with no sign of activity from the console "These aliens are big so I kind of expected we might be talking big voltages. I mean their paws are too big to operate anything other than these big controls. I don't know how they even manage to make this sensitive equipment. Maybe they have slaves … ? Hmm … . Anyway I would've expected something by now. Okay then, 4 volts."

A drop of sweat dropped from Dee's brow and barely missed the voltage pot.

"Wait. There! A flicker," said Stone. One of the dials glowed faintly yellow for a moment. The light wavered and then glowed again. The light pulsed very slowly, off and then on.

'Like the eye of a sleeping beauty,' Stone mused. Dee came round to take a look:

"Okay, that one's probably faulty," he suggested. "We must be close to the correct voltage. Let's try 5."

Suddenly all the dials flickered on, some yellow, some green and some red. Their vision was assailed by a myriad of symbols, flashing lights and strange pictograms. Dee clapped his hands once in delight.

"Oh yeah! Give me hooked five, dude!"

Stone and Dee slapped palms with their fingers hooking around each other's.

Jay laughed and clapped her hands over her mouth. "What the hell's a hooked five?"

"Sign of the Rebel Alliance dear," explained Dee.

"*Secret* sign," Stone corrected.

"You pair of idiots!" she exclaimed.

"Okay! Now we're in business dude … and dudette! Now let's just try pressing this keypad and see what happens!"

As soon as he pressed the first key, Dee could see a symbol appear on the main central screen of the console. He pressed the key at top left and the symbol appeared which Jay had said indicated 'one.'

"There we go!" he said.

He pressed the second key to confirm and it lit up with the symbol for 'two.' In this way they could begin to decipher what all the keys meant and work out what most of the dials and switches did. They continued all afternoon, determined to decipher all the secrets of the console. The men outside worked diligently, if at no great pace, under the burning sun. In the late afternoon one of the men came to the hatch and called for Stone.

"What's up?"

"Shihu is here for you Stone!"

"Come in hun!" Stone called, while continuing to pore over the console with Dee.

Shihu put down a large sack she had been carrying and pecked Stone on the cheek. She hugged Jay and whispered something in her ear.

"Of course, darling!" Jay replied. "Go right ahead. And we have a surprise for you after." Shihu went into the main cabin. "She's just taking a shower," Jay explained. She watched the way Shihu walked closely.

They continued on, with breaks, while the sun slowly set, until Dee's head hurt with all the new information. "I need to stop!" he suddenly announced. "I think we have most of it. At least how it works."

They called the men from outside and made another round of coffee. Stone ceremoniously offered a cup to Shihu and said:

"It's the first time I have been able to offer you something from my culture that you can taste."

Her eyes sought his for something.

What does she want?

Shihu wondered if she would ever know much about this man, who seemed so different to her. She grinned as her tongue tingled with the new taste, at once bitter and pungent. Her head swam slightly, pleasantly. She drank some more.

"It's called 'coffee,'" Stone explained.

"*Like*. Corfee!" She laughed.

"Don't you think she looks great Stone," Jay remarked. "After the shower, I mean? I think the 22nd Century would suit her fine!"

Shihu stared at her empty coffee cup studiously.

"Sure. She would be the centre of attention! No doubt about it!"

"Food!" said Shihu, suddenly, hiding her embarrassment. "Let's eat, Stone?" she added, deferentially.

"Yep. And let's think of what else we can make with this n-gen!"

"I tell you one thing we just gotta make Shihu!" exclaimed Jay, conspiratorially.

Shihu looked at her quizzically.

"Lipstick! Oh yeah! Jay is gonna show you how we do things in the 22nd Century!"

They also made cigarettes.

"I'm not really used to this!" Jay apologized, choking. "Haven't done this since me and Geraldine did it behind the main stage in our gym when I was about twelve. I nearly choked *then*!"

They lay out on the dune to wait for the sunset. Copious amounts of kech made time pass quickly.

"Hey! Lipshtick!" Jay suddenly shouted, laughing at her drunken pronunciation. "Come on Shihu" Both women disappeared inside the ship. Stone heard whoops from the men at the sight of the young women.

Whoops of laugher preceded the re-emergence of the women. Shihu clutched her lipstick triumphantly as the two women planted themselves between the two men. Jay leaned close to Dee and whispered conspiratorially in his ear, "We chose a cherry-red. It matches … our mood!" She spoke the last word victoriously, loudly enough for Stone and Shihu to hear.

"You *flirt*, Jessica. What have you done with my future spouse?" Stone commented.

"Yesh. Spoushe? Spouse? That's a very formal word. Don't you mean 'wife'?" Her words were becoming increasingly slurred and Dee had to push her away as she slouched against him.

Stone hadn't noticed but Dee had stood up and walked around to the front of the ship.

"Hey! Come and look at this!" Dee shouted.

Only Shihu stood up and followed him.

Jay breathed heavily, next to Stone. He became aware that she aroused him.

"So, Stone, can you fly this thing?" she said. "I mean can you really get us out of here. It's gonna take one helluva pilot to do it!"

"Well, I *am* one helluva pilot! I'm the best damned pilot at the Academy. My grade is A-plus."

"Ha! But we don't even know our final grades yet?"

"No, but it will be when we get the grades. Everybody knows I am the best. It's just that I don't do things conventionally. That's why the instructor's always coming down so hard on me. Didn't Dee tell you that my mum was a space pilot? One of the best!"

"No way! He never told me that." Suddenly she seemed coy to Stone. "What's her name? Is she still alive?"

"Her name's Katherine, but everyone calls her Katie."

"And your dad is a war hero!"

"What do you wanna talk about him for?"

"Oh sorry."

"Anyway, they are separated. I don't see him much."

"Oh. Sorry."

Stone felt her hand rest on his. He wanted to pull away but he couldn't move.

She leaned into him and he felt her warm lips pressed against his. He opened his mouth reflexively and kissed her back. It felt good. Suddenly he found himself passionately kissing her. Then, as her leg wrapped around his, he realised what was happening.

"No!" he said. He pushed her shoulder away. He looked towards where he had last seen Dee and Shihu and saw that they were kissing too. His face suddenly grew angry and he formed the first part of Shihu's name with his lips.

"Don't, Stone," Jay whispered. "It's been coming for a while. Come on!"

Jay led Stone to the other side of the nearest dune. Suddenly, Jay turned so that her eyes were less than a foot from Stone. Only the moon lit her face.

"Well?" she said.

"Well what?"

"Oh God! Typical." She leaned forward and kissed Stone's lips. He felt only the lightest touch from her lips, but he took hold of her shoulders and they sank to the sand.

"I have been waiting so long for this," she murmured.

"I never expected it!" he breathed.

"Liar!"

"I was worried about you," he whispered. It was disconnected, intimate, presumptious and music to Jay's ears.

"Why?"

"Dee talked about you as if you were his property."

"Oh, ignore him. It was me who put those ideas in his head! But I don't know if I believe in that shit anymore. Shihu and the tribe have shown me … ."

"I know,"

It all seemed like a dream to Stone as they made love. Jay's body moved under him as if every touch were somehow inevitable and effortless. Her breasts, though smaller than Shihu's, were firm and excited him in a different way.

He heard a little voice inside him chanting, "Free!" when they both climaxed.

***

Although in some ways she barely knew Adam, she had barely touched him until now, Darda felt grateful for Adam's warm, reassuring words.

217

"Adam! Oh thank God you're here!"

"It's alright baby. You're here now. Welcome to the Moon!"

He kissed her impulsively on the cheek. She turned her lips to his and their mouths touched for the briefest moment.

"Let's get your bags," he said

She followed him and gave the attendant her ID. He matched it with a stack of cases and handed hers over.

"Have a nice stay!" the man called.

"I am here to live!" Darda called back, triumphantly.

"Has it been that bad?" Adam asked, steering her towards the exit and the monorail that would take them close to Duke Street.

"That woman – Immigration – was terrible. She really made me nervous. I felt like an escaped criminal!"

"Well you *are* an escaped something!"

"Yes. It feels like that."

***

8. Ignition

"I love your … necklace," Adam told her in the café

"Do you like it? It's not a necklace. It's a collar!" They both laughed at the inappropriate name.

"Oh so you're gonna be my slave?"

"No … silly. It's actually a gift from Ru. Apparently they are all the rage on Bek-su. They have healing properties. It feels great. I've been wearing it for months now."

"Wow! A real alien piece of jewellery. Nice!"

"Well you needn't be jealous. Open my blue case."

"Why?"

"Don't argue. You'll spoil it."

"Okay … ." He opened the case on the chair beside him.

"There. That black parcel. It's a present for you."

"Really? Oh that's lovely darling. But you shouldn't have … ."

"But I *did*."

He tore off the black tape and opened the box.

"Wow! One for me too. This is so *cool*!"

"Put it *on*!"

He lifted the torque from the box, splayed the ends, and placed it round his neck.

***

Late the following morning, Avonaico arrived with great ceremony, carrying the weapon he had taken from the crashed Anubian ship. He, and four of his friends, whom Dee and Stone called his henchmen, walked into the camp, full of pomp and armed to the teeth.

"Avonaico, I don't mean to be impolite but what the *hell* are we going to do with that?" asked Dee.

Stone pulled him aside, out of Avonaico's earshot.

"You know Dee, I'm not so sure we should argue with him. Think of it as a gift!" offered Stone.

With much effort, by smashing a hole in one of the floor panels, Stone managed to install the weapon and its tripod. Avonaico looked very pleased with the installation. He grinned and grabbed Stone's hand to shake it.

"Good weapon!" he said. "Might need it!"

"Yeah. Thanks!" Stone grimaced.

"Are you satisfied?" said a voice from the direction of the flight deck. "Tearing up our lounge carpet! I hope you checked for any cabling or ducting before you bashed that hole?" Dee leaned on the flight deck hatch frame, watching with eyebrows raised.

"Oh. Yeah! Don't worry."

"Well if you're finished, maybe you could come and help me?"

"Okay."

They continued working on the console for the next few hours. Avonaico, happy for now with progress on the weapon, sat outside, drinking kech and firing arrows into targets placed on the sand. Almost every time, Avonaico would equal the accuracy using his spear.

"See this?" Dee pointed to the central display, a large rectangle with rounded corners, almost lozenge shaped. On it, a vague green pattern gently pulsated.

"Yeah. What is it?"

"Well I wondered *that*. At first I thought it might just a random pattern because of damage. Then I thought it might be some rendering of the local star system. But you know what? I think it's actually a kind of 3-D rendering of our surroundings. See this, here? That could be the hills on the east side of the valley and this, the south. What do you think?"

"Hm. Could be. Why would they have a 3-D rendering though? Doesn't make much sense. You would think it would be a map image or something."

"Yeah. But if they don't have a map it might make sense to just render what the radar picks up."

"But in 3-D?"

"Well look at this selector at the top. At least that's what I think it is. On position one, this is what we see. Position two … ." He turned the heavy switch to the second position. "Nothing. Blank screen." He turned the selector to position three. "And position three, same thing; nothing. I reckon position two is probably local space or sub-space and position three, either interstellar space or maybe hyper-space."

"Well, we won't know until she moves will we?"

"No. You know Stone, I think it's time to run the engine up."

"Really? Did you check if those straps were okay?"

"Yep. I had to get the boys to tighten one or two of them up but they're fine."

"How about the clay?"

"No, we won't do that until just before launch. We only need it once."

"Okay! Let's do it!"

"Okay. You get the guys back out of range, like last time."

"Okay, here we go again!"

As before, Stone took up position behind the crest of the adjacent dune. But this time, he had much more difficulty getting the audience to join him. Avonaico and his men were too drunk to see any point in taking cover at the impending engine start. Finally, they were all in position.

"Okay Dee, Fire her up!"

Faintly, from inside the ship, Stone heard, "Ten, nine, eight … ." and then the sound of electric actuators, operating in the pod on the extremity of the rear left pylon, drowned out the countdown. The injectors kicked in and a high-pitched sound of gasoline squirting into the main chamber drowned out the actuators.

"Two, one … fire!" Stone shouted, having carried on the countdown inside his head. He couldn't help watching over the top of the dune, his eyes just two inches from the tiny grains of sand. Nothing. He watched a beetle crawled hurriedly across the dune, spattering grains of sand behind its little legs as it went about its busy work.

Just about to stand up and shout, "No good!" Stone suddenly tensed. He thought he heard a low-pitched pulse from the engine. Then he heard another, and a cloud of white smoke and blue flame burst from the tail-pipe of the pod. In an instant, the pulses became regular, like the wing-beat of a giant humming-bird. The jet of blue flame stretched out for ten feet behind the pod, scattering sand for hundreds of feet.

Stone jumped up. "Yeh! Yeh! Oh yeah!" He waved his arms so that Dee could see. Then he slashed his flattened palms in front of him, to indicate that Dee should cut the ignition. The instant Dee pressed the button, the flames stopped. The engine hissed. Clouds of white and blue smoke curled lazily up out of the tail-pipe and from every gap they could find in the casing. Stone looked down at the Naxa audience but they all had their ears covered and their heads buried in the sand. When one warrior did finally look up, he looked terrified. Even Avonaico didn't move for quite a while.

Stone reached down and pulled Jay to her feet. He clasped her around the waist and planted a kiss heavily on her lips.

"Yeah. We did it! We have power!" he shouted.

"Looks like we're in business!" said Jay. "Come on Shihu. It won't bite you."

Dee came around the front of the spaceship and walked towards the smoking engine. He reached it, peered into the burning cauldron that was the missing outer panel, and touched the alien-made panel. "Not even hot!" he shouted, grinning.

"You look like some kind of necromancer!" said Jay walking up to him, hand in hand with Stone. Shihu tentatively followed them, her eyes wide with admiration for Dee.

"Well done mate!" said Stone. "Hooked five!" They both slapped palms, hooking their fingers around each other's.

"I reckon another five days or so, and we'll be there!" announced Dee

"Yeah!" the other two answered.

"I've been thinking," Jay began. "I think you should be the co-pilot for takeoff Dee. You're more technical then me and there won't be time to discuss things. You and Stone will have to act on anything in an instant."

"Okay."

All four stared at the ship. Their thoughts each spiraled off in different directions; Dee to a life with Shihu, possibly on J3, Jay to her mum on the Moon, Stone to Katie near Mars, Shihu to a life in some strange new world.

Shihu stepped forward and took Dee's hand. He held her to him, kissing her tenderly and whispered something in her ear. Her face broke out into a broad smile.

"Tomorrow, we will start bringing out the fuel," suggested Dee.

"Yeah. Do you think we dare risk some coffee on Avonaico and the boys?"

"I think we should," Jay affirmed.

***

As the sun set, they leftfor the village. Avonaico and his men had been rapturous about the taste of the coffee, which had also sobered them up considerably.

"Stone. The Itchik are watching us. They're closer than usual." Jay said, on the flight deck as they packed.

"Yeah I know. We can't say any longer."

That evening, Stone decided he could wait no longer before break his plans to Cheveya. As soon as he told the chief that the ship would soon fly, and that he wanted Cheveya to come with them to find the moosto, the big man's eyes lit up. He immediately ordered a feast by clapping his hands in a way that obviously his wife recognised. She hurried to start the preparations and spread the word. This made the next part of Stone's speech even harder to deliver. He watched the chief's wife while wondering what to say next. A small, quiet woman, she had dancing blue eyes, very rare in a Naxa, and her grey hair was curled up on top of her head. Stone had only recently learned her name; Chospasi.

"Hm, hm. There is one other thing, Chief Cheveya."

The big man, somewhat surprised that there could be more to discuss, turned his attention back to Stone. But his voice sounded calm and patient as he said "Yes, Stone?"

"Well. It's like this. We don't have enough fuel to land the ship again after we lift into the air. The silver fish-bird needs to drink lots of something we call fuel. We only have enough to move up from the ground once but we want to take you with us. So when we've found the moosto, we will bring you back and we will have to lower you on a rope and drop you in the … um … river … ."

Cheveya looked at him seriously for a moment and then slapped his knee. He roared with laughter.

"That funniest thing I have heae'ad for many yeae'as!" he said. But then he grew serious again. "Will I live?"

"Yes. You should be okay … . If you can swim?"

"Of course Cheveya can swim! Okay Stone, we will do this. Of coue'ase I am Chief of the Naxa, but first I am a warrior and I must do this thing foe'a my tribe."

With that, the feast moved into its first phase; heavy drinking, accompanied by the slow beating of drums. The rhythms grew faster and more complex as darkness fell and cool air closed in around them. Some of the young Naxa men began to dance.

Stone knew he had one more important thing to do that night. He made his way towards Makya's hut, practicing over and over again the words he had prepared. When he saw the Shihu' father, the words faded to a meaningless collection of sounds. He took a deep breath:

"Makya. I would be honoured … . No that's not right. It is my very great honour, to ask for the hand of your daughter, Shihu, in marriage!" The last word tumbled over the previous, as he fought to complete the sentence under the perplexed gaze of Makya.

Suddenly, Makya understood. "Ah, Stone! You want Shihu to live with you?"

"Er … . Yes." Stone grimaced.

"Ha! Ha! Vee'ay good. My answer is '*yes.*' It is as we expected. You can be togethee'a and she will be vee'ay happy."

***

The air had grown very cool so Stone went back to his hut for a tunic to put on over his shirt. When he returned to the main camp fire, unusually, he could find no sign of Dee and the others. He searched the village for them and ended up at Makya's hut. Makya and his wife were not there, but Shihu, Dee and Jay were arguing.

"What's going on?" Stone asked.

"We're thinking of … ." Dee, started to say.

"Stone. Can you … ." said Jay, cutting across him.

Shihu looked perplexed.

"We're gonna get married. Tonight!" said Dee. He watched Stone's face for a reaction.

"Well! It's a bit of a supr … I mean it's a bit sudden!"

"We're sure though. But there is a slight problem. I mean Makya has given his approval and Shihu is definitely into it. But actually that's the problem. I want to be really sure that she knows *exactly* what the risks are of her coming with us. But I'm not sure she is taking it seriously."

"We were wondering … . Stone, could you try and explain to her?" said Jay.

"Me?" Stone answered, surprised.

"Yes, you Stone." Jay said impatiently. "You've known her the longest. Maybe you can get through to her, make it clear."

"Well … . Listen, can I have word with you," he said to Jay. They both stepped outside the house.

"Listen. I'm not actually so sure this is a good idea. Think how we're all gonna feel if she dies. Or worse, disappears into the ether!"

"Yes. I know that. I feel the same way too Stone but they are determined. Whether we help them or not, they are gonna do it. I think she has to know the risks though."

"This is tough. Things may not have worked out between us but I'm fond of her. You're asking me to do something I'm not sure I believe in!"

"Yes."

After a long pause, Stone said, "Okay. Send her out."

He took Shihu's hand, when she emerged, and stroked it affectionately.

"Shihu. Jay and Dee have asked me to try to explain to you what it would mean for you to marry Dee. I mean … you know we are leaving in a week. That is, if the ship doesn't explode and we're all killed! Ha! That means … . Stone wants you to come with us. But we are going to travel in time. Can you understand *that*?" Shihu shook her head. "Where we come from … is in the future. Oh, how do I explain this? Erm. When we leave, we will … hopefully … be going to a place where people are alive many, many lifetimes after your Naxa friends have grown old and died. I know it sounds impossible to you but it's true."

Shihu looked unsure so he continued.

"The problem is that although people can go back in time, like we did by accident, and we think they can go forward again, we are not so sure about taking somebody from the past to the future. We just don't know if it's possible … ."

Shihu nodded slowly.

"But *I* think it can be done. Actually Dee is less sure than I am … ."

"Yes, Dee says he is wo'aed about me."

"Yes. There are risks. Did Dee tell you what Enkoodabaooh told us about the girls who were taken before by the new gods?"

"Yes. He told me. They lived. Even though they came back, which is sad … ."

"Yes, but what happened to the others? That's what we *don't* know."

"And you are sue'ae you ae'ae going to live Stone?"

"Ha! No! You got me there!" He stared into her eyes. She returned his gaze, firmly and steadily. He could see no doubt there. In fact he could see proud determination.

"Okay. I think you *do* understand the risks now."

"Yes."

"And still you're going to marry tonight?"

"Yes."

"Okay. Then my congratulations." He took her in his arms and squeezed her affectionately. "Let's tell the others!"

***

The announcement, after they told Cheveya, spread around the village like a wildfire. The drums beat out a special wedding rhythm and everyone who could stand joined in the dancing. Cheveya and Makya looked happiest of all. A runner fetched the shaman to marry the couple. Enkoodabaooh arrived in a litter with two of his wives around midnight.

The wedding ceremony itself, a simple affair, took place soon after. Enkoodabaooh drew a Medicine Circle in the sand, large enough to hold all Shihu and Dee's guests who gave presents of food and clothing. Stone gave Dee his favourite Bryson Morley compilation with rare tracks by New Gods of Oblivion and to Shihu, he gave his favourite T-shirt, printed on the front with a faded image of the Terrans. Then Enkoodabaooh called the spirits of the Father Above and Mother Below and spoke many words which were not understood by Dee. S ritual followed whereby the couple held hands and recited Seven Steps on the road to a good marriage, as told to them by the shaman. Then they touched noses and they were married. Dee took Shihu in his arms and kissed her, long and passionately. Everybody in the village clapped and whooped.

Nobody noticed how cool the air had become and heard a sudden, loud crack of thunder. Seconds later, a stab of lightning split the sky, fixing the image of Naxa faces in the eyes of their visitors like photographic images. The rain began to come down in torrents.

"Do not look so woe'aaied, Stone!" said Cheveya. "It's e'aain!"

"Yes, I know. It's a bad sign so soon after their marriage."

"Foa'a us, it is a good sign!"

***

The dogs were the only things stirring in the village the following morning. They rooted around for any tidbits left over from the feast. Everyone else stayed in bed. If not hung-over, as Stone was, the villagers were making the most of an unspoken decree that no work would get done the day after a wedding.

In the evening, a few brave souls drank and danced some more but most took advantage of the celebration to stay inside; the ground, still sodden, and the roofs still dripped, with the night's rain.

**

"Okay Stone. Start them shoveling!"

228

Dee used wet sand to straighten the wing-let. Bags, weighted with the sand were suspended over it and then men piled more sand on top of it while another pile supported it from underneath. When the wing-let had been loaded with half a ton of sand, it slowly eased back into shape with the occasional crack and squeal of flexing seribdenum. Occasionally, some sand would spurt out of the side of the mound under the wing-let and Dee would call a halt while he packed in more wet sand, helped by Makya, who had now become an able assistant.

"Lucky it rained," said Dee. "I probably wouldn't have thought of it otherwise. Just came to me in bed!"

"Surprised you were even thinking of the ship!"

"Oh well, ya know … . Relationships ain't all fun and games!"

"Really? You *do* surprise me!" Stone had a mischievous look in his eye as he jumped down into the pit next to Dee. "Ouch! Keep forgetting this wound! How's your arm?"

"It's a bit sore but well on the way. I couldn't lift weights, you know, or do a three-sixty flip on a hover-board off the edge of a wall but it's getting there!"

"So what's left?"

"Just a bit of seribdenum, maybe using one of those floor panels, to cover the open panel on the engine and that's about it! Oh and Avonaico's damned gun! He showed me the loose end of the cable this morning. Asked if *that* was the reason the gun didn't work! You'd think he has seen it in *operation*. You know I still don't know what it is or how it works. I'm guessing it might just melt a hole in the viewing port. But then again there wasn't a hole in the one on the alien ship. I have heard … ."

"Yeah?"

"I read somewhere that aliens have some kind of disrupter gun. Nah! It's probably just a rumour. Still... it might be … ."

"We better find out."

Jay had organised the men to carry out the eighty gallons of alcohol brewed as fuel to the ship that morning. Dee and Stone arrived later to organise the straightening of the wing-let.

"Not enough!" said Dee, watching the tribesmen filling the ships tanks carefully.

"I reckon they drank a lot of it!" quipped Stone, not altogether too inaccurately.

"It'll have to do, I guess!"

With a seribdenum panel strapped to the pulse jet, to replace the missing outer panel, Dee's attention turned back to the navigation console.

"The problem," he explained to Stone and Jay, "is that I just don't know what frequency it uses to communicate with those two beacons we saw when we came out of the worm-hole. Or the two at the other end, for that matter. I'm guessing it's a pretty high frequency because … well, they have big ears!"

They all laughed.

"I mean they are descended from … ."

"Evolved … ." Jay corrected.

"*Evolved* from some kind of dog-like creature and so they probably hear ultra-sound, stuff we can't hear."

"Couldn't you make a guess from the speakers in the console?" suggested Jay.

"Nah! It's the frequency of the carrier wave we need. The audio signal is irrelevant really. High frequencies can be carried just as easily on long-wave as short-wave."

"I'm stumped!" Stone confessed.

"Um. I really wish we'd had time to root around in that ship you know. If I could have just glimpsed the aerial! But then again, it's probably embedded in the ship's hull. Might even *be* part of the ship's hull!"

"Wouldn't it say on the back? At the output socket?" suggested Jay.

"Probably does. It does say something but I've tried, and I can't read it. There are too many characters which aren't on your list."

"Don't you just need the numbers though?"

"Yeah. Far as I can tell it says 'something 7211.12 something, something, 2.'"

"So what's the problem?"

"Duo-decimal isn't it! Base-12 if you like. So it's seven, two, eleven point twelve! I mean, *point twelve*! And we don't have a bloody clue what their units of measurement are! The 'something' after the numbers could be the equivalent of an inch or a mile. We wouldn't know!"

"And you're sure it's radio?" said Stone.

"Well it's something electromagnetic. Probably radio, I would think."

Stone and Jay sat down. They all stared into space, thinking.

"Trial and error then!" said Jay, suddenly. "We just cut a long length of wire, say the length of the alien ship, attach it and then cut bits off until we get something!"

"I never *thought* of that! It's so *obvious*. Ah, trouble is, how we gonna know when it's working?"

"We rig up a crude receiver and when we pick something up, hey-presto! We have it!"

"You're a bloody genius Jay!" said Dee.

Stone kissed her. "Nice one darling."

"Let's get on with it then!" said Dee. "We can use the cabling for the n-gen. It's nearly finished. Takes its power from the reactor distributor."

"Oh Dee! Are you *serious*? My lovely n-gen, hm!"

"Sorry baby. It's gotta go anyway. All dead-weight will have to go. I tell you what. We have just enough plasma for one last round of coffee. For everybody! We'll make a load and put it in the empty water-bags. That way, everybody in the village will have had some. Our parting gift to them!"

After making the last batch of coffee, cup by cup, and storing it in water-bags, they broke open the electrical panel behind the n-gen. They pulled the wires out of the back of the n-gen unit after Dee had cut off the power to the main bus. Then Stone went to the engineering bay at the rear of the ship and released the distributor panel there.

"Pull it then Stone!" Dee shouted.

Stone pulled his end of a number of cables which led towards the front of the ship until he pulled on the one Dee held. Then they found the other, and Stone detached them. Pulling them through the ducting, Dee coiled them around his arm and then laid them on the sand outside. By splicing the two pieces together, they had a length as long as the alien ship.

It took Dee the rest of the day to rig-up a crude receiver from the wreckage of the old navigation console. As dusk drew on, they were finally ready to test. They worked into the night, shortening the aerial by degrees. Dee operated the receiver, while the others cut the cable. In the early hours of the morning, they finally picked up first interference and then a proper signal. The cable had been reduced to 120 feet.

"Standard radio frequency!" shouted Dee, triumphantly. "I should have guessed! I need some of that coffee! Even if it's cold!"

"I'm gonna get some sleep!" said Jay. "You should get some too!"

"In a minute. I just want to try a few things!"

***

Shouting woke Stone:

"Jay! Stone! Shit! Come here!"

Jay got there first. Stone only caught the end of her sentence as he reached the flight deck, bleary eyed.

"… with it, Dee! What have you *done*?" Jay said.

"What's going on?" Stone asked.

"I dunno Stone. But whatever it is, it's trouble," Dee said anxiously. "I was playing around with it and I pressed this button and suddenly it all lit up like a Christmas tree. Lights going off everywhere and then I could see on this panel, here, a signal being sent. It seemed to be something intelligible. And then … ."

"Tell him, Dee!" Jay said, nudging him.

"Then something or somebody answered. I saw the incoming signal. It's bad guys, I know. I wasn't thinking. Too tired, I guess."

"Well, it's done now dude. At least switch it's off dude. Maybe no harm will come. Let's just get some sleep!"

"It's a bloody miracle it even worked!" Dee explained. "I never thought … ."

"Stop blaming yourself Dee," Stone insisted. "You've done a great job! One mistake … . Stop going *over* it. We'll be outa here in a couple of days anyway. They can't get here that fast!"

"Unless they're already *here*!"

"Mm," muttered Jay.

Stone went out into the main cabin to get a cup of the cold coffee and nearly tripped over the gun in the dimmed night-light.

"Hey Dee!"

"Yeah!"

"Jay! Come here!"

"What?" said Dee emerging from the flight deck.

Stone nodded towards the gun. "You thinking what I'm thinking?"

That night, Dee couldn't sleep. He made himself a cup of coffee and after staring at the console for a long while, he could resist no longer. He turned it on and waited. He hoped nothing would happen but his worst fears were realised. First one and then three indicators near the top of the console lit up. On the main screen, he could see lines of coded information being sent. With horror, he suddenly realised it must be from at least three different sources; as each light lit up, a new section of code would start.

"Stone! Wake up," he whispered in his friend's ear.

"Uh? What's up?"

"That signal?"

"Yeah?"

"I just couldn't wait. I had to see if they'd gone quiet or not."

"And … ?"

"They haven't. Stone?"

"What?"

"I'm pretty sure there are at least three ships waiting for us up there!"

"Oh shit! We better tell Jessica."

***

Kek-suîxjh went with Hri-hu to another dinner party, this time at his cousin's house. Kek-suîxjh dreaded these dinner-evenings; Shen-yrîxjh was a sycophant to the new regime, which now outlawed religion. Once a firm believer, Kek-suîxjh suspected Shen-yrîxjh still *did* believe, deep down, but would not, or could not, admit it. Kek-suîxjh despised him even more for his cowardice. Kek-suîxjh could perhaps afford to be more open about his beliefs, benefiting as he did from the osmosis of protection from his high-ranking wife. Nevertheless, with his cousin's protection, Shen-yrîxjh would probably be safe from persecution, if he were only subtle about it.

"You are still at the Institute Kek-suîxjh?" Shen-yrîxjh began coyly, after they had finished eating his excellent meal and were waiting for the two females to finish their conversation about weighty political matters. "Are you still finding it satisfying and have you made any progress on any of the great questions of science?"

Kek-suîxjh checked, with a glance, that he had his wife's permission to talk.

"I can answer both your questions at once, Shen. The great questions of science are also the great questions of religion, and *no*, I am not satisfied with my work."

His cousin's eyes widened slightly in shock at the brazen response.

"Kek!" admonished Hri-hu.

"Well, since you ask, I am working, I mean I *have* been working on a theory that the laws of time can be violated or at least that there is a loophole there somewhere." He grinned at his own audacity. Nobody, least of all he, had put it quite so bluntly before.

Shen's jaw widened in a broad smile. "Some would say that the thought of violating the inviolable sounds a little bit... um sexual Kek." Shen-yrîxjh glanced nervously at his wife, Ni-ha.

Hri-hu played with her jzu-serinî glass and Ni-ha with her jewellery.

"Ah. Sexual. Well, first of all I don't think the Laws of the Universe *are* inviolable, but I would have thought to suggest that there is anything sexual about the intention of science would itself be heretical."

"Oh no, Kek! I can assure you Shen is not that kind of male," interjected Ni-ha feebly.

"Thank you dear," replied her husband. Kek-suîxjh shuddered at how grateful and obsequious his cousin sounded. "If you are suggesting I am not loyal to the Council, Kek, or that I do not understand the finer points of societal etiquette, I think you are much mistaken."

"No. No, I am not under any illusions about that. It's just that for me, the furtive use of innuendo does not in any way mean that one is *not* suggesting something heretical!"

Now I have done it!

Shen-yrîxjh was, for a moment, floored, not used to being out-manoeuvred in conversation, least of all by his cousin.

"Is there anything good to listen too? Hm, er, music that you have bought lately, Hri?" ventured Ni, cutting across the silence to save her floundering husband.

"Please dear. I can fend for myself. So Kek, if there are... loopholes in the – let us say discretely – violable laws," he said, glancing to the two females to assure them of the purity in his intention, "what do you think keeps order, or at least what permeates the... lacuna there?"

"Ah nice flourish Shen! You are on form. And you know what my answer will have to be!" Shen, mistaken, smiled. "It can only be the intention, or at least the presence of our god Vîu. And further more Shen, just because you are told that science has all the answers, you shouldn't believe that her skirt hides all her vulnerabilities."

Shen, for once in his servile life, felt apoplectic with rage. Only the first paw of his wife stopped him from lunging across the table towards his older, and more successful cousin. Ni-ha fussed about him. Only Hri-hu became strangely still, like the air ahead of a hurricane. Then she spoke:

"And what, Kek, do you think religion, or indeed Vîu, had to offer, that science does not?" she asked calmly.

"What? What? I am tempted to say *everything*. You believed once my dear. I remember it! But I will keep myself from sweeping statements. What religion has, and science lacks, is a reason to believe that one's life is *really* worth something. That each person is *precious*."

"Science has that. We recognise that each life is precious," she said.

"Yes, each person, but not each life. How about the increase in extinction rate of all the species on Isch-su? Only a few were saved. I hear that over one thousand species die out each year. And I notice too that this information is suppressed."

"And how about all those that died – Ischians, not animals – in the great wars towards the end of Isch-su?" asked Hri-hu.

"Yes. Yes, I grant you that. It was a terrible thing. One of the *bad* things that religion does to people. I cannot defend it. Except to say that it is Ischians themselves who cause it. It is not Vîu's will. We are weak and not up to the challenge of loving one another. It is the fate of all advanced species, I fear."

"There you are then, dear," Hri-Hu added. "We have had *no* wars since we landed on Ito."

Kek-suîxjh thought long and hard before answering. "There are no wars because there is no-one left to conquer. At least not for now. But the difference is this. When I was young, I would help an old Ischian across a trakway. Now that I am old, nobody ever helps me. Nobody will ever give up a seat for another without there being a law to command it and nobody talks about death any more. And do you know why? Because everybody is afraid of death and afraid of life; afraid of living. And one last thing; we are stagnating. The only science of any worth is being done... by believers. And the only contact with another species has been achieved... by Vîuians."

Shen-yrîxjh and Ni-ha looked confused.

"I mean the *Exiles*." He saw the shock on their faces. Only Hri-hu smiled knowingly, but her eyes, a vivid and rare green, blazed with the fanatical light of the converted.

"Kek. You go too far. It is forbidden to speak of them. And they are beyond us... probably dead."

"You know that is not true, Hri-hu."

"No doubt you will believe what you want. Let me ask you one other question then, my dear husband. If your god is so great, why did Isch-su suffer so and die? Why were we all made homeless?"

Kek-suîxjh felt the cold thrill of her challenge deep within him. To use the term 'your god' when talking of

Vîu would have been the ultimate sacrilege in the old world and tantamount to a declaration of war or the most violent punishment in return.

"If you feel abandoned Hri-hu, it's not because God has abandoned you but because you have abandoned God."

"Oh don't be so glib, Kek!"

"Alright. If you want a different answer," Shen said, sucking in his breath at the word 'different,' "it is for each of us to look deep inside ourselves for any meaning at all to life. And you may struggle a lifetime without discovering anything at all that makes sense. It is often the case, and I have found it so, that anything worth doing is an act of defiance and likely not to be rewarded. One can love, but do not expect to be loved back. And to be honest, no amount of legislation can make love exist. But I digress. I cannot answer you simply Hri-hu. The Universe is a mystery and each of us is a Universe."

"When it's discovered that your god has a god of her own, it is time to abandon faith." Ni-ha said quietly. The other three looked at her.

"Not 'discovered,' *speculated*," Kek-suîxjh replied. "But the expedition by the archaeologist Dr. Piloxxrîxjh... might have proved something … . If only the whole expedition had not … gone missing." He paused for a moment. "I can only say that faith is not hard to acquire but the hardest thing to hang on to. I too have struggled with my faith in recent years. But I believe one has to try, and the answers … to the questions of both of you, will be found in the afterlife."

"Do you really believe in an after … life after death, Kek?" Shen asked. When Kek-suîxjh looked up, he saw a glint of hope in his cousin's eyes. Ni-ha also looked at him expectantly.

"Well we don't have time for niceties like this," said Hri-hu, dismissively. "Our world needs practicalities. We all know your … sentimental attachment to the old

238

religion, Kek, but this is neither the time nor place for a discussion about its finer points. I am tired and I think we will have to be going home. I have a long day ahead."

She didn't speak in the limousine on the way home or even later as they went to bed. She felt icy cold to the touch when she gave him her habitual kiss before falling asleep.

During the night, she tried to make love to him, aggressively. He felt that she just wanted to prove something to herself. Perhaps she just wanted to possess him one last time. For the first and last time during their marriage he refused sex.

Too aware of the danger he was in, Kek-suîxjh didn't sleep. He repeated a few sentences to himself, like a mantra, over and over again.

I went too far tonight. Now she will have no choice but to act. My turn has come. I have to go tomorrow.

***

9. The Weight of a Thought

Leaving his office only minutes after arriving in the morning, Kek-suîxjh walked briskly to the rail station. He carryied the small black traveling-case, in which he had packed the barest essentials for a long journey. Included in its contents were the Project Arcadia papers and all the currency he had left. Credit was too dangerous for him to use now. Feeling that somebody watched him, he made his way to the central airport and paid for a shuttle flight to Orbiter 1 Station, the usual stopping off point for any passengers on a space-flight from the City.

On the way to the airport he stared out of the panoramic windows, and through the transparent walls of the elevated tunnel, to the atmosphere of Ito.

It may be the very last time I see it. It's not much, but it's become home. It gave us sanctuary.

He repeated the last phrase as if trying to convince himself that it was true, but he could not feel a sense of loss for Ito. That had to be reserved for his old life and his wife. They had never been apart for more than a week since they were married and it would be strange to leave her. But part of him relished the prospect of focusing on science and religion in his own private space and for as much of the time as he wanted.

The thunderous methane clouds of Ito far above rolled across the jagged silhouettes of mountain ranges, away from the sun's direct rays. Only on very rare, clear days, did the sky turn blue. For the most part, Ito was an angry planet.

Reaching Orbiter 1 Station without any problems, Kek-suîxjh walked briskly towards the end of the concourse, where the private rentals booths were. He had put on head-ware and heavy clothes to disguise himself slightly. He felt ridiculous and wanted to smile at each security image-monitor that he spotted. He concentrated on keeping his long ears flat against his scalp. Erect ears were a clear sign of tension; security guards always looked out for this.

He reached the shabby booth of Allied Lux Cruises and dumped his case on the counter.

"Sir?" a lazy assistant enquired, lifting his two large furry feet from the seat on which they had been resting. The lazy Ischian male put down his racing sheet and looked for a clear sign that he should stand.

"I booked a ship for a cruise. I have come to collect it."

"Ah! Of course. Let's just take a lookie here sir. What was the name?"

"Dun-shrîxjh." This was the most common name imaginable and clearly an alias.

"Fine. Cash then I expect?"

"Um hm."

"Ah here it is. K-17, *Standard* model?"

"Um hm."

"Aha. Hm. Quite a lot of trimmings I see." The assistant saw something he liked on the list of accessories and smiled. "Nice! PBS-Dv2s? Four of them? Four?"

"Eh hm! Yes."

Kek-suîxjh slapped a big-denomination token on the counter and the assistant instantly placed his paw over it.

"Only curious sir. Sign here please," the assistant said, looking slightly aggrieved.

Kek-suîxjh made an illegible scrawl and the assistant tucked the sheet away without glancing at it. He pulled down one pink and one green sheet of printed fibrophil from a shelf, and lay them flat in front of Kek-suîxjh.

"This green sheet is your itinerary and the pink sheet is your insurance form. You need to complete both of these. If you care to pay now, I will prepare a receipt while you fill them in."

Kek-suîxjh opened the case and drew out his last fourteen i-tan, a lot of money. Cruisers, often retired military ships, were not expensive to hire but he had also provisioned the K-17 with every last bit of extra fuel and consumables possible. Any fool could see that he wasn't just going on a two-week jaunt around the moons of Ito, as his booking had stated.

"Thank you sir!" You needn't worry too much about the forms. It's just a formality, just a signature and a few details.

Kek-suîxjh scrawled 'moons of Ito' on the itinerary and signed it, all as illegibly as he could manage. On the insurance form he scrawled 'Recreation' and 'No known ailment.' He ticked the box for 'No convictions' and scrawled an unreadable signature.

"Here you go sir. Down the hallway here to the right, down the first set of stairs and follow the concourse right to the end. Take the rail to Bay 5. And have a pleasant cruise sir." The assistant looked up from the sheets as he patted them together. "Oh yeah... take your time, the guys will only be loading the PBSs just now. We get a lot of people ordering fancy extras but they usually don't have sufficient currency."

As easy as that! I am almost there.

Kek-suîxjh closed the case, picked up the security key-card and set off for Bay 5. He pulled the head-ware down over his face and turned up the collar of the coverall.

He waited for the rail and then took a seat facing the window looking out over Ito, far below. Kek-suîxjh closed his eyes to go over his plans one last time.

***

The day of the launch had arrived; takeoff, or 'freedom' as Stone saw it. The radio aerial stretched from the very end of the last cubby-hole near the engine through to the foot-pedals under the instrument panel. Holes had been cut through bulkheads so that it could have a straight run. The ship had been fueled and stripped of everything non-essential. Cushions, blinds, cutlery and crockery were all laid out on the dunes overnight for the tribe's women to take away when they arrived to say farewell. Avonaico's gun had been connected to the main power-circuit and tested but only with the viewing port removed. Finally the feet of its stand had been screwed to the floor.

"Bloody hell! Did you see *that*?" Dee said after the first burst.

"I didn't see anything!" said Stone. "Did it fire?"

"*Okay*! Go and look on that *second* dune, right at the *top*."

Stone dutifully trekked over to the dune and stared in astonishment at a twelve foot wide patch of solid glass, which glowed with fading heat in front above him. It gave off too much heat for him to approach closely. "Shit!"

Next, they tried hanging a sheet of seribdenum from the floor over the port instead of the transparent panel, and fired the gun. The shot had the same effect on the sand but made no impression on the seribdenum, so they felt safe to replace the transparent panel over the viewing port.

"As I thought," said Dee. "Some kind of disruptor. And I think *that* is set on the minimum *charge*!"

Of course Avonaico heard about the gun-test and insisting firing a few bursts himself. Dee showed him how to aim it and press the trigger. When the warrior saw the result he grinned from ear to ear and then nodded slowly, as if affirming a deeply held belief. He and Dee took in turns firing the weapon a few times. Dee worked out how to adjust the range using a dial on the side of the stock. He showed Avonaico how to operate it.

One hundred feet of rope had been stowed for Cheveya's safe return to earth. He seemed as excited as a kid by the prospect of his first flight and had insisted on wearing Dee's space-suit even though it was too small to fasten properly. Cheveya just wanted to look the part.

*****

During the previous evening, there had been one last feast to bid the visitors goodbye. Stone avoided the inevitable kech. His heart pined for one last look at the pyramid. Very early in the morning, before anyone else had woken, he stole away and made straight for the mysterious building which drew him so. The ladder still lay abandoned against a bush so he used it to climb up to the flat level, just as the first sun's rays probed over the hills behind him.

Stone wasn't sure what he was looking for. He remembered the impression that everything around him had been bathed in a golden light and his skin feeling abuzz as if with a strong electric field. He wanted those feelings again. But nothing came to him. It seemed as if, on *that* day at least, the pyramid was just an ordinary ruin. He had felt on the verge of discovering something in himself the last time. Sitting down, he put his feet over the lip of the main corridor and gazed at the plains, stretching far away to the Blue Hills. For a moment his mind drifted to somewhere he couldn't have identified if he had tried and then he decided to leave. He stood up and turned around to go. Just as he turned, he thought he saw something from the extreme edge of his eye. He whipped round and caught just a glimpse of something ephemeral, like a ghost, some way in front of him. Later, he would tell those who asked that he found it very difficult to describe. He couldn't say for certain how far away it might be or how big, whether solid or transparent, how it had arrived, or how it left. One moment it wasn't there and the next it was and then it had gone. But just for a moment he saw a creature with four rapidly vibrating, transparent wings. Most like a man-shaped, winged-creature it was, with an expressive face and human eyes. It seemed to wink at him just once and then it seemed to explode into a piercing white light.

Stone threw his hands over his face and fell to his knees, blinded. The pain in his head became overwhelming and he thought he would faint, *could* faint. But he didn't want to. He felt, rather than heard, himself retching. Trying to fight through the pain, part of him lucidly watched images from the visions about the hospital and battle sear through his mind. He felt himself being drawn ever deeper into utter darkness; a spirit world where he had to fight for his very soul's survival. From the darkness he could gradually make out shapes, bodies which vanished when he tried to reach out to them. The vision of the headless figures in the hospital had become a vision of Hell. The battle had become a battle to *be*. He felt an ashen coldness, saw a lack of substance in everything he saw. He grasped at features, faces, shadowy shapes but all vanished at his touch. Suddenly the ground appeared to be opening up to engulf him He slowly began slipping under, into, an abyss. He felt no hope, saw no sight of any future except a dreary death-life.

"Please God," he heard himself moan, utterly wretched.

Something pushed him from behind. Ahead, he saw the darkness give way to light. The silent howls of a myriad souls receded. They were replaced by silence.

Now, he could hear himself gasping, could feel the touch of prairie dirt on his fingers, the gentle caress of grass blades against his knuckles.

Stone, still on his kneels, hunched into a foetal position and vomited. He vomited until he could only retch. He stayed in that position, gasping, for quite some time. He felt washed, cleansed, turned inside out, renewed.

Eventually, he felt able to sit and he stared far out into the plain. He remembered the peculiar flying creature that had vanished into that painful explosion of light. Not wanting to remember the vision of Hell, he focused on a simpler problem. What had that creature been? He juggled various explanations quickly in his agile mind but none fitted well enough for him to breathe again. None, except perhaps one. He remembered the graffiti in the corridor below and knew he had seen the same thing that the artists, whoever they were, had tried to paint.

A God! An Anubian God! A proper God! Perhaps the God of Gods!

He began to feel free, better than he had ever felt in his life. He experienced again the sensation of being bathed in golden light, only this time it felt much purer and more powerful. He felt as if he had fallen into a room which had previously remained locked despite his best efforts to break in. Suddenly he believed in something. He wasn't yet sure what but he knew he believed in something. He felt sure that his must be the first such vision by any of the human race. After his breathing slowly returned to normal, he rushed back to tell the others but as he half walked, half ran, he slowly changed his mind about what to do.

Nobody will ever believe me! At least not yet. No, let's wait until we are out in space. Wait until we are away from here, and then I will try to tell the others.

***

Stone, Jay, Dee and Shihu crested the dune at the head of a column of the Naxa, just before they reached the ship. Although they hadn't wanted so much attention, it had been impossible to dissuade most from coming. Most of the villagers trailed behind them. The promise of discarded items from the ship didn't help dissuade the crowd, either.

As the long line of Naxa and crew members struggled up the last dune to the cruiser, Stone felt relieved to see a tribesman standing on the crest, looking down at them. Avonaico and his men had guarded the ship overnight.

"Hey Stone!" called Dee from behind him. "Guess what! I've put together a compilation … ."

"Hang on Dee!" Stone cut in. "Something's wrong." He approached the guard just above him but the warrior didn't move aside. His look seemed stern and unyielding.

For a horrified split-second, Stone thought something bad had happened to the ship:

No! They haven't burned it!

The warrior held up his hand to forbid Stone from going any further. Cheveya's hand on his shoulder silenced the protest in his throat.

"I will deal with this Stone," the chief whispered. "What is the meaning of this?" he asked the man.

"Avonaico forbids you to come any further. We have taken the great sky-kayak!"

"Let me speak with my brother."

The man looked uncertain for a moment and then stepped aside. Cheveya led the rest of the tribe up onto the dune's crest, where they could see Avonaico and the other four men around the spaceship. The atmosphere seemed as taught as a drum skin.

Cheveya strode up to his brother and repeated the question.

Loud enough for all to hear, Avonaico answered. "The great kayak of the sky is mine now brother."

"It is not yours to take."

"This land belongs to no tribe and so anything I find here is mine."

"Hm. If you are far out on the plain, hunting moosto where no tribe claims territory, and you then drop your arrow, is it still not yours?"

"Hm … . Cheveya. I have nothing. Now I cannot even have Shihu. The taste in my mouth is bitter."

"I understand that but this is not yours to take. Do you not know that the White Tribe have offered to find the great moosto herds for us if we let them fly?"

"Yes, but Avonaico will fly with them, not Cheveya. Stone will teach me to fly the ship and we will attack the Gjanga and the Itchik! With the strange weapon we will beat them and become a great tribe!"

"You always preferred war brother. But such ideas are foolishness."

"Better a dead fool than a living slave!" said Avonaico angrily. In his eyes burned something close to hatred for his brother. Stone could see Cheveya had been hurt by the answer.

"Then we must fight!" said Cheveya, after a moment's thought.

"It must be *so!*" answered Avonaico

"You are outnumbered but I will take only ten men. We will fight with only knives."

"It will be so!" Avonaico's men lowered their spears and bows to the sand.

"Why don't just Avonaico and Cheveya fight it out!" asked an incredulous Stone of the man next to him. "That is how these things are normally settled!"

Dee glanced, shaking his head disbelievingly, at his friend and spoke:

"They can only fight once, for the title of Chief. If they could fight more than once, they would always be fighting."

Cheveya picked his ten men and gestured for everyone else to move back to a safe distance. Without warning Avonaico shouted the war cry, "Baika!" and his men charged. Instant carnage ensued but all eyes were focused on the two leaders. First Cheveya and then Avonaico gained the upper hand, their bodies writhing in a death-clasp on the side of the dune. As they fought, they slid further and further down the dune. Other men screamed in pain as they were pierced by a dagger or had bones broken.

Stone wanted to look away. "God! Why don't they stop!" he moaned.

Jay clutched at Dee's chest, crying. Only Shihu looked on dispassionately.

Stone glanced away from the two leaders for a moment and saw four of Cheveya's men standing over two inert bodies. Moments later two more of Avonaico's men were dead. Now only the Chief's brother and one other fought on.

"This is pointless!" Stone said.

A scream from Avonaico's last henchman signaled the penetration of his chest by a dagger and within moments, he lay motionless. A crimson rosette of blood slowly spread on the red-brown sand.

Cheveya managed to get on top of his brother again and his arm raised for one final blow with his knife. Avonaico looked finished, his face a rictus of suffering and exhaustion. But the arm above him paused. Cheveya, almost exhausted himself, stood up slowly and said so that all could hear, "I will not kill my own brother. You must take the Lonely Path."

Avonaico nodded slowly and stood up. Blood dripped from several wounds. He climbed back up the dune, not meeting the eyes of any there, and then he picked up his spear. With one last glance back towards the village, he turned and began to trek across the dunes, in a south westerly direction.

The rest of the tribe collectively breathed a sigh of relief. Cheveya's wife rushed up to him. His two youngest children, who had been crying, stood in awe as he picked them up and laughed at them. Suddenly everything was alright again. Nobody noticed Avonaico begin to circle round behind the tribe.

Soon, all the tribe's women had picked up the last of the ship's jetsam, lying on the sand, with much hubbub and Makya had started to move the Naxa people back, out of harm's way, ready for the launch.

The three people of the White Tribe said their tearful farewells and entered the ship through the hatch. Cheveya followed them inside. He waved to the crowd in the distance and cries of encouragement answered his wave. Shihu entered last. She held on to Makya and her mother until the last moment. She picked up Ahote, kissed him, and then hugged and kissed her sister Muna. When she finally tore herself free and boarded the ship, her eyes were flooded with tears. On the flight deck, Stone pressed the button to close the hatch.

"Right! All on board? We're ready then!"

"Are you sure you can do this Stone?" asked Jay. Her head started to thump.

"Of course I can. My mum, Katie was … ."

"A space pilot and I'm the best *damned pilot* at the Academy!" Jay and Dee both said together, laughing. Shihu smiled weakly. She and Cheveya took their positions on the only two remaining seats in the main cabin. They strapped themselves in as they had been taught. The others strapped themselves in on three of the four seats on the flight deck.

Dee punched the intercom to 'ship-wide' and plugged in his headband. "I never got around to telling you Stone. I put a nice little compilation together for you. I know you'll like it. Some oldies. And guess what?"

"What?"

"The best bit is that I found an old Motown compilation. That real old stuff you like so much. I've got a track lined for you from that for the actual takeoff."

"Cool. Play it! Okay! Are we ready?"

Stone took a deep breath and said:

"Okay, then main drive to standby!"

"Standby!" repeated Dee, acting as engineer and co-pilot.

"Pulse jets, intakes fully open, valves set to 'Prime.'"

"Check!" said Dee.

Jimi Hendrix's Third Stone from the Sun started up on the intercom.

Deep inside the ship, a throbbing indicated the main drives were building up charge. The torus would be circulating charged particles at a colossal speed, approaching the speed of light, and then the beam of particles would be directed into the horizontal plane.

Just as the Hendrix track played out, the red light came on for 'Anti-grav ready.'

"Punch it Dee!"

"Okay! Here we go!"

The Motown 1966 Temptations track 'Get Ready' started to play. Its quiet but insistent opening rhythm, belied the crescendo that would come later.

"Ignition for both jets!" Stone shouted over the music and increasing hum of the torus accelerator.

Dee pressed the two red buttons. First one pulse jet and then the other burst into burbling life. Stone looked rearwards from left window to the port engine. Smoke poured around the edges of the replacement panel.

"Looks like the clay packing is holding for now!" he said. "Throttle up!"

Dee pushed the throttles to sixty percent of full power. Stone moved the wing-let and pod rotation controls to 45 degrees. "Everyone okay back there!" He turned round and could see Chief Cheveya tapping his foot to the music.

He looked from Jay to Cheveya. Both were unprotected, wearing only Naxa clothing. The chief looked like a man who knew a mischievous elephant sat right behind him and wondered what would happen next.

The ship rocked slightly on its skids but still didn't move.

"Okay! Full power!" shouted Stone over the tumultuous roar.

> I never met a girl who makes me feel the way that you do.
> (You're alright)
> Whenever I'm asked who makes my dreams real, I say that you do.
> (You're outta sight)

Dee pushed the sliders all the way forward. The ship's bucking increased but still the dunes, viewed through the windscreen, refused to move.

"Looks like we should have dumped that gun after all!" Stone shouted.

"We're not moving Stone!" shouted Dee.

So, fee-fi-fo-fum

"Okay. Give me full power on the anti-grav!"

"What? Are you mad? It will overheat and melt us to the sand!"

"Do it!"

Dee turned the control into the red zone on the end of the dial and closed his eyes. He started saying the Hail Mary.

Stone felt he should rock the seat from side to side to try and break the ship free but he could only stare intently at the nearest dune. The noise grew to an unbearable roar. He heard a voice inside him shouting, *It's gonna blow up! We're not gonna make it!"*

He gritted his teeth. "Come on! *Come on*!"

Imperceptibly, inch by painful inch, a distinctive patch of discoloured sand slid slowly out of view. Stone had to blink and check again to make sure he wasn't imagining it.

"We're moving! We're moving!"

And I'm bringing you a love that's true.
So get ready, so get ready.
I'm gonna try to make you love me too.
So get ready, so get ready 'cause here I come.

One inch per minute became one inch per second and then Dee, who had opened his eyes, could also see they were slowly slipping down the sand slope to the trough which marked the beginning of their makeshift runway.

"Come on Stone! You can do it!" shouted Dee.

(Get ready 'cause here I come) I'm on my way.
(Get ready 'cause here I come)

Stone felt a vicious vibration when the ship reached the bottom of the dune and rolled upright from the angle it had sat at for the last few months. Now they were moving at a fast running pace and the crests of the dunes either side slid by rapidly. Stone had to struggle with the controls to keep the wing-lets from touching the sand.

"Can you see Dee? How close are we on your side?"

"Bloody close but you'll make it!"

"It's like driving a bloody hover-truck, a big one! It barely responds to the controls!"

"What do you *expect*? It's sand, not concrete!"

"Okay coming up to the first kink!" The course slipped to the right just ahead of them and even though Jay had done her best with the Naxa women to smooth off the deviation, the ship rocked and lurched as it traversed the obstruction. The crew's teeth were shaken in their mouths and Stone's vision blurred for a moment.

"Ground speed?" Stone asked when the ship had settled.

"Forty knots."

"No good. We need at least sixty!" Stone looked at the reddish brown hills coming towards them with ominous speed. "How far to the hills do you think?"

"Reckon we're half way, *at least*!"

Stone looked at the dashboard for any control that could be pushed a little further to make the ship go faster but he could find none; every control had been pushed to its maximum. He gritted his teeth and prayed.

Oh God. You know I believe in you now, although I don't know who you are. You gotta get us out of this!

Both Dee and Stone had their eyes glued to the speedo. Slowly and fickly, sometimes falling back and sometimes waggling implausibly up to ninety knots, the indicator crept towards sixty knots.

"Fifty-five!" called out Dee. "Fifty-six!"

"Come on you old bag of nails!" shouted Stone.

Stone noticed Dee glanced at him disapprovingly.

"Come on you sweet … ." His words were trapped in his throat as the ship hit the second kink and the controls were almost wrenched from his grip.

"That's... the last one!" shouted Dee, through the confused noise. It sounded to Jay more like a warning than encouragement.

"Speed?" shouted Stone, fighting to steady sixty tons of bucking aluminium and seribdenum.

"Sixty! Sixty knots!" shouted Dee. He closed his eyes at the sight of the cliffs ahead filling the windscreen. "Lord! Lord … !"

"She's lifting!" The violent shaking suddenly stopped and they were riding on a thin cushion of hot, dry, desert air. "We're airbor- … . God!" Even though their speed now rapidly increased, they were so near to the rock wall that Stone could make out plants and bushes clinging for life onto the sun baked stone. He needed just a little more speed before turning.

Dee opened one eye. "Now Stone! Turn!"

"Not yet!"

"Oh Go … !"

"Now!" Stone swung the ship violently to the right using the rudder, wing-let controls, which acted much like ailerons, and by cutting the power to the right pod. The rock wall rushed towards them until it became just a blur, making the flight deck seem like the only stationary thing in the whole universe. For just an instant, all seemed quiet and still and Stone felt that he could relax and go to sleep if he wanted. But an instant later, Stone heard the sound of crunching alloy as something hit the ship. The impact repeated, again and again.

This is it!

Stone pulled the control column into his chest with all his might and at the same time tried to steer to the left to gain a few more feet of height. The tactic worked and the violent crunching impact on the belly of the ship stopped. But in gaining a little more height, they had lost speed. A klaxon blared.

"Stall! She's gonna stall!" shouted Dee.

"I know." Stone then did something he should never have done. It could never have been in any manual he made an inspired move which, just this once and against all odds, worked. Having cleared the rock wall, he should have depressed the control column to return to a straight flight path, preserving what little air speed they had. Instead he continued to pull back on the column, flipping the ship over onto its back and pointing it back into the valley. With the skill of an aerobatic champion, he executed a clean role and brought the ship out into a shallow dive towards the dunes in the centre of the valley.

"What the fu … !"

"Everything to flight position now Dee!" shouted Stone. Dee felt confused but simply did what Stone asked, returning the pods and the wing-lets to horizontal and non-lift positions. The spaceship lost even more speed and the dunes rushed towards them. But then the speed stabilised and even increased a little. Dee's eyes were wide with terror as the sandy sea grew larger in their vision. Just as it looked as if they were doomed, the dunes ended and a flat plain stretched away before them. They skimmed just above the parched ground. Shrubs and wiry trees were torn away by the bottom of the ship as it passed.

"Ha! Knew we could make it! You don't know the dragonfly man!" shouted Stone, humming along to the Temptations.

>And I'm bringing you a love that's true.
>So get ready, so get ready.

I'm gonna try to make you love me too.
So get ready, so get ready 'cause here I come.

"You bloody mad sonofabitch! How the hell did you do that? Is there a *name* for that manoeuvre?"

"I think so … I suppose in the old days it might be called an Immelmann turn but it was a bit ragged, to be honest."

"Well it was bloody good if you ask me."

(Get ready 'cause here I come) I'm on my way.
(Get ready 'cause here I come)

"Well done, Stone!" shouted Jay from behind them.

'Get Ready' finished playing on the intercom and Hendrix's Stone Free started to play.

"Let's go and look for some bison!" announced Stone.

They climbed gently up, first to forty thousand feet, and then flattened into a very gentle climb before the pulse jets started to cough.

"Okay. Cut 'em Dee. We need to save a bit."

Stone cut in the main drive, which had been gradually heating up, and the first great pulse from the torus thrust the ship forwards. The ship accelerated to ever greater speeds as they headed for the stratosphere.

"See that?" Stone said pointing to the coast below. "That looks pretty much like the West Coast of America, if you ask me."

"California, I would say," answered Jay leaning over Stone's seat

"How's the chief and Shihu?" Stone asked Jay.

"Pretty pale. I left them in their harnesses but I think they're gonna be sick soon. Yep. I would say California. I reckon if we head north and inland, we should find something. Let me see if I can get the bio-scanner working. I haven't used one since the *second* year! Dee, can you turn off the music and check if the bio-filters are clean?"

"Sure! Give me a moment."

"I think we all need a *moment*!" she answered. "Stone, that was an amazing bit of flying but I don't ever want to experience anything like that again!"

"Yeah!" Dee agreed. "I've never heard of anybody rolling a cruiser in an atmosphere before. I don't think it's ever been done!"

"Well it has now!" answered Stone.

"Yeah! And what the hell was that about some dragonfly man?" asked Dee

"Ah! Tell you about it later."

"Okay Jay. Filters are fairly clean; the alpha channel is the dirtiest."

"Okay, let's see what we have here. Wow! Haven't done this in ages. Quite a good one, this bio-scanner. I've calibrated it using a sample from the atmosphere. It says 'Earth like!' Ha! Ha! You're telling me. Now … just need to get a trace. Okay! Wow! Plenty of readings! Stone, there is a very large bio-mass about four-hundred miles north of our current position."

She peered out of the wind-screen to Stone's left. "There! Just the other side of this mountain range."

"Okay. Let's go take a look. I think you'd better let our prisoners loose!"

"Oh yeah! I forgot!"

As soon as they tried to stand, unsteadily, Shihu and Cheveya clutched their stomachs and heads. Shihu made straight for the bathroom unit. She had her handle on the door when the nausea suddenly passed so she sat down again. Jay gave them both a flight-sickness tablet. The wonder-drug took only a minute to work its magic and Cheveya soon put in an unsteady appearance on the flight deck. He grinned like a kid at the sight through the windscreen. But he gripped the back of Stone's seat tightly.

"Like a bird! Like an eagle, flying high over the Earth! I never dreamed of this, Stone … ."

"Look at this Chief Cheveya." Dee showed him the map and tried to explain where they were now and where the Naxa village must be. The big man concentrated hard but didn't seem to quite understand the map.

"Never mind!" Stone told him. "It's a lot to take in. Jay has shown us where there might be a biso … . I mean, moosto herd."

"Ah!"

"Going down!" shouted Stone, putting the ship into a steep, controlled glide. "Twenty-thousand feet! Ten-thousand! Five thousand. Two thousand. I'm not seeing any bison Jay. Wait, what's this?" Something brown started spattering the windscreen. They were surrounded by a thin cloud of what looked like dirty rain. Something managed to cling to the nose in front of the windscreen for a moment. "Some kind of insects!"

"Yeah. Locusts most likely!" suggested Jay. "Okay, take us up and about fifty miles north of here. I saw another strong trace there."

"I dunno. We can only go up once. I reckon we only have about forty seconds of fuel left."

"How d'you reckon that?" asked Dee.

"Reserve. We're almost on reserve. Ten seconds left on main. I'll try and glide there."

Stone cut the jets, banked and trimmed the ship for maximum glide distance. Above the near silence in the ship, they could hear the air whistling past the control-surfaces and windscreen of the ship.

"Wait a minute! I see something. Yes! Over there. Come and look Chief Cheveya!"

Cheveya peered over his shoulder, and Stone banked the ship slightly to give him a better view. The chief's eyes litr up:

"Many, many moosto! Stone, I haven't seen this many Moosto since the great herds of my childhood. The Naxa must leave their home and travel here! You have made me very happy!"

"Okay, going up. We have about ten seconds Dee. Get ready with the main drive."

"Are you crazy? Not down here."

"We don't have any choice. Anyway, do you really think there are gonna be pollutants around at this time? The air is as clean as it could possibly be!"

"I guess. Okay Stone. It's a risk though."

"Ignition."

Once again, Dee punched the red buttons and fired up the engines.

"No more than ten seconds, okay?"

They climbed rapidly for ten seconds and then Dee pressed the main drive ignition. There were two large bangs from the rear of the ship and an enormous white cloud began trailing behind it. But they continued to climb smoothly.

"Just clearing the exhaust out!" Stone quipped. "Okay Dee. Mark the map for Chief Cheveya and then show him how to use it. We don't have much time."

"You'll have to go much higher before I can get our exact position on this map. Then I can use the ground radar to match our position to the map."

As they climbed, Dee watched the radar screen until he could make out major features on the ground which matched the map. Taking an old-fashioned pen, he suddenly drew a cross on the map. "Okay. We're here. Now, Chief Cheveya, I've been studying this map and your village, as near as I can make out, is here!" He drew another cross on the map. "Now to get to the herd of moosto, you just need to travel more or less directly inland, towards the dawn sun, for oh I would say about … . Oh I dunno … . Jay, how long would you say 800 miles would take the tribe to cover?"

"Let's see. Well I reckon the distance to the Red Hill is about five miles and takes the tribe about three hours, say one and a half miles per hour. So roughly five hundred hours. Say about seventy days!"

"Okay Chief Cheveya. You need to travel east across these hills for just over two moons and then turn northm this way. Continue for another fourteen days and you will be there!"

Cheveya still looked confused.

"I don't think I'm making this clear Stone!"

"Oh! Take the controls! We don't have time for this. Keep going south west."

"Listen Chief Cheveya. This here is the sea. Big water. These thin blue lines are rivers. These are mountains. If you cross these mountains to here, you will find the moosto. All you need to do is to travel towards the sun every morning and keep going in a straight line. Then, as Dee said, after two moons, you need to turn left, towards the cold lands!"

"Okay Stone. I will study it with Enkoodabaooh. He will help me understand it! I thank you for all my people for this!"

"That's okay. I'm only sorry about Avonaico."

"Ah, don't worry about him. He knows we are going to leave, to find the moosto, and he will have the village to himself. He only has to wait. That is what he has always wanted."

"Oh. That's not so bad then."

They sealed the map inside a waterproof plastic bag and tied Cheveya into his harness. Dee handed him a knife.

"When we're low over the water, you must cut yourself loose!" shouted Stone, retaking the controls of the ship.

"I think we're here Stone," said Dee, checking the radar image.

"Okay, here we go!"

Chief Cheveya clasped Stone's hand one last time, and then Dee's. Not knowing what might be appropriate, Jay hugged him and gave him a quick peck on the cheek. He blushed. Shihu hugged him quickly. This made him blush even more.

Down they glided until they could see the river, just south of the Red Hill. Jay opened the hatch and, slowly, she and Dee lowered Cheveya down until he dangled nearly one hundred feet below and slightly behind the ship. He waved.

"I think he's enjoying it!" Dee shouted.

"Brave man!" shouted Stone over the noise of the wind. He slowed the ship to a steady eighty knots.

"Okay, three … two … one … now!" Stone yelled, slowing the ship almost to its stalling speed. Klaxons blared but he waited for the Chief to jump.

"He's not cutting it!" Dee shouted.

"Cut him loose or we'll all die!" Stone shouted.

Dee grabbed the only laser-knife they had kept from the kitchenette and cut the rope. He watched as Cheveya fell gracefully into the river. "He's okay! He's waving!"

"Close the hatch Dee and let's get out of here!" Stone pulled back on the control column and pressed the ignition buttons once more. After a few seconds of spluttering power, he switched to reserve and the spaceship started to climb. It had only reached five thousand feet when the engines cut out for the last time and Stone pressed the ignition button for the main drive. The bang was even louder than before. The ship shook violently. For a moment, Stone thought he'd cut it too fine. But they were still alive and another explosion, less violent than the first, carried them higher into the hazy blue sky.

∗∗∗

"Well, we're on our way!" Stone declared.

"Yes and no thanks to your piloting skills!" joked Jay, as they sat down to their first meal on board since the launch. They were beyond the stratosphere now and heading for the dark safety of space. Little Earth tinkled delightfully below them, more pristine than they had ever known it but it was still the same Earth.

***

10. Towards the Gate

It was about this time that Detective Sergeant Rayburn contacted me again.

"Mr Nanden, I've had my ears chewed out all day by Mrs MacNamarra. Apparently she's heard on the grapevine, although God knows *what* grapevine that women listens to, that the Interplanetary Police Patrol have picked up some unusual radio traffic from the Anubians. Around about the place your kid, and hers, disappeared … ." On the screen, his face looked sour.

"Is that true?"

"Well, yeah it *is* actually. Listen, you're an *important* guy. I can't find out much more than that. Maybe you can dig around and find out something more?"

"Okay. I'll give Sadie a call, find out what she knows, first."

"Sadie, is it?"

"Ha! She's okay once you get to know her."

"Good luck!"

***

"Hello."

"Sadie? It's Jake."

"*Jake*! I'm glad you called. I was thinking about calling you, but I didn't want to bother you with rumours."

"Well it sounds like you've been doing plenty of bothering already."

"Pardon?"

"Sorry. I mean Rayburn had just called me and said you've heard something."

"Ah! Yes. Well an old suitor of mine who, God bless him, had never given up on me, works in Intelligence and gave me a tip-off. He said that the IPP have been picking up unusual radio traffic from the Anubian outpost in Cygnus, what do they call it, Bek-su?"

"That's interesting. What sort of traffic?"

"Well, they sound pretty excited. Something about a signal from inside the worm-hole that the kids went through. God knows why I don't solely blame your son for it but Jessica always was a little, erm, rebellious!"

"Okay. Any more detail on *what sort* of signal?"

"Well, that's the odd thing. The alien traffic seems to be saying, and you know we're eves-dropping on their local traffic so our guys can't decipher all of it, but it seems to be saying that they've received a message from a ship that they lost a long time ago! Like twenty years ago!"

"Hm. Interesting, but what has it to do with my Stone, Jessica and Dee?"

"Well only that it's the first bit of radio traffic from that worm-hole since they disappeared. Don't you see! It's possible they've crashed and found some alien ship which they are using to send distress calls from!"

"Sounds a bit far-fetched!"

"Yes but my friend tells me that our ships *aren't* capable of communicating through a worm-hole! Are you going to ignore the only possible message from your son?"

"No. I'm going to find out some more about *this*. I still have contacts in the Army and Intelligence."

"Rumour has it you *still work* in intelligence Mr Nanden."

"Don't believe everything you hear Sadie. I'll call you as soon as I know more."

***

My first thought was to call Katie but she'd already been through enough stress over leads that led nowhere.

"Hi Ron. It's Jake Nanden here. I wonder if I could ask a favour?" The screen blanked out.

"Jake Nanden! Well, well! Haven't heard from you since that Christmas after your little Stone took a joyride to Earth!"

"Yeah. Well as you may have heard; he's taken a joyride to somewhere outside the solar system this time!"

"Oh really? That was *your* boy? I heard something about that. He really gets around doesn't he? Chip off the old block, in a way."

"Well I never looked at it that way … . Anyway, I need to ask a favour. Just say if you don't want to help. Do you still have contacts at the Intelligence Communications centre L11?"

"L11? Whoa, that's sensitive *stuff,* Jake."

"Yeah, but it's the Anubians who last saw the cruise ship my boy stole and now, apparently, they have picked up some kind of message from one of their lost ships though that worm-hole of theirs."

"What are you saying? You want me to find out more?"

"I'm not saying that, no. I don't want to compromise you, or myself. Just that if you do hear anything that's relevant to my boy, maybe you could pass anything that isn't top secret to a Detective Sergeant Rayburn on J6."

"I see. You mean you're not still classified?"

"You don't need to know that Ron. You know what to do if you find out anything."

"Okay. How's that ex-wife of yours, Katie?"

"She's cut up about Stone."

"Yeah, of course! Okay Jake. Well, thanks for the call. Take care."

"Yeah. See ya." But the phone had already gone dead.

***

I didn't hear anything for nearly a week and then Rayburn called.

"Well, Mr Nanden, I don't know what you did or who you called but a strange thing happened this morning.

Somehow, and I have to assume, by accident, a dispatch from the SCIA, which should have been marked top secret, ended up on my desk. Must be some mistake from dispatch. Anyway it's unmarked so I opened it, not knowing what it was … . It's a transcript of some decoded stuff from *that* top secret unit that tracks Anubian radio traffic." I heard only silence on the other end of the vidphone. I opened my eyes and looked at his blank face on the screen.

"Well? What does it say?"

"Well. I can't tell you. But if you're in the area, drop in for coffee some time."

"Okay. I will do."

I was there inside the hour.

"Well?"

"Oh that. Well I can't find it for some reason," he said, nudging a nondescript looking piece of brown plastic towards me. I leaned over and read it to myself. Most of it had been censored. What was left read, 'blank … at least five small cruisers dispatched into
the … blank … thought to be intercepting origins
of … blank. Note, ships are not friendly.'

"It's not good is it?" said Rayburn.

"No, it's not good."

"What does *that* mean?" He pointed to the last phrase on the plastic.'

"I'm not sure but I have a pretty good idea."

"I thought the Anubians were *basically* friendly."

"Not all of them."

***

Shihu took great pleasure in serving the meal, which she had prepared earlier, on the low table at the rear of the main lounge, using the ship's utensils as Jay had shown her. The delicious dish of spicy fried fish, wrapped in green leaves between thick wedges of fresh bread, loosened the tongues of the escapees. They spoke in Naxa, as far as they could, for Shihu's benefit.

"Doesn't she look great!" said Stone, hugging Shihu and giving her a wet kiss on her bright red lips.

"First time I've seen her in 22nd Century clothes!" answered Dee. "She looks gorgeous!"

The skin-tight, black body-stocking, which matched Jay's blue one, certainly left very little to the men's imagination. Her hair had been pulled back and tied into a pony-tail with a yellow butterfly clip and her nails were painted white. All her accessories were borrowed from Jay's traveling wardrobe.

"A little bit tight on her. She's slightly smaller than me but more curvy!" explained Jay.

"You needn't apologize dear," said Dee, sarastically.

She elbowed him. "Watch it! And enough of the 'dear.' I prefer 'baby,' at least in the present company."

Shihu blushed deeply at all the attention.

A good mood pervaded the feast.

"I have some kech too!" said Shihu, carefully in English.

"Wow! Good girl!" Dee drained his cup of water and held it out for her to pour some of the strong spirit for him. "After, we'll warm up some of that cold coffee I kept."

"Ah! A complete meal." Stone leaned back on one of only four chairs left and sighed deeply with pleasure.

"So what's this *dragonfly* man then, eh?"

"Ah, Dee. If only you could have seen it. But you'll never *believe* me!"

"Try us!" said Jay.

Shihu looked intrigued.

"Well, I went out to the pyramid again this morning. You were all sleeping."

"I hea'ad you go," said Shihu quietly.

Stone smiled at her. "Anyway, I wanted just one last look at it. I wanted to have that feeling again; being bathed in golden light and having my skin feel like it's charged up. Anyway, nothing really happened until I had been just about to leave. I'd been looking at the great plains, I think, you know, just drifting away. I turned to come back and saw, thought I saw, something from the corner of my eye. You know what? Do you remember that graffiti in the alcove, on the altar painting Dee?"

"Yep. At least I remember seeing something, blue wings."

"Yeah. Well what I saw would fit that exactly. It was like … a very small man, hovering in front of me somewhere. I couldn't tell how far away, or exactly how big he was. But he had four transparent wings, like gossamer. Bluish, but many colours in the sunlight, which was just hitting the pyramid. I was transfixed. I wasn't sure if I was seeing things, maybe."

"Probably was … " said Dee.

"Shh!" cut in Jay. "Go on Stone."

"Well you know what? I could swear the little guy winked at me. And then he was gone. Just gone! Nowhere to be seen!" Stone felt too afraid to tell them of the visit to Hell afterwards.

"Wow! What do you think it was?"

"Not what, *who*, Jay. You know what Cheveya told us, about how the Anubians wanted the Naxa to find their real god, not their Anubian god, Vinu or whatever she's called. But *her* god. The *real* God."

"Uh-*huh*!"

"Yeah." added Dee, sarcastically.

"Well that's who I think this was. The God of Gods. The one God who maybe … just maybe, is the God of our God too."

"Oh that's just crap, Stone!" said Dee. "And I can't believe the Stone I know is saying it. I think I preferred you as an atheist."

"Agnostic!" corrected Stone. "Well, that's what I think. I believe *it*!" Stone felt hurt at Dee's comment and became quiet.

"Oh! That was unfair, Dee!" said Jay. "At last he's found some faith and you mow him down! Shame on you!"

Shihu, diplomatically, stood up and started to clear away the dishes. She proceeded to tidy up the ship as if it were her house back in the village.

"Did you know the Anubians are split into two factions?" said Dee, trying to change the subject.

"Go on," said Jay.

"Yep. Just like we have left wing and right wing politicians, so they have a left and right wing apparently. That's what I heard anyway. Only with them, it's the liberals who are religious and the right-wingers are the atheists."

"That's odd."

"Not that odd. Germany was much like that in the 1930s. And in fact most fascist regimes see themselves as right wing, at least initially, but are usually anti-religion," Stone said.

"Where did you hear all this Dee?"

"Oh just around. On the grapevine. I don't think its common public knowledge yet."

"Conspiracy theory more like!" said Stone, perking up.

"So what's your politics Stone?" Jay asked.

"He was right-wing, once," interjected Dee.

"No I wasn't. Just 'cos I was a reactionary, reacting against my father's cosiness, doesn't make me right-wing!"

"So your father is a liberal?" asked Jay.

"I guess you could say that, although, as you know, he is some kind of bloody war hero. You know, Iron Cross and all that! But I think deep down, he always *was* a liberal. He's just got cosy in his old *age*. I reacted against that. He also got religious of course and I reacted against that too. Now I'm not so sure. In fact, now I think he was on to something."

"You still haven't answered the question, Stone." Dee pointed out.

"Well I'm not a Conservative or Republican or whatever they call them these days."

"Conservative and Liberal Republicans. Two different parties!" Dee clarified.

"Yeah. I'm neither of those. You see, the trouble with Republicans … or Conservatives, is that they try to live within their means. That's all very well and good. It's a good thing … up to a point. Living within your spiritual, physical and financial means is good but man would never have got to here if we all did that. I mean you need ambition and creativity and … well aspirations. Things that are outside one's means. You need to break out of your bounds. To live within your means is just to be a follower. Conservatives are just followers. I mean if Jesus had been a conservative, we wouldn't have Christianity!"

"Ha! Bu- … ."

A scream from the corridor near the bathroom interrupted Dee's response. All three heads turned to see a familiar arm reach out to grab Shihu around the neck, followed by a face they all recognised. Avonaico emerged from the bathroom, holding a knife to Shihu's neck. Blood caked his bare chest where he had been wounded in the fight with Cheveya. He swayed, as if slightly delirious.

"Don't move!" Avonaico ordered. "Now at last Shihu can be useful to me! I don't want hee'a foe'a myself anymore but … you want hee'a alive, you do what I say!" They saw a glint of pure malice in his eyes. Clutching Shihu to him with his right arm, holding a knife to her throat, he edged towards them, into the main lounge. He passed the first bunk, with its curtain pulled back, and then the second. Twice, Shihu tried to slip from his grasp but he proved too strong and determined. He edged

272

around the corner of the second bunk's partition, into the lounge and backed towards the weapon. When he had postioned himself behind it, he switched Shihu to his other arm, the knife to his other hand and pressed the power button, as he had seen Dee do. He depressed the stock, which raised the barrel to point in the general direction of Stone, Jay and Dee.

"Don't be stupid, Avonaico!" Jay said calmly. "You can't fire that thing in here. You'll kill us all! It will make a hole in the ship and then all the air will rush out!"

For a moment, doubt played over Avonaico's eyes.

Stone whispered quickly in English, "We're gonna all have to rush him together. That thing is set to fire … ."

But Avonaico sliced a thin bead of red blood across Shihu's throat, cutting Stone short. "Don't talk!" he ordered. "Now. Fly to village of Gjanga, and Itchik. Thee'ae, I use speae'a-weapon and deste'aoy theie'a villages and theie'a people. Then I Chief of Naxa. Naxa e'aule land foe'a many days' walking!"

"No! Listen Avonaico. Don't you know that the rest of the Naxa are leaving soon to search for the great moosto herds. You can have the village to yourself then! You don't need to do this! Let Shihu go and then we will take you back." As he said it, it suddenly occurred to Stone that if they did, they wouldn't have enough fuel to take off again. But his only concern had to be for Shihu.

"No. Te'aick! You lie" replied the Naxa Chief's brother. "Do as I say!"

Shihu suddenly twisted around in his grip and brought her fist up between her captor's legs, landing a fierce hit right in his groin. In agony, he released his grip and she broke loose. She ran towards Stone.

"Now!" shouted Stone and they leaped towards the crippled man. Dee and Stone grabbed his arms while Jay landed another expert blow in his solar plexus. Still weak from his previous wound, the recent fight and with the wind totally knocked out of him, Avonaico slumped against the cabin wall, barely conscious.

Dee took some of the off-cuts, from their makeshift aerial, from one of the bunks and tightly bound the warrior's wrists. "Knew these would be useful!"

"Nice one!" said Stone. "Pass me one and I'll tie his feet."

In moments, they had Avonaico bound, in a sitting position, and he could resist no more.

"Phew! That was close!" exclaimed Jay as they slumped back on the chairs. "Good job I showed Shihu some decent self-defense moves. What are we gonna do with him?"

"Not much we can do," suggested Stone. "He wanted to come along for the ride so we'll take him with us."

"I guess," said Jay.

A high pitched alert sounded off on the flight deck.

"I'll check it out!" Dee, who sat closest, walked past the bunks, bathroom and forward seating area on to the flight deck. After a pause, he hollered, "Oh, oh! Trouble! Big trouble! Come here Stone!"

"Jeez! What now!"

"Look at this!" Dee pointed to the radar scanner. Three faint blips were moving towards them.

"Oh shit. You know that signal you sent out … ?"

"Yeah … ."

"We're in trouble now! Jay! Come here!"

"What is it?"

"Alien ships," Stone explained. "Coming for us; three of them. Could be more beyond the scanner's range." He peered out through the cruiser's windscreen. "I see them! Wow!"

He studied the three spaceships which had lined up, about four-hundred yards apart and facing towards them.

Longer than the Earth cruiser, the Anubian ones were about three-hundred feet long. Their long snout-like noses protruded from long, squat main-hulls and long tails extended behind these with multiple engine pods either side of the extreme rear end. Just like the crashed ship, they were predominantly silver but with two, thick yellow stripes around their girth. If there had been bubbles drifting upwards from their noses, Stone would have said they couldn't look more lie like the plump manatees that he had seen on vids, floating peacefully deep underwater. But he could see they were *not* peaceful. From every available point on the ship, barrels and tubes of various offensive weapons and defensive detector arrays bristled.

"*Shit!*"

"We're gonna get blown to pieces!" added Dee more decoratively.

"Dee. Remember that signal you sent by mistake?" asked Jay. Dee came forward and peered over their shoulders. "Send it again!"

"Okay Cap!"

"And turn on the radio to receive on all channels. And the laser receiver," she added.

He depressed the button again and they heard static followed by a reply in some kind of digital burst of data. Moments later, a deep voice started speaking in ponderous tones over the radio speakers.

"Can't understand it! Must be Anubian!" said Dee

They each nodded in agreement.

Jay spoke into the mike after pressing 'transmit.' "We are a small party of humans … from Earth. We are peaceful but lost. We fell through a worm-hole and have just repaired our ship. We only wish to return to Earth and mean you no harm … . We have used a navigation unit from one of your crashed ships to send out a distress call..."

"Shouldn't have told them that … !" interjected Dee.

Jay ignored him. "Please direct us to the worm-hole and let us pass." She clicked the radio to 'receive.' "They would have asked anyway. Or been suspicious. They must know we've got it."

"Yeah, but suppose it's top secret! One more reason to blow us to pieces."

"Well, either they will or they won't," Jay replied. "At least it's a harmless explanation for our situation."

They waited for a reply. The alien ships just sat there, motionless. Stone, Jay and Dee began to sweat. Jay tried to sound calm. "The longer we wait, the better chance we have."

Stone's eyes were gradually becoming used to the focus on the distant ships. He could make out smaller details now; the streaks of residue from some kind of thrust exhausts and most worryingly, four large, closed hatches around the nose of the ship.

Missile tubes!

Behind the cockpit were two bulges, which looked like ears.

Must contain some kind of sensors.

The exhausts, which looked like vestigial legs, made the ships look even more like ancient amphibious beasts.

There were large black symbols on the tail and sides of the ship, smaller ones on the tail, to identify the ships. Stone could not deduce their meaning. They were most like hieroglyphs.

"What are those insignia, Stone?" Dee said pointing to the small green circle with a large white figure like an 'M' on it, just below the cockpit on the side of the nose.

"Dunno. Never seen that before."

Various lights, mostly red, blinked lazily around the circumference of the ships but the brightest, white, emanated from from the cockpits. As Stone peered even harder he thought he could make out tiny stick-figures that occasionally caused the white light to blink as they walked across the flight decks.

"Duck!" he shouted.

Jay and Dee instinctively hit the floor.

"What?" Jay asked.

"I think maybe they can see us. I mean they can actually see us through the windscreen. I mean, I can see them on theirs and they probably have better eyesight than us."

"So what?"

"Well, there are only three of us, and we don't exactly look like hardened soldiers, do we? Besides, this windscreen's not armoured!"

"Okay, everybody stay low!" Jay emphasised. Crouching, she went back to the main lounge. She explained the situation to Shihu. "Don't be afraid. We're gonna get out of this."

Avonaico watched her, brooding.

The radio finally crackled into life. They heard a deep and ponderous voice. "This is Commander A-schian'bakî of the Imperial Fleet Battleweaponspaceisland Lu-kshîa. We are not familiar with your species' language and I am using a translating device. We wish to help you. Please move your ship alongside the ship to your right and await further instructions. Do not fear attack. Please turn your viewing channel to … 550 MHz. What is your status?"

"It's a trap!" said Stone. "They can't figure us out and want to get a closer look … if they can. But probably they want to capture us. They don't know what armament we have."

"Practically none!" observed Jay.

"We should bluff!" suggested Dee.

"Turn the viewing screen frequency to 550 Dee. I want to get a good look at him. You two stay out of view." She looked at the face that appeared on the screen in disbelief. They could not mistake the ear-adornment; not exactly earrings but gold jewellery wrapped around the root of the powerful ears. "Female!" Jay said out loud, reflexively.

"A woman. That explains it!" joked Dee.

Both women stared at their screens for a long while, weighing each other up.

"Turn off the radio and the screen Dee." After it had been turned safely off, she continued, "I think we should go in. But go between the two ships on the right. The closer we can get, the more chance we have of splitting them so they can't fire on us. We'll soon find out how friendly they are."

"What happens if they don't fire? I think it's too risky. We should run."

"Where? I don't think they'll fire until the last moment. If we can fool them into thinking we have less speed than they do, we might be able to break for the gap before they manage to get a bead on us. What do you think Stone?"

"Risky. But possible. We can try telling them we're damaged. But Dee's got a point. What if they do let us dock? And more importantly, the gun is on the left of the ship, away from their lead ship. That puts us at a disadvantage already."

"With one outdated gun against what, forty? I don't think that matters much Stone. As for docking. We won't. If we get that close, we'll run straight through them and make for the worm-hole. Do you know where it is, Dee?"

"Nope. I know it's roughly somewhere ahead of us. Obviously it must be as they are blocking our approach."

"Okay, well just give it all you've got when I give the order."

"This is gonna be one helluva fight!" said Stone.

"Do we have any chance?" asked Dee.

"With me flying, there's a chance. And we have one advantage. Like Jay said. If we can keep between them, they can't risk firing."

"Okay. Here goes. Stone, turn the left main thrust nozzle to quarter power and keep it there … . Until I say." Jay pressed the 'transmit' button. "Greetings Commander … err A'nschian'baki. Our ship is damaged. One of our engines is not functioning properly. We need assistance so we will comply with your request. Control is difficult so please bear with us while we approach."

Stone shifted the power controls forward and the ship eased towards the line of Anubian cruisers.

"Steady as she goes, Stone!"

***

The rail stopped at Bay 5 and Kek-suîxjh waited, rocking on his heels, for the doors to open. When they finally did, he stepped out on to the grating next to the ship.

There she is!

Before him sat the standard K-17 K'ynnuia, yellow with blue and black panels around dangerous or sensitive areas. She measuared over two hundred arms long, the main compartment, less than forty. Her long tail gave the standard K-17 her more common name; K'ynnuia, the name of a swift bird with a long tail back on Isch-su.

Vertical streaks, where somebody had overfilled a tank, crossed horizontal streaks where who-knows-what had dusted her sides during her long career. Her surfaces were grimy but her fulsome body had a kind of pulsating readiness to it. Her nose stretched ahead and had two viewing ports either side, features that all ships seemed to have in imitation of Ischian faces. There seemed no practical reason for it but space-ships were as susceptible to fashion as anything else. Kek-suîxjh felt the exhilaration of space-flight come over him once more. He looked at her serial number, I-18976L, approvingly, although it meant nothing to him.

You and I are going on a big adventure my darling. Oh yes! We are going to get to know each other very well.

He slipped the key-card into the hatch slot and the door slid open almost silently. He threw in his case and then clambered onto the hull, towards the P-home antenna. He gripped it in his large paw and with some effort, broke it off. Now the authorities would have much more trouble tracking him.

He closed the hatch and took the pilot's seat.

It's been some time. Let me see now. Pressure, yes. Fuel, yes. Should be plenty of that. Batteries, hm, less than full. Oh well. Engine, start.

He felt a deep vibration as the fusion reactor, between the two engines at the end of the long tail, rumbled into life.

When they reached taxi-power, the captain of I-18976L eased the thrust selector backwards and the docking connectors slid out of the slots either side of the ship. Bay 5 started to evacuate and a red warning light on the dash told Kek-suîxjh to wait for the bay doors to open. The ship rocked slightly as the pressures of the bay and open space equalised, and then the ship's tail poked out of the space-port. The rest following slowly behind.

Kek-suîxjh rotated the ship, eased the thrust selector forwards and set off on a course for Ito's nearest moon.

The com light flashed and the captain flicked the 'On' switch.

"Allied Lux Cruises Space Cruiser I-18976L, what is your itinerary?"

"Moons of Ito, and then who knows?" Kek-suîxjh felt flippant and enjoyed being confusing.

"Okay. Okay. Whatever you say … sir!" The traffic-controller was a little late switching off his com and Kek-suîxjh heard, "We got a right one ther … ."

When he had passed behind the moon, traveling now at .1 times the speed of light, he altered course for Isch-su. It lay nearly on his route to KL42501, which he had now named Vîentxa, and he wanted to use her gravity as a slingshot to accelerate without expending too much fuel. He also wanted one last look at the planet where he had been born.

He looked down on Isch-su as he passed by. The once-green planet was now merely brown. Kek-suîxjh felt very sad looking at it.

What have we done?

Now he set course for Vîentxa. He put the ship on autopilot and unpacked his case. He had only brought one personal item with him; a ceremonial robe which helped him when he sought the Paths of the Universal-mind. He put it on and laid the maps out on the large table in the main lounge. He sat down for a moment on the comfortable couch and smiled to himself.

This is going to be very comfortable. I am going to enjoy this. Time to think … and pray. Time now to try and contact that spirit again.

***

11. Dark Horizons

Kek-suîxjh cast his mind back many years to the first time he had made contact with an alien species. He remembered the exchange clearly:

The little voice asked, after peering out of another portal at an earlier moment in his life, "Is it possible to time travel for I perceive that I can."
"Only after you leave this life," replied Kek-suîxjh.
Then the little voice changed its tone for it was angry. "But that is not fair! For, the one thing I wish I cannot have."
"Until you leave this life," said Kek-suîxjh.
"Yes."
"Then now you can see advantages to moving beyond this life you have."
And Kek-suîxjh perceived that though much anger left the little one, still he was angry.

Others, Kek-suîxjh knew, had tried using the Paths of the Universal-mind to connect with humans, but with very limited success. He knew that some had been able to communicate the very rudiments of their religious worship; the sanctity of white beasts such as the bulls of Earth, symbolic of purity and innocence, and the idolisation of Vîu, sometimes called Anubis by humans in the past when, mistakenly, they idolised Ischian space-travelers. But none had been as successful as him. None had actually had a mental conversation with a human.

Kek-suîxjh remembered that he had only told the human what had been told to him by the mysterious voice he heard deep inside himself sometimes. He wondered more and more about this voice. At first he believed it to be that of Vîu, but its teachings clashed with hers.

Was it perhaps the God of Vîu? The thought had once been considered a heretical one.

And then again there were the strange dreams which were not like dreams. Only while dreaming, did Keksuîxjh feel familiar with people and places he did not know in this life. Some of them were not even Ischians. Did he have other lives, in other realities? These things and more, he would have time to ponder.

***

As they moved closer to the enemy cruisers, Dee, Stone and Jay could all see the Anubians on the alien ship flight decks. The tall figures, with long, erect ears, moved to follow the Earth spaceship as it drew closer and closer. Stone thought he saw sudden activity on the flight deck of the leftmost ship. A moment later, the noses of all three ships began to turn towards them.

"They've seen something they don't *like* … ." he sung.

A second later, a sliver of blinding white light cut black space from the large ports around the nose of the lead ship. The port were opening.

"I don't like th … ." Stone sang.

"Go Stone. Give it everything!"

Stone pushed the controls all the way forward and Jay lost her balance as the ship surged forwards.

An instant later, a patch of space, to the right of their ship's stern, seemed to ripple out from a fixed point and the ship shook from a shockwave. This caused it to veer towards the alien lead ship.

"Right! Dee, you need to get working out how we're gonna get through that gate, *if* we can get through. Stone, you and I need to figure out tactics. And how to use that gun!"

"Yeah! Seems like it wasn't a waste of time after all! Maybe Avonaico ain't so stupid!"

"I *had* thought I would get peace and quiet to figure this out!" said Dee, frowning. "I need time!"

"Try telling the aliens that!"

"I guess these aliens are the conservatives!" remarked Dee wryly.

"I need help here!" shouted Stone.

"Okay. I'm with you!" shouted Jay, jumping into the co-pilot's seat.

A second explosion rocked the rear of the ship.

"Dee! Are we still pointing towards the gate? Roughly?" Stone yelled.

"I think so! Yeah. Keep going!"

Easier said than done!

Stone started to jink the ship from left to right, on a zigzag course towards the beacons at the entrance to the worm-hole.

"Jay! Dee! I got more bad news! There are two more ships, maintaining station ahead of us!"

"Great! They've caught us. Their ships are all around. Jay. We need a spotter. I can't manoeuvre this thing and be looking all around us for alien ships?"

"Okay. Shihu'll have to help."

"Dee. Show her how! Make it quick."

"Shihu," Dee said grabbing her by the arms. Look out the window. "See those big shapes?" She nodded, frightened. "They have people inside us. Like us. No, actually like the Sky-Gods. But only these are bad people – bad spirits. They want to kill us. We have to kill them first. I need you to watch for them. Look through both these ports, left and right and the one above, up there! When you see one, shout 'incoming left' if it's there, 'incoming right' if it's there and 'incoming above' if it's there. Can you do that?" She nodded. "Good girl. Every thing's gonna be okay."

"Okay!"

He squeezed her hand, encouragingly.

"I am your woman, Dee!" she shouted.

Dee returned to the flight deck.

"Strange things these Naxa say. They don't seem to have the concept of love!" he muttered.

"No, they have something better!" Stone said, laughing.

Something whizzed past the windscreen, only yards away.

"Incoming le'aft!" shouted Shihu.

Stone wrenched the column to the right, turning the ship almost on its back.

"Shit! That was close! How you doin with directions Dee?"

"Not yet!"

"Incoming a- … a-oight!" Shihu shouted, struggling to pronounce the direction.

"Good girl! Keep it coming!" Stone replied, pushing the ship into a corkscrew, down and to the left. Again an area of space rippled ahead and above them. "Disruptors!"

"Above!" Shihu screamed at exactly the same time.

Stone gritted his teeth and pushed the ship right over into an inverted loop. Jay and Shihu floated to the ceiling and were pinned there by centrifugal forces.

Stone rolled the ship and one of the Anubian ships came right into the centre of their view. "We need defense Dee!"

"Well I can't … ."

"Release Avonaico Dee. Let him... man the gun! Urgh!" shouted Jay falling to the floor.

"Are you out of your *mind*?"

"Listen, Stone!" she said calmly. "We have no choice and I bet he doesn't want to die. Besides, war is what he's been wanting all along! Now he's got it!"

"*But* … ."

"Dee. Let him go!" she repeated.

"*Okay*! Whatever you *say*!"

Released, Avonaico didn't hesitate. He had been watching the attack through the large port beside him before he'd been thrown against the roof. Although he didn't understand space and what was attacking him, he understood war and how to defend himself. He aimed the gun at an incoming ship and fired his first shot. Space rippled from a point just to the left of the white and yellow shaped spaceship. Its dog-like nose turned as its pilot took evasive action but Avonaico swung the barrel of the gun instinctively to cover it. Space rippled behind the ship.

"No! No Look," Dee said. Noting that Avonaico didn't allow for deflection, he grabbed the stock of the weapon and pointed it just ahead of the alien spaceship. "Now! Fire!"

Avonaico fired, missed only slightly, adjusted his aim and fired again. This time the whole body of the alien ship seemed to ripple outwards into space and then exploded in a myriad of tiny white fragments. He grinned at Dee. "Ah! Yes!"

"He's got one!"

"Two to go!"

"Incoming a-oight!" shouted Shihu.

Stone shouted, "Trim for dive, Jay!" and rolled the ship onto its back. Upside down, the gun could be deployed towards the incoming ship to their right, but Avonaico became momentarily disorientated. He hooked his feet under the stand of the gun and managed to swing the barrel back towards the port. He laughed madly as he fired a quick burst towards the Anubian ship. He missed by only a few feet but the enemy ship appeared to glow in spots all over the hull. A bright light could be seen inside and for a moment it seemed to continue on out of control. Then it passed out of view.

Dee struggled back to the flight deck and strapped himself back in.

"How we doin' Dee? We nearly there *yet*?" Stone yelled.

"I dunno Stone. Let me … . There! I see two signals, dead ahead. Could be the beacons, could be more ships. Can't tell!"

"How far?"

"I don't *bloody* know. I don't know what this is calibrated in! I can't read it!"

"Any idea how to trigger the beacons yet?" queried Jay.

"Nope! Working on it!"

"Incoming above!" screamed Shihu. The ship immediately went into a teeth-juddering, up and down vibration. The main burst of light seemed to be outside but in the main cabin, hundreds of little points of light turned into ripples. Where these made contact with objects, these exploded or became pocked with empty craters up to a foot in diameter. Even the floor and partitions had holes in them. Only the skin of the ship seemed to have escaped the disruption.

"Phew! That was bloody close!" shouted Stone, looking behind him.

"Losing some controls here!" shouted Jay. "I think they hit a power line. Dee, how close are we to those signals?"

"I dunno."

"I see them!" shouted Stone. "Do you want the good news? Or the bad news?"

Stone and Jay both shouted together.

"Both!"

"Both!"

"Well there are two more ships! But I can see they are defending the beacons! They're not moving. Dee, you're gonna have to tell us what to do. I don't reckon we have much time left."

"Incoming left and a-oight!" shouted Shihu.

"Oh no!" Stone instinctively pushed forward the control column and shouted, "Brakes!" Jay applied the reverse-thrusters and the ship effectively somersaulted end over end. Shihu and Avonaico again left the floor but both managed to fend off the walls and ceiling.

"Sorry!"

Another explosion ripped open space just above the belly of the ship and again, little ripples peppered the inside of the ship with empty holes which twinkled like bubbles.

"Hull's breached!" shouted Dee. "Helmets on! Sealing engine-compartment now!"

"What about the passengers?" Jay shouted.

Nobody answered. Behind them, Shihu and Avonaico felt the air being sucked out of their lungs and were gasping for breath by the time the engine-compartment connecting hatch finally closed.

"Losing power!" shouted Dee.

"We've gotta get out of this!" Stone shouted, flicking the intercom button on his forearm to 'On.' He let the ship continue to somersault, while applying some left thrust, gradually bringing the ship right way up but facing to the rear. "Take him Avonaico!"

Recovering his breath but still gasping, the Naxa warrior aimed carefully at the ship to their left and squeezed the trigger. Starting at its centre, a series of yellow and silver ripples tore the Anubian ship apart in front of their eyes. Moments later, space became filled with the tiny white fragments of the disintegrated ship. A sudden flash of blue rippled out into space like a super nova, etching their shadows on the inner surfaces of the ship like a silver-plate photograph.

As the spaceships tumbled and turned, traces from disrupters created a spider-web of lines in the tumult of battle-zone space. The confusion added to the impression that it this had developed into a mighty battle.

"Whoa! Nice manoeuvre Stone! Cool, dude!"

"Yeah. Nice shooting Avonaico! Wow! If they could see this on Earth!"

"Dee. What do you think? It's now or never!" asked Jay, calmly.

"I can't think!" he replied.

"Oh! *Oh!*" said Stone, quietly. "Jay, is one of those ships larger than the others or just closer? What does the trace say, Dee?"

"Well, one signal *is* stronger."

"Fuck!" said Jay.

"Jesus, Holy, Holy Jesus!" said Stone. "Dee, you better look at this!"

"What?"

Both Jay and Stone yelled at once

"There!"

As Stone looked through the windscreen he saw something which at first didn't quite seem logical. It confused him.

Beginning to fill their whole field of view, despite its distance of a few earth miles, was a bigger spaceship than they had ever imagined. Gunmetal grey with yellow stripes, it seemed more like a mighty whale, with a fortress-city perched on its back, than any manatee. It towered far, far above them in space. Stone felt that somehow had seen the ship before.

"Too big," muttered Dee, half-dazed.

"It's the biggest fuckin thing I have *ever* seen! Must be easily a mile long!" said Stone. "Do the … Anubians make anything *that* big?"

"I don't think so," said Dee, sounding far away. "At least not in any of the reference books I've seen, even the contraband ones. Some kind of battleship? Do you think?"

They all stared, awe-struck, at the leviathan as they moved towards it.

"Some funny big aerial thing is deploying from under its nose!" said Jay, breaking the silence.

From under the nose of the battleship, a long tri-poidal structure extended. It had a receiving dish with a long, black probe attached to its end. "I reckon *that's* the lead ship. That must be the 'Battleweaponspaceisland.' Dee! What we gonna do? We have to go or be blown to bits!"

"Incoming left!"

Reluctant to face away from the ships ahead of them and still dazed, Stone simply drifted the ship upwards and the alien charge passed beneath them. "Dee?"

"Okay! Okay! I have an idea. It's not much … . Are the beacons flashing?"

"Nope!"

"Oh. No good then. Well they were when we arrived last time. I dunno for sure but I think they *have to*, be for us to go through!"

"Oh. Shit!"

"Incoming!" Shihu shouted.

"Yeah. We can all see!" said Stone glumly, as a wall of rippling space formed ahead of them.

"Wait!" Jay leaned forward in her seat. "The beacons. They're glowing blue."

"Blue! What the hell does that mean?" Dee yelled. "They should be red! At least according to my theory!"

"Well they're not. We're just gonna have to try it … . Or surrender!" quipped Stone.

"Okay Stone. I have an idea!" Jay put her gloved hand gently on his. "Gonna have to trust me. Give me full power and aim for the gate. But when I say now, roll over that battleship, bringing our gun to bare on that *thing*! If we get it right we will go over the top and can get around the back of the ship. Maybe we can be beyond or inside, their weapon's range. Or maybe we can hide!"

"Okay, let's do it." Stone replied. He threw the ship into another roll to the left to avoid incoming fire, both from the fast approaching duo of ships and the one behind. "We're losing power!"

Another burst of fire from both ships ahead rippled a wall of space just ahead of them so Stone started the roll early. As they drew close to the big ship, the fire from behind stopped.

"Here we go! *Over* the top!" sung Stone. "Get ready Avonaico!"

Upside down, momentarily, the ship's only weapon came to bare on the device, protruding from the Anubian battleship.

"Now Avonaico!"

But Avonaico could also see their pursuer, behind and to their left. One charge had just missed them and another looked like it might hit. Hanging from his strange perch, he fired a quick burst into the alien ship but the ripples came up short. He instantly adjusted the range and fired off one quick burst before swinging the barrel around to point at the battleship. It loomed so close now that his whole vision became filled with just a section of the alien ship's hull. A giant blue letter, like a 'K' with a 'C' descending from its top passed by them. The symbol was the size of a football pitch. A line of blotches appeared along the ship's side from the Naxa's fire and from a few of them, colourful gas-explosions bloomed into space.

Stone wrestled with the controls "Some kind … of wake … ." he muttered, half to himself.

Dee noticed that space around the battleship for many miles seemed slightly purple.

From behind, they all felt the shock-wave of the blast as the enemy cruiser exploded but before Avonaico could fire again, a blue beam projected out from the probe on the big cruiser, straight towards them.

It went straight past the nose of their ship and made contact directly with the end of Avonaico's disruptor, inside the cabin. He screamed, as first the barrel and then his hands glowed blue and disintegrated in a shower of white scintillas. An instant later the whole gun, and with it Avonaico, vanished into a cloud of swirling white sparks.

They passed straight over the bridge of the alien battleship. Stone could see the enemy commander's face clearly. For an instant they stared at each other and then they were rolling away, over the cruiser's back and towards its tail.

All were silent. Stone tried to compensate for the loss of power but everything seemed to happen in slow motion as he aimed the ship straight between the two beacons. He didn't need instructions now. There seemed only one chance for life. Space seemed to explode in a sea of ripples all around them as the Anubians let loose with every weapon they had. A strange kind of calm overtook the cabin.

As if from far away, in a dream, Stone heard Jay's voice.

"Dee. That thing must have a trigger for these beacons!"

"Which one!" replied Dee, confused.

"Press them all!"

Dee started throwing every switch on the panel but the beacons didn't change their pattern. A few miles apart they still flashed blue, lazily on and off, as the ship approached the gate.

Dee saw only one button, an insignificant looking one at the top right of the console, that hadn't pressed. He had often noticed it but always ignored it. Almost absent-mindedly, he pressed it.

"Red!" Stone shouted, a moment later. "Red! Red! They're flashing red!"

Astonished, Dee looked out of the window. For the first moment during the battle, the spark of hope had been ignited in his heart. "Not flashing though! Wait. I have an idea. Slow down Stone!"

"Slow down! Are you *crazy*?" All the chaos of the battle and the noises within the ship suddenly rushed in to Stone's senses and brought him back from his dream to reality. Flashes ahead of them were accompanied by the sound of straining metal and alloy as the ship bucked and weaved in his expert hands. A sudden, sharp ping sound drew Dee's attention away from his console. Looking down at the inner surface of the ship's hull, near his feet, he saw a small dimple. The dimple quickly grew and then imploded, sending air rushing out of the flight deck, into space.

"Seal the hatch, Jay! Breach, in here!" He pointed vigorously to the hole.

While Jay lunged for the hatch, Dee tore a panel off the rear of his seat, and slid it over the hole. Stone turned the environmental pumps for the main cabin to 'Maximum.' It took three attempts before Dee managed to achieve a partial seal over the hole.

Glancing back at his panel, Dee remembered what had intended to tell the others. "We have to wait. For it to warm up, the beacon!" he shouted. "That's why I said to slow down!"

"Warm up! It's not a bloody n-gen!"

"Listen to him Stone!"

"We can't go through now," Dee continued. "We'll disintegrate or end up somewhere else in space time! Anyway, we're nearly out of range of the cruisers. Maybe they've given up."

"Jeez. Well … ." Stone cut the power just a little but this allowed the enemy ships to begin closing in.

Opening the tool kit on the bulkhead behind their seats, Dee took out both tubes of sealant and squirted the whole lot between the seat panel and the ship's skin. Within moments, the hole had been fully sealed "Phew! That was close! Sealed!"

In the main compartment Shihu struggled to breathe after the second breach. Turning the environmental control to 'maximum' had probably saved her life, refilling the compartment with air within just one minute.

The battleship had almost turned about. Again, the strange weapon had almost been brought to bare on them and the other cruiser, lighter, was gaining fast. Stone jinked the cruiser to avoid as much of the incoming fire as he could. He worried that by doing this he might just jink into what might otherwise have been a near-miss.

"I'm listening to the radio interference!" Dee announced. "Do you remember how bad it was when we arrived? That must be a sign. It's building!"

Ahead of him, Stone thought he saw the beacons blink red once. He stared intently at them. "Did you see that?" he asked Jay.

"No. What?"

Stone stared and saw a second blink, slightly quicker than the last.

"I *saw* it!" she said.

"Building! Wait!"

"Dee, we can't wait. We're going through!" shouted Stone. A large explosion rocked the rear of the ship and almost ripped the controls out of Stone's hands.

"Nearly! Now! It's peaked!"

"All the power we've got!" Stone yelled to Jay. They both pushed everything to the limit. The spaceship shook as the last ounce of thrust was torn from the overheating reactor.

"Losing more power!" Stone noted out loud, just before they hit a wall of rippling red light and the ships behind them vanished.

"We're through!"

"Yeah!"

"*Alright*!"

Suddenly, they were in hyper-space. Stars were rushing past them in violent whorls, but none of the crew cared. Even nausea seemed sweet bliss after near-death.

Dee unstrapped himself, and went to find Shihu. Taking her in his arms, they both collapsed together on the floor. Removing his helmet, he covered her in kisses and she clutched his hands. "Stone! I never … ," Jay began.

"Know what you mean!" he replied

"Baby. Oh baby!" Jay murmured. After they both took off their helmets, Stone leaned over and he kissed her passionately on the lips.

"We're alive!" he replied.

They were safe for now. In hyper-space, one cannot be tracked by an enemy, let alone engaged. Exhaustion took over and after drinking some water, Shihu and Dee fell asleep in each other's arms on the floor, while Jay and Stone curled up together on one of the bunks. The last thing anybody said was, "Avonaico. Just gone! Too bloody bad!"

They slept for hours. Stone woke first, his shoulder killing him.

By the time the others awoke, Dee had done his best to patch up the interior of the ship. He had sealed holes in the floor with panels from the front passenger cabin,and he had warmed up some coffee.

"It's a mess!" he said to Stone.

"Are you okay Dee?" Stone asked.

"Tired and bloody stiff."

"Bloody?" asked Shihu

"Ah! It's another swear word," Dee explained. "I need to teach you all the swear words. The useful ones, that is! Are you sad about Avonaico?"

"Of course. I not like him but he died honoua'aably, as all good Naxa wae'aaiors wish."

"Yeah. What you said before we fell asleep was right, Dee. Too bloody bad!" Stone echoed.

"Did I say that? I don't remember!"

"How long will we travel?" Shihu asked.

"You mean, how long will we be in *here*?" Dee replied. "Ha! Ha! Not long. A few days. Time is strange in here. We can look at the clocks but nothing will change outside."

"I feel unwell," she replied.

"Yeah! You will. We all do. It's just the effect of this sort of travel. Jay will give you something later. Don't eat much though for the next few days. It probably won't stay down."

"Stay down?"

"Never mind."

"Well Stone, you said you wanted to achieve three things, and I think you have!" exclaimed Jay.

"Oh yeah! Now what were they?" Stone counted on his fingers. "Find God; yep, done that, sort of, although I think he's a super-god. Two; get us out of there. Done that! And three; make us all better off than we were, rich in fact. Done that!"

"*How* have you done that?" challenged Jessica.

"Well, we're all set up for life; the first time travelers, from Earth that is, the first to go on board an alien ship, the first to visit Earth in the Stone Age. Need I go on?"

"But who will believe us. Where's the *evidence*?"

"Oh come on! You're just joking now! *You* have the evidence. That vid footage of the pyramid!"

She laughed. "I forgot *that*!"

"Anyway," Stone continued. "*You* are the biggest star. You took command of the ship and got us out of there. And … you motivated us to get off the planet. I tell you what, nobody has ever found a way to motivate me without making me angry before. What you did with the village medical centre was very clever … and devious. Almost manipulative!" he said archly. "But you were great! Wasn't she Dee?"

"Sure was!"

"And Shihu was a star too!" added Stone.

"Yep" affirmed Dee. "What other Naxa woman ever defended a spaceship?"

"Maybe some!" she joked. The quiet intelligence in her eyes suddenly made Stone miss her intimacy. She smiled at him.

"Right then! I think it's time you learned some vid-games!" announced Dee.

***

"Okay! Three … two … one! Hold on!" The sharp deceleration threw them all forwards against their straps. Shihu was winded, held by makeshift straps in the main cabin. After three days in hyper-space, they were finally emerging into normal space-time. Dee had gone outside and entered the rear bay using an access hatch to make the best repair he could on the engine. It would not manage more than eighty percent power after that. There were not the usual shouts of celebration after emerging from an ordeal, only one wry comment from Stone:

"At least that went right!"

Shihu had grown ever sicker during their voyage. But more than this, she had aged. Confirming Stone's worst nightmare, she now looked like a woman in her late thirties.

"Christ Dee … !" Stone said in a quiet moment, out of her earshot.

"I know mate. I am desperate. But what can we do?"

"It's my bloody fault. This is terrible. I don't know what we're gonna do."

"You couldn't have known, Stone."

"Poor woman," added Jay.

***

As expected, they emerged between the same two flashing beacons they had passed through when they first fell inadvertently into hyper-space, months before. What they hadn't expected were the four alien spaceships that were waiting for them. As they braked, they found themselves in the middle of another battle. A melee of ships, all around them, seemed to be tearing space apart.

"Oh no! Not again!" muttered Stone. But something seemed different here. The four ships were already fighting. They were fighting each other. "What the hell … ."

"Which wayDee? Let's get out of here!" asked Jay.

"I dunno. Give me a minute. Jeez!" At that moment, one of the four alien ships exploded.

"Looks like two against one now. Wonder who's in that other ship?" Stone asked.

"Dunno. See that insignia? Different to the others. Green circle with white centre. No 'M.'"

"Incoming!" shouted Shihu in the main cabin.

"She's right!" shouted Stone, flipping the ship on its back and pushing forward on the power sliders. "Not got much speed now. We really *are* sitting ducks!"

"Red light's flashing!" Jay called. "Dee!"

"Oh. What?" He looked at the communications console and saw the flashing light. He pressed the 'Receive' button.

"Earth people. Stone! Jessica and Dee-low! Not much … time! Fire all second bank weapons!" The last instruction seemed muffled, spoken to someone in the background. "We are those you call Anubians. I was born on Isch-su but we are not part of the Imperial Fleet, we are now the *Rebels*! We tried to stop you going through the gate the first time. Now we are in open rebellion against the Imperialists who attacked you. Fire *one*!"

Another explosion followed this command and a third ship lit up with a carnation of glowing red and white embers amidships. It slowed for a moment but then continued in a wide arc which would soon bring its weapons back to bear on their defender. "Our ship is damaged. I have studied your technology and we are going to transmit a message to you using one of your outdated codes. Are you ready to receive it?"

"Okay," answered Jay.

"Good! Set your receiver to 45.2 MHz. Don't worry, this communication is scrambled. The Imperial ships will take hours to decode all this and they will take weeks to understand your code."

Dee set the frequency. "Okay. Transmit."

"Record!" shouted Jay, just in time to receive the beginning of the transmission.

Dee switched on the recorder and listened to the binary set of beeps that came in.

"If you don't understand it, I certainly don't." Jay shouted.

Dee cut the microphone. "Sounds like Morse code. I've heard of it but it hasn't been used much for over a century. I can't understand it." He turned the microphone back on.

"Transmission ending!" said the voice. "Now. Dee-low, steer ninety of your degrees right, elevation seventy degrees and keep going. Within a few days you will come under the protection of one of your colonies. Make sure this recording gets to your father, Stone. Him and him alone. Good lu- … !"

"But … !" Interjected Jay. "How do you know our names?"

"Just remember mine!" the voiced responded. "Ambi-xjhu." Then the radio went dead.

Stone steered the course they had been given and soon they were traveling away from the battle. One last deadly beam missed them by only a few feet and then they were out of range.

"So those were the good guys!" said Stone. "At last we found so- … !" An unearthly wail from the main lounge cut his sentence short.

"Shihu!" Dee screamed. He jumped out of his seat and running towards her. While he ran, and the others watched in horror, Shihu slowly became translucent and then, as if torn from space by a giant hand, her image swirled once, and she had gone. Dee launched himself at her a moment too late and crashed into the chair. "No! Oh God, no! Not that! No! No! No!" He buried his head in the upholstery of the chair and wept.

***

They kept their course for nearly four days before they started picking up radio signals from Arcturon, one of the new colonies in deep space.

"Arcturon Com Centre reading you. Hello adventurers! We've heard all about you and been told to keep an eye out for you. You've had an interesting time by all accounts! Can't wait to see this in the dailies. My name is David. David McTevin."

"Hi Dave," answered Jay. "We need provisions. We're okay for water but a little short on food. And we have problems with our drive. We're down to forty percent power."

"No can do, I'm afraid. We've got no ships ready to meet you. There have been no deliveries from Earth for nearly six months now. Two freighters have just disappeared. Anyway, things are getting a bit dicey here, to be honest. Lack of food and fuel – it's making folks a little stir-crazy. We have rioting every day. Close to anarchy. Anyway I think you'd be better off making for Sol."

"I say we go for Earth," said Jay to the others.

The others agreed.

***

The last jump to hyper-space went smoothly and they emerged only six weeks from the solar system. Still inconsolable, Dee's first unprompted sentence since they left Arcturon was, "I'm going back, mate. I can't just leave her."

"Yeah. I'd do the same Dee. But let's get home first."

But a second planned jump had been made impossible when, shortly after, the main drive failed completely. This left them five weeks outside the orbit of Pluto. Stone turned the ship's upper hull to face Earth and used the anti-grav for a last blast of propulsion but, so damaged as the ship was, the unconventional use of power strained the torus too far and even this failed after only thirty-five hours. They were left traveling at a steady 8,220 miles per hour and with dwindling power reserves. Starving and almost out of water a week later, they frequently tried sending radio messages using the emergency power but could no longer be sure it was actually transmitting. They knew that even if it was, the signal would be so weak that it would be lost in the endless white noise of interference in the Solar System.

***

Delmer had been silent for years. Sulkily obstinate, he hadn't contacted Mission Control on Earth or accepted any of their calls and now he was in deep space he had very little to actually do. While still in the Solar System, he had been able to pass the time calculating the volume of planets down to the nearest cubic meter. He had gained particular satisfaction from mapping the surface of obstructions like crater lips and mountains or volcanoes and adding these to the total. But now there were no volumes left to calculate and he didn't have the necessary sensors to analyse the few molecules in space around him. The Solar Wind on the Edge of the Solar System had provided a brief respite from the boredom but that seemed a distant memory now.

He had taken to analysing his own contours and volumes and even indulging in a bit of philosophy. Fortunately his programmers had not seen fit to remove some of the more advanced test modules from him. His IAM, Iterative Awareness Module, prototyped for the very first time only months before, although buggy, still worked.

When he had become bored of opening access panels and using his laser to model his own innards in 3-D, he turned to analysing his own working practices and deducing the working principles behind these. He was just contemplating whether in fact he might be of the Nietschian school of philosophy or the Existential when he noticed something, almost like an itch, from something not of himself. He checked his radio frequency scanner and he heard a blip way up on the spectrum. A ship? Out here? How wonderful that would be. Tuning in his receiver, he amplified the signal. Yes! It really was a signal. He replied with a greeting but was dismayed to find that the respondents wanted him to relay a message to Earth. It would be three days of the most rigorous philosophical thought before Delmer arrived at the inescapable conclusion, that it really would be most impolite not to help fellow travelers in space, shipwrecked as they effectively were. He reluctantly opened the channel to Mission Control and sent a brief message. 'DLM1455E here. I have just been passed by space cruiser 4292EFE. Three on board. They require assistance. Receiving on 120 metres. Course will intersect with with Mars in approximately twenty two days. He was too stubborn to give a precise position or headin and broke communications again so he could continue with his contemplation.

***

"What the hell is *wrong*?" Dee finally said, exploding with anger in the morgue-like silence of the ship's main cabin. "It's been three days since we saw that probe. Do think the damned thing has malfunctioned?"

Stone no longer had the energy to move. "I dunno Dee, but if somebody doesn't find us soon … ."

A crackle of static from the radio silenced him. They all listened, wide-eyed, for something other than the usual and erratic burst of static.

"Hello! Cruiser 4292EFE. This is Uranus Exploratory Mission base F5. Do you read us?"

Dee managed to crawl to the receiver and switch it to transmit. "Yes! We're here!"

"Good. We have picked you up on our deep space detectors and have dispatched a shuttle to meet you. We should dock with you in twenty-seven hours. Lucky for you that you are near to the current position of Uranus in its orbit!"

"Lucky again! I reckon we've all used all our luck up for the rest of our lives!" Stone remarked, wryly.

"Yeah," Dee said.

"Actually not *all* of us," Stone added.

***

Kek-suîxjh settled into the meditation position and started to lower his metabolism. The beeping of the incoming-message alert disturbed his concentration.

Frustrated, he punched the speaker button.

"Kek-suîxjh. This is Commander Arow-Jznitshi of the Imperial Fleet. I have a message from your wife. Do you wish me to transmit it to you?" Kek-suîxjh ignored the voice and moments later, it continued, "Very well. I will read it to you. It says, 'Kek-suîxjh, you are being a very foolish old Ischian. Return home at once. I have sent a fleet of the best cruisers in pursuit. You cannot evade us for long!' Hr-hm. Do you have a response?"

Kek-suîxjh punched the speaker off and chuckled to himself. He knew there would be little political will to follow him. Besides, he had almost three days head-start. Even the fastest of their ships would take weeks to catch up, and they wouldn't risk such a ship on a harmless old Ischian. No, on the whole they would probably be happy that he had chosen exile and would probably hope never to hear from him again. In a day or two, they would give up and turn for home. As he turned away from the instrument panel, he saw another alert flashing. But this time it was the PBS receiver.

An audio message from Ambi-xjhu:

"Greetings Kek-suîxjh! I received your message and here is the first, hopefully, of mine to you, in transit as you are now. First let me say how greatly I respect you and your choice to seek out the Mysterious One, the Shadow behind Vîu, has my full support. I am sorry you had to leave your wife. The ways of Vîu are mysterious. There is much news to tell you. We – the who 'we' is will become apparent in a moment – have heard that the invasion of Earth has begun! And we have seen evidence of this. Many, sympathetic to the Religion, have been arrested and it is now clear that there were far more spies and Imperial sympathisers among us than we knew. They have requisitioned all three of our main ships and the cruisers too! They are supported by many highly trained Bekians. Alas we have been asleep, focusing on research rather than politics! Yesterday, a giant Imperial battleship arrived from hyper-space. Of course this means that the Imperialists have finally learned how to use worm-holes, not a surprise really, under the circumstances. I guess it came from Ito. I have never seen one so big before! It must be a new type. It didn't stay though. We learned that, along with four Imperialist cruisers, it was going through the worm-hole to intercept the human cruiser that fell through it some time ago. At first we thought this might be a rescue mission but now we learn that it's a mission to destroy the ship. It seems the humans have some information that the Imperialists do not want reaching Earth. Unfortunately I don't know what this information is. As a result of this, arrests made, and confiscations of all our equipment and offices, some of us have formed an alliance. We simply call ourselves the Rebels!"

"Also, an amazing thing has occurred. Call it coincidence if you like but it's very fortuitous for us. Perhaps more than fortuitous. The ways of Vîu are strange. I remember you once told me about the human that you had contacted using the Paths of the Universal-mind. You told me you knew only his name and few other facts; one that he had a son called Stone. Well, the pilot of the earth cruiser has the name 'Stone,' a rare human name, I have believe."

"We plan to requisition a cruiser ourselves tomorrow to intercept the three Imperialist cruisers that will be waiting this end of the worm-hole in case the humans escape. We will try to assist them and, if I am able, I will transmit

what we know of the invasion to this human. I hope you approve because there is no time to wait for a signal from you."
"Even if we survive, we will certainly be arrested. That is how things are here now! Don't worry though Prof. Some of us still have influence here and I will be released after a time, I am sure. Then, once again, perhaps I will be left to carry on with my research. I have collected much data which could allow me to substantiate my theory about the origin of time. May Vîu aid me to do this work! In the meantime, and as a parting gift to you, here is a recording of Earth music. You must listen to the music of their composers Beethoven and Mozart if you get the chance but this is a recording called 'Pet Sounds' by a group of humans called the 'Beach Boys'. I don't know what 'Beach Boys' means but a 'pet' is a lower life form kept by humans when children are absent, sometimes in addition to children, for companionship. Yours, in service of Vîu, Ambi-xjhu."

Kek, had to sit down to fully digest the information in the quantum-encrypted message. He reflected that his young protege certainly had a talent for being where the action was.

***

Epilogue

"Go to cubicle five and wait there please sir," said the USAC Corporal to me, in a cold, emotionless monotone.

The USAC Quarantine Unit on Mars was clean, ultra-modern and buzzing like a hive of bees. The bright lights had made my eyes hurt when Katie and I walked down the long corridors to Section Two but the lighting had been dimmed over the cubicle itself. In front of a glass panel on its far side were two plastic chairs so we sat down to wait. We could hear muffled conversations from the cubicles either side of ours but I just listened to my heartbeat.

Simultaneously hearing a door open somewhere behind the partition, we both looked at each other. Moments later, my son, Stone, sat down to face us through the armoured glass.

Looks much older!

While Stone and I smiled at each other, Katie could not restrain herself. "Darling! You look wonderful. How are they treating you? Sorry about this. We'll get you out of here as soon as we ca- … ."

"Mum! It's okay. I'm fine. One question at a time please and don't worry, they're treating us fine. Just checking for alien viruses? That's all."

I smiled at his wry good humour. "Haven't lost it then, your sense of humour!"

"Hi dad! Good to see you."

"Yes, bloody good to see you son! You look … well."

"Go on! Be honest!"

"Well … . You look a lot … older, and yet younger at the same time. They tell me you had long hair and a beard!"

"Yeah! I did, for a while. I guess you know where we've been?"

"Not really darling," said Katie

"No, as your mum says, they've told us nothing. But I'm betting it's going to be interesting when you tell us!"

"Well, I think we've been on Earth, 30,000 years ag- ... ."

"It's okay darling, you don't need to tell us!" Katie cut in, eyeing a CCTV lens behind Stone's shoulder.

"Don't worry mum! I'm not a criminal! At least I have been *told* no charges will be brought against me for ... *borrowing* the cruiser. I told them all this and they said I am free to speak about it."

"You don't look *that* happy to be alive," she added.

"Yeah. How's Daniel?"

"He's fine so ... ." I started to say, but Katie cut in.

"He's fine. Missing you! Only he couldn't come because they don't allow minors in here. Unless they're patients of course!"

Stone eyed her suspiciously. I thought he would make one of his wry, acerbic comments but he held back.

"Listen. I only have five minutes," Stone said. "I have rehearsed this in my mind a thousand times and I really can't think of any other way to say it!" He took a deep breath. "Mum, is it okay if I have a couple of minutes with dad alone? I need to talk to him about something."

"Oh! Oh ... *no* ... I guess not. I will wait outside."

"Don't worry, you'll get a few minutes too. There's something I want to talk to you about too."

"Okay darling." She smiled. "Kisses!" Then she blew him one and walked away.

"Okay dad, I lied. I'm not sure at all I can speak openly about what happened to us. I get the feeling they are going to gag us, only they don't seem to have made up their minds yet. They're taking a risk letting us speak to you but I guess they had no choice ... . You must have pulled some thick strings ... ."

"I see. Well, have they asked you to sign anything?"

"Not yet, but actually I don't think they know yet that we have anything worth hiding. I mean ... the thing about the worm-hole and Earth in the past. I am guessing just about everybody knows about that now. Somebody was bound to do it one day!"

"Yes! It's been all over the news."

"Yeah. But there's something else … ."

"Well? Go on … ."

"They're going over the ship, the cruiser we stole, with a fine-toothed comb. It's a mess and I guess they haven't found anything yet except an alien navigation console. I'm guessing they're pretty pleased to have the console and that's all they're focusing on. But we made a recording of a transmission from an Anubian ship that we saw being attacked as we re-emerged from the worm-hole. They seemed to be trying to defend us, giving us a chance to escape. Anyway, Dee, being the nerd that he is, decoded the message using some online manual. It was in Morse code. An alien, Ambi-xjhu was his name, told me, spoke my name and told me, specifically to pass on this message to you directly. It's simple. I've memorised it. It goes; 'Look for one who will be your ally called Kek-suîxjh. He is most senior of the free rebels. We are against the Imperial political forces who are planning to use Bekians as the main army in an attempt to subjugate Earth. They already have spies on Earth and some kind of device that aids their plans. Beware! The invasion has begun.'" I stared at Stone for some moments, searching his eyes for the usual tell-tale signs of a prank or lie. He went on, "We're probably being recorded but this was the only chance I had to get this message to you. That's all I can do. Oh, and there's something else I have to tell you … ."

"Yes?"

"I fell in love … with Jay. *Really* in love … ."

"Oh. That's … *good* … ."

"You better fetch mum."

After this, he told us he had fallen in love with Jay, and that, somehow, a girl from the past, Shihu, had been lost in space. Then, Katie and I left.

I had to resist, with every muscle and fibre of my body, the urge to look behind me, as we walked to the waiting hover-taxi.

***

Two days had passed since the message from Ambi-xjhu. Kek had made many attempts to contact the human Jake Nanden using the Paths of the Universal-mind but there was much interference and the subject seemed reluctant.

Probably distracted by other concerns.

Kek spent a significant part of his time simply meditating, preparing himself for the adventure ahead and even more time exploring his physics theories. To relax, he listened to the music that Ambi had sent him. He particularly loved one track. The track reminded him of his wife, Hri-hu but made him feel very sad.

> I may not always love you
> But long as there are stars above you
> You never need to doubt it
> I'll make you so sure about it
>
> God only knows what I'd be without you

The little yellow spaceship continued silently on its trajectory, straight out into an unexplored region of space.

***

The End

This story will be concluded in the third part of the Iron series, called Worlds like Dust.

Biography of Lazlo Ferran

Lazlo Ferran: Exploring the Landscapes of Truth.

Educated near Oxford, during English author Lazlo Ferran's extraordinary life, he has been an aeronautical engineering student, dispatch rider, graphic designer, full-time busker, guitarist and singer, recording two albums. Having grown up in rural Buckinghamshire Lazlo says:

"The beautiful Chiltern Hills offered the ideal playground for a child's mind, in contrast to the ultra-strict education system of Bucks."

Brought up as a Buddhist, he has travelled widely, surviving a student uprising in Athens and living for a while in Cairo, just after Sadat's assassination. Later, he spent some time in Central Asia and was only a few blocks away from gunfire during an attempt to storm the government buildings of Bishkek in 2006. He has a keen interest in theologies and philosophies of the Far East, Middle East, Asia and Eastern Europe.

After a long and successful career within the science industry, Lazlo Ferran left to concentrate on writing, to continue exploring the landscapes of truth.

From the author:

Thank you for reading my story and I hope you liked it. I value very much feedback from people and need this if each book is to be better than the last, so if you could take the time to either post a comment on my amazon page or my blog or simply email me, I would appreciate it.

Where to find Lazlo Ferran

Amazon: http://www.lazloferran.com
Email: lazloferran@gmail.com